Kendler followed closely on Caltha's heels. With each step, her feet slipped in the fine dust that covered the incline. If she fell, there would be little chance of saving her.

She paused, turning slowly, as though trying to locate the source of the emanations. "Its desperation is growing. Can't you feel it?"

Kendler moved after her as she raced down the passage then disappeared around a sudden angular turn. Her voice echoed back to him. "Nils, in here. It's in here!"

He rounded the corner and stepped into a chamber.

Caltha stood at the room's center, turning in uncertain circles.

"It's here, Nils, I can feel it." Tears streamed down her cheeks. "It knows we're here."

They had found, in that room, what man had searched the stars to discover. . . .

Fawcett Gold Medal Books
by Geo. W. Proctor:

☐ FIRE AT THE CENTER   14417 $2.25

☐ SHADOWMAN   14350 $1.95

FIRE
AT THE CENTER

by

Geo. W. Proctor

FAWCETT GOLD MEDAL • NEW YORK

FIRE AT THE CENTER

Copyright © 1981 Geo. W. Proctor

Published by Fawcett Gold Medal Books, a unit of CBS
Publications, the Consumer Publishing Division of CBS Inc.

ISBN: 0-449-14417-8

Printed in the United States of America

First Fawcett Gold Medal printing: July 1981

10 9 8 7 6 5 4 3 2 1

This one is for the original members of *The Turkey City Neo Pro Rodeo*, whose *esprit de corps* helped keep the words coming. Friends then and now:

> Lisa Tuttle
> Joseph Pumilia
> Jake "Buddy" Saunders
> Steven Utley
> Howard Waldrop

And in memory of our lost member, whose words ended just when they began to flow:

> Tom Reamy.

ONE

Excitement mounting, Nils Kendler endeavored to contain his anticipation of this moment. His fingers methodically pinched along the two seams of the surface suit. Liquid adhesive welled from the plastic, sealing him within a second skin. Mentally counting off the thirty seconds required for the solution to solidify, he matched the edges of the faceplate to the grooved lips of the suit's cowl. He repeated the adhesive-releasing process and secured the transparent bubble over his face. A sharp metallic taste immediately filled his mouth as the chemical filters incorporated in the faceplate cleansed the air rushing to his lungs.

Other than the obvious delay required to get into the suit, postponing his exit yet another few minutes, Kendler's dislike for the surface attire equaled his enmity for the claustrophobic confines of a space suit. While he accepted the life-giving necessity of a space suit, he failed to comprehend the purpose of the red sheath of plastic he now wore.

According to the mathematics and reality of time travel, his presence in this time period could in no conceivable way alter the future. The primary law governing the temporal dimension was the simple maxim that what is past is past—unchangeable history. There was absolutely nothing the

Retrieve teams could do to erase a portion of the past, even if they had any intention of doing so, which they did not. Fifteen Retrieve missions had proved the unalterable relationship between points in time beyond a doubt.

A fact that provided no deterrence to the bureaucratic mind of a lone LofAl Council member who envisioned the Retrieve Program as an instrument designed to annihilate the development of Man. A belief that contained more than an irrational concern for the possible destruction of the breeding line that eventually produced that fearful council member, Kendler suspected.

Despite protests by Retrieve officials, the bureaucratic fears prevailed, resulting in the instigation of surface suits as a "precautionary measure designed to protect temporal environments from potentially harmful microorganisms carried within the bodies of Retrieve personnel."

The flashing digits of a chronometer on the wall confirmed Kendler's mental calculations. The adhesive had had time to do its work. He gripped the elastic fabric on each side of the waist seam and wrenched with decided determination, vainly hoping the material would rip. It did not. Nor did he receive any more satisfactory results from the neck binding or the faceplate. The suit's strength only increased his annoyance.

Cursing in displeasure to no one but himself, Kendler strapped a hunting knife to his thigh, then stepped into the exit compartment's cramped interior for the last phase of decontamination.

The hatch secured itself behind him. Kendler positioned himself dead center atop a black bull's-eye stenciled around a drain grating in the floor. A cloudburst of chemicals erupted from high-pressure jets in the chamber's ceiling, bathing every centimeter of the suit's exterior in a torrent of sterility.

Abruptly as it began, the chemical rain ceased. The exit hatch swung outward. Anticipation honed to a keen edge, Kendler briskly covered the distance to the exit and ducked through the circular opening.

As with all the generations of men who had lived with the radiation-imposed exile from Earth since the Holocaust of 2123, Kendler shared the desire and dream of one day returning to the planet that had spawned Man. None of his daydreaming ever produced an imaginary world to rival the one he stepped into. It defied what inadequate descriptive abilities he possessed.

A wall of green were the only words that moved through

his mind. He stared at the tangled mass of vegetation surrounding the camp, his eyes unable to take it all in at once.

The jungle forest stood before him like an experiment in creation gone wild. There were ferns and evergreens, but they no longer dominated the landscape as they had during the earlier periods. The prehistoric jungle around him flourished with deciduous trees and angiosperms, the highest order of plant life Earth would know.

There growing side by side, as though battling for the precious nutrients in the soil, were magnolias, figs, beeches, poplars, birches, maples, oaks, walnuts, planes, tulips, sweet gums, breadfruits, and ebony trees. Even the dense undergrowth of grasses and shrubs of laurel, ivy, hazelnut, and holly were essentially the plant life that existed during Man's brief stay on this planet.

"Fantastic, isn't it?" A voice crackled over the receiver lodged in Kendler's left ear. "The Cretaceous forest . . . perhaps the most significant advance in evolution during this period."

Kendler turned, locating the source of the voice. Val Tarkio sat behind a compact control console six meters to his right. She wore a bright-red suit similar to his.

Monitoring the force shield enveloping the camp was not the type of duty he expected the renowned biologist and camp director to draw. Shield watches were a necessity that team members shared equally. The force shield, unlike the surface suits, protected the camp from the hostile world outside the camp's perimeter. The Earth Kendler now walked was a dominion still ruled by reptilian giants. It was a world that had no suitable niche for Man, nor would it prepare a place for the pinnacle of its evolutionary processes for millions of years.

"I didn't realize it was anything like this." Kendler made no attempt to conceal his awe. "It's unbelievable!"

"I know." The woman laughed while he walked to her side. "We have the habit of giving Earth the face of planets we've grown to know. For sixty mornings now, I've walked from the huts and experienced what you're feeling now. That feeling doesn't lessen, no matter how many times you've seen it. I've been a member of expeditions into primitive forests of at least fifteen planets. But this forest is like a maturing womb, preparing to conceive a wondrous child."

Reverence filled the woman's tone. The etched lines of age

9

softened on her weathered face, which, despite two faceplates distorting his vision, Kendler could see easily. He smiled. "I believe there's a touch of poet hidden within the heart of the biologist."

"Perhaps," she replied, her gray eyes alive with the morning's light. "Maybe I'm just becoming sentimental in my old age. But there's something in this world that can make a true believer out of the most ardent atheist."

"Sounds as if I'm talking with the newest convert." Kendler's gaze returned to the forest.

"You are," she said. "This world won't know Man for another sixty-five million years. The hands of creation are still testing their powers here, searching for the vessel needed to carry life from this ball of clay. While you're in the forest, you might catch a glimpse of a little furry creature scurrying amid the undergrowth. You'll have to look closely to see him. He's terribly easy to frighten, as well he should be. The forest holds innumerable predators waiting to make him part of their day's diet. Despite the hungry jaws surrounding him, that small creature continues to exist and thrive. The forest is in the midst of a revolution, a biological revolution that will unseat the dinosaurs from their thrones and leave that small mammal king. That is, until the next turn of the wheel of evolution."

She paused, glancing at Kendler with a slightly embarrassed expression. "Sorry, I babble too much. You're not interested in the heir to this forest, but the king himself, *Tyrannosaurus rex*."

Kendler's reply remained unspoken. Val waved away his comment, pressing a hand to the left side of her head. "It's Rani."

A sharp click sounded in his left ear when Val cut off contact with him. Kendler watched the woman's lips move silently behind the transparent bubble of her faceplate, wishing he could hear the conversation between the biologist and the Retrieve field leader. However, without a link to the receiver outside the force field, it was impossible.

"Rani says they're ready for you." Val's voice returned to his earphone. "They've constructed a platform in an oak near the lake. It's an easy walk, no more than two kilometers from here. Just follow the yellow-marked path."

Kendler followed the woman's pointing finger to a broad splotch of yellow dye splattered on the trunk of a palm beyond the camp's perimeter. Similar dye patches marked other trees and bushes for as far as his gaze could penetrate the thick vegetation. The path appeared well defined, probably more so than routes normally used by the Retrieve team. They were taking no chances on their special visitor's losing himself in the Cretaceous jungle.

"You'll also need this." Val lifted the silvery form of a compact rifle from one side of the control console. "It's a pulse-beam laser, maximum setting of two hundred bursts per minute, charged for five minutes of continuous firing. It'll handle anything you might run into out there, including the king. Although we would all prefer it if you brought *rex* back alive and deposited him right in the middle of that grid over there."

"I've no intention of using this." Kendler accepted the weapon, pleasantly surprised by its light heft. He glanced at the circular grid outside the force shield. "I'll do my best to deliver you a prize specimen."

"Good. There shouldn't be any reason for the laser, unless a grazing herd of *Triceratops* blunders into you by accident." Val smiled, her fingers moving over a series of buttons on the panel. "There you go. The field's down. Rani will fill you in. . . . And, Kendler, good luck. We've got our money on you."

He tried to smile reassuringly when he stepped into the forest. But the woman's last comment could not be taken lightly.

The Retrieve Program was staking its life on Nils Kendler and his psi abilities, and Nils Kendler was fully aware of that fact. As with all Lofgrin Alliance projects, Retrieve depended on LofAl Council funding for its continued existence. Not all the council members were amiable toward the program, nor were they willing to consider the benefits derived from delving Earth's past. That the majority of the populace inhabiting the Alliance's forty planets remained totally unaware of Retrieve did nothing to endear the project to the hearts of politicians, who preferred to woo the electorate more than they desired to unveil Man's history.

Faced with growing apathy among council members, Retrieve officials determined that to survive, their program required a full-blown public relations campaign, a crusade specifically aimed at placing their efforts in the public spotlight for as long as possible before the upcoming council budgetary sessions.

Whatever that campaign was to be, it had to be big and spectacular, something to capture the fickle imagination of a public inured to such wonders as the Aledpa Chameleon Sprites and the Fire Steeds of Kai Lung. Their bid for public approval took the shape of a major exhibit of Earth's prehistoric life; no holotapes or any of the other normal mass-media channels, but the real thing brought from the past.

Psi Corps Director Kate Dunbar got wind of the Retrieve scheme through the usual intra-agency grapevine her intelligence team gleaned each day. The plan held all the prospects of being a miserable failure. Yet it contained just the right amount of color to attract Dunbar. If the circus fanfare was loud enough, it held the possibility of being one of the most successful pieces of showmanship to rock the LofAl planets since the Yrielian Alien Intelligence Hoax.

That slim possibility of success sold Kate Dunbar. If glory were to be gained, she would make sure the Psi Corps received its fair share. If the valiant venture fell flat on its face, the corps would be none the worse for having offered a helping hand.

The helping hand Kate Dunbar magnanimously extended was Nils Kendler and his abilities as a mind-merger. Retrieve officials eagerly accepted the unexpected assistance. And Kendler found his ambition to walk on Earth's surface fulfilled, even though he was some sixty-five million years too soon, give or take a few thousand years, to glimpse the civilizations of which he daydreamed.

Kendler's job was relatively simple, as Dunbar had gone out of her way to explain to him. He was to merge with a target, gain control of its mind and body, then maneuver the target to a force grid, where the target would be transported to the future. That the target was a giant reptile from Earth's late Cretaceous period, bearing the ominous title *Tyrannosaurus rex*, played no part in his task. A merge was a merge was a merge, whether it be with a dinosaur or a glowslug inhabiting the radioactive sludge of Apan's World.

"Kendler," the voice of field team leader Rani sounded in Kendler's ear, "Panburn's sighted a *rex* eight kilometers from our position. He estimates it's four to five meters in height and moving toward the lake. It looks like what we're looking for."

"How long should it take me to reach your position?" Kendler skirted around a tangled web of ivy, following the yellow-marked path.

"A half hour, forty minutes at the most," Rani answered. "No need to hurry. Panburn says the target is sluggish. Apparently it spent the night in the rocks near the mountains south of our position and still hasn't warmed up. Should take *rex* a full hour and a half to reach the platform area. You've got time to spare."

"Sounds good." Kendler picked his way over the trunks of two uprooted pines. "If everything goes this easy, we should have your specimen caged and delivered back to Base One in time to interrupt their lunch."

Rani chuckled. "Perfect! It'll give Beamin and his crew something more to do than slip supplies back to the field camps. I'd love to see his face when he gets his first glimpse of our king."

"I'll see that you get a full report." Kendler smiled, wondering about his own expression when he first viewed the prehistoric monarch.

"Agreed," Rani said. "Got to cut off now. Panburn's signaling again. I'll be back if there're any new developments."

A curt click rudely popped in Kendler's ear, leaving him isolated within the surprisingly silent wilderness. Panburn's interruption was welcomed. Kendler gratefully accepted any solitude before a merge, especially when he found himself immersed in the alien environment of his target. Solitude was a luxury the Psi Corps usually ignored, relying on the merger to adjust to his surroundings via his host's memories.

No matter how small his personal knowledge of a target's world, it eased the intellectual and emotional shock of a merge for both the host and himself. The full impact of two minds melting together could be an experience of tornadic sensations. When the goal of one of those minds was to dominate the other, insanity or even death could result.

During his twelve years with the corps, Kendler had been lucky. He was unscathed by the two hundred plus merges he had undergone. The same could not be said for twenty of his hosts. In five cases, the damage he caused had been accidental. The other fifteen had been a matter of design.

The forest undergrowth thinned before Kendler; he quickened his strides. His annoyance with the surface suit returned. Not only was it uncomfortable, but it hindered his assimilation of the world around him. Instead of the jungle's flower-scented breath, there was only the metallic bite of chemical filters. Instead of the varying textures of leaves and barks, there was only the elastic sheath covering his hands. Even his vision was occasionally obscured by the sun's glare on the faceplate bubble.

He covered a kilometer before pausing for a short radio check with the field leader. Then, hefting the laser to his shoulder, Kendler once more took up the dye-splattered trail, only to pause again before several uprooted oaks strewn across his path. He eyed the situation, speculating which of the jungle's gargantuan denizens had created such havoc. The fallen trees bordered a glade that stretched at least ninety meters to his right.

Stepping atop the first oak trunk, Kendler leaped to the second, then the third. Poised for the jump to the fourth toppled tree, Kendler glanced down. A flurry of brown erupted beside his right foot.

Kendler jerked away from the movement. The startled reaction cost him his balance and sent him sprawling backward. He reached out for nonexistent support. His right elbow cracked against an overturned trunk behind him. Painful fire shot through his arm. The impact jarred the laser from his grasp; it flew into the entangled foliage about him. Air rushed from his lungs as his back struck the ground.

Chagrined at his awkwardness and overreaction, Kendler pushed to a sitting position with his left arm. A small rodentlike creature scurried down the trunk to disappear in the fallen tree's tangled roots.

Kendler shook his head. It was one of Val Tarkio's early mammals. The animal had almost lost its life beneath the heel of a creature who would not walk Earth for millions of years to come. Most definitely an ignoble end for an heir apparent to this primitive world.

Gingerly lifting his right arm, he carefully felt along its throbbing length with his left hand. There would be an ugly bruise and probably some swelling, but as far as he could determine, nothing was broken. He placed his palm on the ground and gradually applied pressure. Fresh flames of pain seared out from his elbow, coursing up and down the arm.

Kendler grimaced. The arm would be useless for a day or two. Shifting his weight to the left side, he pushed to his feet and glanced around for the laser's silvery form.

The silence of the clearing behind him was shattered by thunder. A bellowing roar vibrated within the marrow of his bones. Kendler twisted and froze, staring across the glade. There, poked above the needle tops of a clump of pines, hung a head. Móre than a meter in length, the elongated oval symmetry of that head was split lengthwise by gaping jaws filled with saberlike, recurving teeth. Sunken and set far back on that awesome head gleamed tiny eyes that surveyed the forest below.

The mighty scissor-hinged jaws snapped shut with traplike precision, then ripped open again. The dewlap hanging loosely from the neck beneath stretched and tautened. Thunder once more roared from the creature's lungs, an alien roar not meant for the ears of man.

There was no further need for Kendler to follow the yellow-dye-marked path. He no longer sought his merge target. The target had come to him. *Tyrannosaurus rex,* the tyrant lizard king, the largest predator ever to walk Earth's surface, stood before him.

TWO

Kendler broke through the numbing shock clouding his brain and dropped to a crouch between the uprooted trees. Eyes riveted to the massive reptilian head, he edged back to seek the security of the leafy boughs and his lost laser.

Rex swiveled its head atop a disproportionately slender neck. Its small eyes glinted in the morning light while the lizard king perused the toppled oaks as though perceiving the man's motion.

Kendler froze again, hoping the carnosaur shared the color blindness that marred the vision of the majority of Earth's creatures below man on the evolutionary ladder. If not, there was no way of camouflaging the red of his surface suit, no matter how hard he tried to blend with the forest. For endless seconds, unblinking eyes peered down, then moved back to the treetops.

Kendler inched backward only to find his retreat barricaded by an imposing limb at least half the thickness of one of the trunks. Cautiously feeling behind him, he sought an exit beneath the obstacle, but could detect no more than a few centimeters' clearance between the bough and the ground. His only alternative route to the shelter of the dense foliage was over the limb, an action that was sure to draw the carnivore's attention.

Kendler glanced over his shoulder, searching for the laser. The gesture was wasted energy. The dense leaves completely obscured the weapon. It would be suicide to clamber over the limb without the guarantee the rifle would be within his grasp.

The ground shook under Kendler, a tremor that had not been spawned by the geological shifting of the Earth's crust. His head jerked back, and he stared across the clearing.

Rex walked.

The forest shuddered as though the ground convulsively protested the ponderous burden of the theropod's weight. A cluster of slim ferns swayed briefly, then snapped like dry saplings before the ten tons of predator that easily pushed through the vegetation and strode into the glade.

No obstacles stood between man and beast now. Kendler suppressed a shudder threatening to run up his spine. He gazed on the full terrible splendor of the Cretaceous monarch. Standing upright on two gargantuan legs, *rex* towered to a height of six meters. Its trunklike tail, stiffly outstretched on the ground behind it, supported the dinosaur in a tripod stance that gave the creature a total length of at least fifteen meters.

The monstrous head with its gaping jaws and small eyes once again moved to the fallen trees and the man crouched between the toppled boles. Kendler no longer doubted *rex* focused on his vulnerable position.

"Rani . . . Rani . . . Rani!" Kendler called over the suit's radio. No response came.

Rex stood immobile at the opposite end of the clearing. Its head tilted as though perplexed by the nature of the creature huddled amid the fallen oaks.

Kendler roughly estimated the expanse separating them at ninety meters. The carnosaur's powerful legs were capable of moving its ten tons of malevolent fury at a speed of thirty-two kilometers an hour. Such speed could close the distance between them in a matter of nine seconds.

Nine seconds—more than enough time to complete the mind merge.

It was either that, or face the reptilian giant armed with only the hunting knife strapped to his thigh.

Closing his eyes, Kendler pulled within himself to subdue the input of his own senses, then completely eliminated

17

them from his consciousness as he drifted into alpha level. Isolated from the prehistoric forest around him, he floated on the streams of unharnessed psi forces. He gathered the random energies, linking them, feeding their power, focusing the gyrating surges until he commanded the full power of his mind.

He reached out.

Shock!

The theropod's brain railed at first contact. Kendler forced himself deeper into the reptile's consciousness.

There was no room for intellect in that brain measuring but twenty-one centimeters in length and five centimeters in diameter. There were none of the sophisticated emotions of love, hate, ambition, or greed. Nor was there the viciousness, savagery, or malevolence the brain of such a predator would be expected to contain. Those were emotions reserved for Man, Kendler knew, for an intellect that mistakingly moralizes nature's killers as evil because they prey on the flesh of lesser creatures.

Rex knew nothing of morals. His brain—it was now a he; Kendler personified the host his mind melted with—was a primitive jungle of raw instinct and basic sensations. There was fright, hunger, and the primal urge to mate. And dominating all was the prime motivation—survival.

That instinct now directed the desperate struggle to expel the invader from his brain. In panicked fear, *Tyrannosaurus* battled a power his own brain had no capacity to comprehend.

Kendler expected this. Every primitive brain he had ever encountered held the same determination. Only Man presented an easy target for a merge. Intellect produced an ego that refused to accept the possibility that minds existed capable of invading and dominating, superior wills that could control. Man even denied contact with the mind of a merger, preferring to believe in insanity rather than admit domination by a superior mind. When a human being finally admitted what was happening, it was too late.

The primitive brain recognized a merge as something alien and contrary to its natural state. It reacted immediately, attempting to repel the power trying to conquer it. Survival could not exist in domination.

This was the driving will Kendler fought while his mind moved into the gargantuan's brain. Flowing and blending, he mingled within every region of the beast's conscious exis-

18

tence. He worked along the lines of least resistance, first matching his will to that of the carnosaur, then exerting himself against the walls of mental opposition.

The *Tyrannosaurus* opened to him. First came the smell-taste, a strange suffusion of odors entering the carnivore's slitted nostrils and the sensations of its tongue as it smelled the air much in the manner of its far-future cousins the snakes would do with their flicking forked tongues.

Next came hearing and the deep thudding of some bass drum beating a terrible tempo to the screaming roar of thunder.

Panic gripped Kendler. He recognized that vibrating beat—the roar! He was suddenly aware of the sensation of motion. He could feel the powerful muscles of the creature's legs cording and stretching in time to the heavy pounding. *Rex* moved! And if the vibrating thud was any indication, he was in full stride.

Kendler rose against the resistance that still met him, suppressing the primitive instincts and gaining control. The last of the beast's senses opened to him. He saw through the eyes of *Tyrannosaurus rex*!

Despite his knowledge of what would come, the sight still jolted Kendler, threatening to unseat him from the conquered brain. He stared down at his own helpless body from the mind of a creature fully intent on snatching him up in its horrible jaws—no more than a light snack before beginning its day's search for a substantial meal.

The merge had consumed more time than Kendler realized. Less than thirty meters separated his body from the yawning jaws of this primitive predator. A distance *rex* would cover in three seconds.

Kendler screamed commands within the brain he controlled. He felt the legs react, but the reaction time of the carnosaur's inadequate nervous system was too slow. *Rex* would stop, but by then Kendler's body would be crushed beneath the creature's taloned feet. The momentum of the ten-ton body was too great to be halted in time.

One avenue was left to him. Kendler withdrew, abandoning the beast's brain, flowing back within his own consciousness. No time existed for the normal readjustment period. Kendler forced will into flaccid muscles. He opened his mind to the senses locked out only seconds ago.

His eyes opened and stared into the face of sheer destruction.

The carnivore charged with his body held virtually horizontal to the ground. The magnificent head was elevated a few degrees, and its traplike jaws stretched wide to expose two rows of sixteen-centimeter teeth ready to snare the human morsel. There were no serpentine writhings of the great tail. Instead the massive trunk of flesh was rigidly extended behind the lizard's body for balance. The ponderous gait was an exercise in precision. Each three-toed foot was lifted and firmly planted before the other foot left the ground. Head and body swayed in an exact counterpoint rhythm to maintain the balance of the reptile's elephantine proportions.

For any other creature such an awkward, wobbly run would have been ridiculous. But there was nothing ridiculous about *rex*. The rippling musculature of his gigantic body, from his blunt snout to the end of his stiffly held tail, was a portrait of titanic locomotion.

Legs tensed and panic eating along his spine, Kendler crouched before the tyrant king, waiting as the carnivore's strides devoured the distance between them. He counted off one frightening second. Then he ran.

His brain demanding every ounce of power from calves and thighs, he ran not backward into the tangled foliage of the fallen branches, but forward, straight toward the wide jaws that waited for him.

It was the one action he knew *rex* would be unprepared for. The *Tyrannosaurus* brain was too slow to react to the unexpected movement.

Under those terrible jaws and fungus-mottled belly, Kendler darted. He rushed between the theropod's pistonlike legs and was out from beneath the extended tail, running for the yellow-marked trees of the forest.

Behind him, Kendler heard an awesome thud and the splintering of wood when *rex* snapped his powerful jaws closed around the oak trunks that had sheltered his prey but a second before.

"Rani!" Kendler cried out while he weaved around a small thicket of ferns. "Rani! Rani!"

The receiver plugged into his left ear remained dead. A thunderous roar of anger ripped from the throat of a carnosaur deprived of its morning meal. The ground rumbled. *Rex* slashed around to locate his elusive breakfast.

"Rani! Rani!" Not even a crackle of static came from the earphone. Kendler tapped a compact case strapped to the surface suit's waist. The radio offered no reply, evidently damaged during his fall.

Ahead, the path wove through a thick grove of magnolias. Selecting a large tree, Kendler ducked behind it and collapsed against the dark trunk. He had sprinted less than a hundred meters, but his lungs burned and his legs ached from the demands placed on them. Even a few seconds' rest provided welcomed relief.

His eyes darted over the forest around him, desperately searching for anything that could be used as a weapon. There was nothing. He was out of his element.

Earth was not yet ready for man, a fact all too apparent to him. This was a world of survival, survival that depended on brute force and sharp senses. His world was that of the mind. His only power was the merge, but the physical exertion drained him of that ability. He needed time to focus his energies. Time he did not have. At the moment, he was willing to exchange a few iotas of his psi capabilities for a measure of the strength and endurance *rex* held in his powerful legs.

He smiled ironically. He was deprived of his own limited senses. The surface suit enclosed him like a death trap.

He grasped the faceplate with both hands and wrenched. The adhesive held, anchoring the transparent bubble to the cowl. He toyed with the idea of smashing the faceplate against the tree trunk, but there was no time to deal with the shattered plastic that would result.

Instead, he used the hunting knife strapped to his thigh, carefully cutting through the suit's neck. The elastic fabric was tough, but the knife's edge won out. Within a matter of seconds, Kendler completely opened the suit's neck and pulled the cowl from his head.

Despite the forest's heavy humidity, the air he sucked into his lungs was invigorating. His body came alive with the exposure to the primitive world. Even with *rex* behind him somewhere, the jungle took on an atmosphere of peace and serenity.

Quiet. He was aware of the silence about him. He no longer heard the carnosaur's bellows, or even the vibrations of its strides. Perhaps luck was with him and the *Tyrannosaurus* had decided such a small morsel was not worth further effort.

Cautiously, Kendler peered around the trunk and found luck had fled his side. Even through the tangled vegetation, he could see the massive form of his Cretaceous opponent. *Rex* held himself in a position Kendler could only describe as a squat. The beast pressed its blunt snout to the ground like some hunting hound sniffing out a lost scent.

Kendler gauged the distance between them at fifty meters. While the space was even shorter than the distance of the first merge attempt, he was now completely hidden from the creature. Again Kendler closed himself to the world and reached with his mind.

The carnivore recoiled from contact. The small, primitive brain somehow made the association between the mental invasion and the prey it sought. *Rex* charged, driving full force in the direction of Kendler's spoor.

Kendler reeled back. He made no attempt at a full merge. Instead, he regained control of his body and did as he had done once before. He ran.

THREE

Angling off the yellow-dyed path, Kendler worked his way among the larger oaks and pines to avoid the heavy under-brush and vines that hindered his flight, yet provided no resistance to the *Tyrannosaurus*. Behind him came the snapping and crashing of saplings, felled before his pursuer's hulking weight.

Covering another hundred meters, Kendler paused amid a triangular grouping of palms. He sucked air into aching lungs and allowed his legs another few seconds' rest.

The carnosaur took no rest. However, his gait was no longer a full driving charge. Like the giant mammals that walked Earth during its last death throes, the theropod's powerful legs were unable to sustain any speed for more than a short time.

But the reptilian predator had not given up the chase. With a steadfast determination, he came toward Kendler in a wobbly, one-foot-at-a-time walk that would quickly bring him to the palms concealing his prey. Adjusting his own speed to a long-strided lope, Kendler abandoned the slender trunks and cut back into the forest.

The new pace of the man-dinosaur chase was much easier to maintain. However, Kendler fully realized that should his gait slow, *rex* would quickly close the gap between them. A quicker stride would leave him exhausted and would result in the same conclusion to the chase. At the moment, it was simply a matter of endurance, a question of which would outlast the other, man or carnosaur.

Weaving back toward the direction of his original forest path, Kendler could not locate the familar yellow-dye splotches that would allow him to lead *rex* into the range of the field team's lasers. The effort to find the path was a waste of precious energy. He had misjudged the distance traveled from the trail and lost himself in the Cretaceous forest.

The situation was some cosmic joke—a man lost in a jungle that existed sixty-five million years before his birth; a man stalked by the largest predator that had ever walked the Earth.

To add a touch of irony, whatever fates ruled this world had stripped him of his technological advantages and ordered, "Prove yourself against nature, prove your worthiness to exist here and now."

It was ridiculous! Had it not been so real, Kendler would have laughed. He had not asked for this duel of man and dinosaur, but he accepted it; not in the spirit of adventure, but for survival. He would see it through to its ultimate conclusion, whether it meant his riding within the mind of *rex* and returning the carnivore to the force cage back at camp, or his own death in those jaws waiting for him to make a mistake. He had no other choice.

Kendler lost all perspective of time and distance. His legs continued their long strides. He matched himself to the deep rhythm of the theropod's thudding gait.

The forest thinned and fell away. A broad grassy plain opened before him. Bordering it to the right, no more than a kilometer from his position, was an escarpment rising at least a hundred meters in the air. From atop the plateau, three waterfalls spilled into a lake that formed the boundary to the far side of the plain.

To his left, Kendler saw a small herd of twenty-five to thirty *Triceratops* scurry from their grazing into a protective grove of pines. Two large bulls turned their three-horned, turretlike crowns toward Kendler's pursuer, hissing a menacing threat. *Rex* paid them no more than a casual glance.

Kendler realized the carnosaur's small brain was capable of comprehending only one task at a time. Kendler also realized he was the focal point of those primitive thoughts at the moment.

After the tangled undergrowth of the forest, Kendler's legs seemed to develop wings, flying across the open, level ground. It was a two-sided situation. *Rex* had the same advantage on the unobstructed terrain. Kendler forced his legs to lengthen their strides to keep time with the increasing tempo of the predator's gait.

The lake loomed before him like a small inland sea. From what now seemed like hours ago, Kendler remembered Rani's mentioning something about a. lake being near the field team's platform. Surely this had to be the same lake.

Glancing over his shoulder, he searched the distant tree-tops for the platform. He sensed a strange relief move through him when he was unable to make out any signs of the field team. An ironic smile played at the corners of his mouth. Whatever the outcome of this chase, he did not want the field team to interfere. He wanted to see it through to the end—on his own. He felt a strong bond between himself and the prehistoric killer breathing down his neck. The creature was not *Tyrannosaurus rex*; it was *his rex*! The Retrieve team had no right, no claim, to interfere with the carnivore's capture.

Thoughts of Rani and his teammates were abruptly dispelled from Kendler's mind. The pounding beat behind him once more increased in tempo. The slow pace had given *rex* the opportunity to gather his strength for another burst of speed.

With each vibrating fall of those taloned feet, Kendler felt the reptile gaining on him. The theropod's primitive muscles were winning over the superior brain of a man from the future—a brain Kendler was helpless to use.

Trying to ignore the cramping aches in his calves and thighs, Kendler drove onward. The lake was his hope for escape. If he could just reach the water!

Rex was not meant for an aquatic existence. His weight would pull him beneath the deadly waters, filling his lungs before his brain perceived what had happened.

The pounding reverberations grew closer and closer. Kendler felt the dry plain give way to moist soil, then slippery mud. Fighting to maintain his precarious footing in the slime, he raced toward the water's edge. His heart threatened to stop in midbeat.

Duck-billed heads appeared to be floating on the surface of the lake. *Trachodons!*

The lake was not the refuge Kendler sought. While *trachodons* were relatively harmless herbivores, a swimming man might draw their curiosity. The attention of a creature that size, no matter how innocent, could cause damage. And what aquatic predators swam beneath the surface Kendler could only guess.

Rex roared. Kendler twisted to face his death.

Death did not come. The *Tyrannosaurus* stood six meters from Kendler. Its massive head cocked to one side as it stared at the man.

Why had the carnosaur stopped? Kendler was confused. By all rights he should now be within those cavernous jaws. Yet he still lived.

Rex, apparently impatient with the situation, stepped forward. The monstrous three-toed foot began to sink in the mud surrounding the lake's edge. Without hesitation, the towering gargantuan jerked his foot back to solid ground.

Kendler grinned while his prehistoric opponent roared his frustration. The slippery slime oozing around Kendler's ankles was no more than an unpleasant sensation for him. For *rex*, it presented a death trap. Ankle-deep mud for a *Tyrannosaurus* could easily unsettle the delicate balance of its strides and topple it. Size and weight were working against *rex*. The creature could not risk a fall. His own ten tons would crush him.

Realizing the effectiveness of the muddy barrier separating them, Kendler casually turned and walked toward the three waterfalls feeding into the lake. On a parallel path just beyond the mire, *rex* stalked his unobtainable prey, occasionally testing the slime, then withdrawing.

Kendler did not understand what compelled the carnivore to maintain his vigil over such a small morsel, but he was grateful for whatever it was. This determined killer that had chased him with steadfast resolution was the one he wanted to return to the future. He realized that should *rex* suddenly turn and abandon the chase, he would follow the carnosaur until a favorable merge situation presented itself. If *rex* held a streak of stubbornness, his ran ten times deeper.

Working steadily toward the escarpment and the three falls, Kendler studied the terrain ahead of him. Some thirty meters from the face of the cliff, the ground turned to solid rock. If he tried for the cliff, he would be open prey for *rex*.

However, just behind the cascading waters of the falls ran a broad shelf of rock. If he was able to reach that ledge and his opponent's abhorrence of water was as great as it appeared, the shelf would be a perfect position for the mind-merge. Something he could not risk at the moment with his body vulnerably exposed.

A thundering roar jarred Kendler from his thoughts. *Rex* answered, the creature's attention diverted from Kendler for the first time since their accidental meeting in the glade.

Again the roar sounded, echoing from the forest. *Rex* thrashed around to meet the bellowed challenge. Kendler jumped back, avoiding the slashing swipe of the carnivore's tremendous tail and a sudden end to their cat-and-mouse game.

For a third time the bellow blared. *Rex* roared back, rising to his full height to await the intruder.

The wait was short. Two palms on the forest edge parted abruptly, their trunks snapping near their bases. From the Cretaceous jungle stepped the roaring challenger, yet another *Tyrannosaurus*. The prehistoric gargantuan lowered his massive head and charged.

FOUR

Kendler stood, frozen by the sight of the approaching theropod. In the same birdlike wobble-run, the *rex* quickly covered the distance from the forest to the lake's edge. Instead of making the attack Kendler anticipated, the newcomer halted ten meters from Kendler's *rex*. The two primitive giants stood staring at one another.

Having no wish to find himself in the middle of the developing battle, Kendler ran, darting toward the cliff for thirty meters before turning back to watch the jungle monarchs duel.

Like boxers squared off, the two titans faced each other. Their vestiges of forearms looked ridiculously inadequate for even the simplest sparring bout. The newcomer, two meters shorter than Kendler's *rex*, began to pace back and forth. His scissorlike jaws snapped, and a deep-throated roar rippled from his cavernous mouth.

Rex imitated the actions, stepping toward the challenger, only to back hastily away when the intruder approached. Neither giant seemed willing to strike the first blow.

At first glance the scene appeared vicious enough; it now seemed the battle Kendler expected was not to take place. However, the reptiles' preoccupation with themselves gave him the opportunity he needed to reach the shelter of the rocky shelf. He pivoted from the carnosaurs and ran.

His flight was not unnoticed, as the rumbling reverberations of the ground announced. Where there had been only one set of pounding feet to contend with, there were now two. *Tyrannosaurus* was not a creature that stalked its prey as a team. Yet a glance over the shoulder revealed what Kendler already knew. Both the carnivores were chasing him.

The walk along the lake's edge had renewed the strength of his legs. Adrenaline flowed into his veins. The ground firmed beneath his feet. He forced himself to run even faster.

The tremors behind him increased in their jarring intensity. His *rex* began to outdistance the smaller newcomer, refusing to allow his prey to escape. *Rex*'s labored breathing hissed like a giant bellows above the pounding of his taloned feet.

Kendler took the small incline to the ledge in three leaps. He maintained his strides, ducking under the first and lesser of the three waterfalls.

Apparently unsure of his footing on the rocky slope, *rex* once more slowed to a walk. He moved up the incline onto the shelf. Each step was slow and deliberate. The creature tested its weight before moving farther along the water-slick ledge.

The smaller carnosaur refused to follow. However, it seemed to have no intention of leaving the scene. Instead, it paced back and forth at the foot of the incline, its small eyes surveying its fellow dinosaur and the creature it pursued.

Rex paused, cautiously eyeing the first waterfall, as though uncertain how to deal with the cascading torrent. Despite his natural fear of water, the arc of the falling current offered more than enough clearance for his ponderous body. *Rex* hugged close to the face of the cliff and walked beneath the falls.

Kendler cursed under his breath and ran on to the next falls. Unlike the first, this torrent lacked an overhang to direct its current beyond the shelf and into the lake. Pressing flat against the cliff, Kendler entered the plummeting stream. His fingers sought and found cracks within the rock, needed handholds to keep him from being swept away by the onslaught of water.

Centimeter by centimeter, he hauled himself through the wall of pounding water, hands cramping under the tension of his grip. The hammering falls gave way to fresh air. Kendler stepped clear of the water and collapsed to the shelf in exhaustion.

Behind him, *rex* roared.

Kendler lifted his head and stared through the white current, barely able to make out the form of the *Tyrannosaurus*. The tyrant lizard king had reached the end of the chase and lost. There was no way *rex* could make his way around, or force his way through the impassable barrier. The cascading falls would wash him from the ledge.

Kendler caught his breath. Apparently the carnosaur's small brain did not perceive that fact. *Rex* was going to attempt the falls!

The theropod raised his right foot and placed it within the thundering stream. For seconds, he stood there, testing his footing. The three recurved talons bit into rock. The left foot rose.

Kendler saw the carnivore totter, precariously balanced on one leg, struggling against the blasting current. *Rex* wrenched his left foot back. There was no retreat. He lost his equilibrium. The carnosaur's massive body toppled, thudding into the face of the cliff and sliding down toward the edge of the shelf.

Kendler stared, unable to halt the course of the inevitable. The water's surface was less than three meters from the ledge, a fall a man could easily survive. However, *rex* would be crushed by his own weight when he hit the water. Even if the beast did survive the fall, he would drown in a matter of seconds.

Kendler was cheated. It was not supposed to end this way. He did not want such a victory.

The awful sound of talon against rock grated in Kendler's ears. *Rex* fought for some foothold to stop his slide. One of those great claws dug in, finding the resistance needed, a small crack in the rock. His massive body halted, one ponderous leg dangling over the side of the shelf.

For moments, the beast lay still. His barrel-like chest heaved in labored breaths. Then *rex* moved. Slowly and with care, he worked his body back onto the ledge. He tucked his legs to each side of his torso and pushed to full height.

If there was a time for a victory roar, this was it, Kendler thought. But *rex* just stood, staring at the endless torrent of the falls and the man standing behind the impenetrable barrier. The king of the Cretaceous world was mute.

The carnosaur's head twisted on his slender neck, examining the ledge behind him. He inched back, eventually moving down the slope to the safety of the rocky shore. The smaller gargantuan approached to resume its challenge.

The two giants began the awkward circling they had started before Kendler's break for the falls. For minutes, Kendler watched them, their monstrous jaws snapping and biting the empty air. Still, neither creature seemed willing to begin the battle.

Kendler's *rex*, as though tiring of the mock battle, abruptly turned from the smaller theropod and started back toward the forest. The other *Tyrannosaurus* followed at a cautious distance.

Now was the time for the merge. Glancing farther along the ledge, Kendler saw a boulder resting near the edge of the shelf. The rock offered the protection his body needed while his mind rode within the brain of *rex*. Pushing to his feet, Kendler quickly covered the distance to the boulder and curled behind it.

He closed his eyes and blocked all his senses. The psi forces within his mind flowed together, forming a swirling maelstrom of power. He reached out.

This time Kendler was prepared for the initial contact and the struggle that followed. He offered no resistance to *rex*. He matched and blended his will to that of the carnosaur, weaving himself into every area of the beast's consciousness. For an instant, he was *Tyrannosaurus rex*. Then he exerted control, dominating the mighty ruler of the Cretaceous forest. His victory was complete.

Solidly merged with the primitive brain, Kendler turned the massive beast back toward the ledge to study his partially exposed body resting on the shelf. He did not like leaving himself so vulnerable, but his ego would not permit him to lose this creature.

He turned *rex* once again, to retrace the path of their chase. However, once more the smaller *rex* approached, repeating the circling and snapping. Searching his host's memories, Kendler found the answer to the strange behavior. If the lips of the monstrous reptile whose mind he now shared were capable of smiling, they would have smiled.

Kendler carefully directed *rex* to ignore the other creature's aggressive advances and continued on the path back to the camp. The lesser *rex* would follow; there was no way to stop him. However, Kendler doubted that the Retrieve team would mind having two specimens for their exhibition, rather than the planned one.

Entering the forest, Kendler kept *rex* at a steady gait, following the tree-strewn path the carnosaur had left in the wake of their chase. There would be no problem finding his way back once in his own body again. The trees were tossed around like jackstraws.

What had seemed like a lifetime now took on an ironic perspective as Kendler stared from the dinosaur's eyes. From his vantage point above the trees, he noted that on several occasions his flight had paralleled the yellow-dye splotches. Now what had seemed like an endless run proved to be no more than eight kilometers at the most.

Eventually the domed forms of the camp's huts came into sight. Kendler-*rex* stepped into the clearing, then moved to the exact center of the force grid. The smaller *Tyrannosaurus* followed.

Even with *rex*'s keen eyesight, Kendler could not see Val Tarkio's expression when she saw the two kings of the forest. But he could imagine it. No matter what her surprise, the woman's fingers quickly scurried over the control console. A blue, shimmering aurora danced around the grid, trapping the two specimens of Cretaceous royalty within the force field.

His task completed, Kendler withdrew. His body, some eight kilometers away, stirred, as though awakening from a deep sleep.

The eight members of the Retrieve team were gathered at the campsite when Kendler came striding from the forest. Somewhere amid the Retrieve team's backslapping and general celebration, Kendler managed to give an account of his accidental meeting with *rex*, the chase, and the successful capture of the two carnosaurs. He also taped a full report specifically detailing the hazards of requiring temporal travelers to wear surface suits. Once the report was in the hands of Psi Corps Director Kate Dunbar, he could almost guarantee results.

"They're a beautiful pair, Nils." Rani beamed, his gaze on the captured carnivores. "The tale of their capture is the shot in the arm this project needs. None of the media will be able to resist blowing it up to heroic proportions. The LofAl planets will be bidding to see who gets the exhibition first.

"However, there's something I still fail to understand." The field leader paused and turned to Kendler. "I never realized a psiotic could merge and control two minds at the same time."

Kendler grinned, catching a similar smile of amusement

on Val Tarkio's face. "I can't. And I don't believe there's a psiotic around who's developed that talent yet."

"But . . . what about . . . how did you get the second *rex*?" Rani's face twisted with confusion.

"The capture of our second king had nothing to do with Nils's psi abilities," Val said, her amusement growing. "In fact, Nils had absolutely nothing to do with the smaller *Tyrannosaurus*, except being in the right brain at the right time. As it is, everything boils down to a simple matter of biology."

"Biology?" Rani stared at the woman.

"The big one, my *rex*, Dr. Rani," Kendler said, his grin widening as he turned to the two carnosaurs, "isn't a *rex* at all. She's a *regina*."

FIVE

An annoying buzz like the drone of swarming insects wedged its way into Kendler's ears. It grew louder, drowning out the sound of the waves that gently lapped the clean white sand of Rochelle's Point. Questioning, Kendler rolled to the black-haired girl stretched on her back beside him on the beach. The sun played over her lithe young body, its light fracturing into a myriad of blazing jewels on her nude, oil-slickened skin. He reached out, his fingertips nudging her bare shoulder.

His sister's eyes opened. She pushed to her elbows and smiled a bit dreamily as though she had been drifting near sleep. Her lips moved, but the words they formed did not penetrate the wall of noise filling Kendler's head. Concern furrowed her forehead. She sat straight. Her right hand rose to him.

Blackness descended, blanketing the beach, his sister.

The dream ended.

Kendler's eyes blinked open to stare vacantly about the surroundings. Nothing registered. He allowed his leadened eyelids to close of their own volition, only too willing to drift back into the dream's peaceful comfort. It had been a long time since he . . .

The annoying buzz persisted.

He groaned-grunted and slowly dragged a hand over his face in an ineffectual effort to wipe away the sleep. He forced his eyes open again. The unfamiliar surroundings remained. He blinked, once, twice, three times before the disorientation passed to be replaced by the realization that he lay on his back atop a bunk within one of the Retrieve domes.

The buzz rang in his ears.

Lifting his left hand, Kendler groped along the wall behind his head like a drunken five-legged spider until he located the intercom. "Kendler here."

"Sorry to wake you, Nils." Val Tarkio's voice replaced the nagging buzz. "Just got confirmation from Beamin at Base One. You're to jump up in ninety minutes our time."

"Uh-hmmm." *Jump up*—it took a second or two for the biologist's meaning to sink through the sleep-cotton still muffling his brain. He had ninety minutes before he was transported back to *real* time, or base time as the Retrieve project dubbed the temporal coordinates for Base One.

"You sound like you're at the bottom of a well." Val sounded too cheerful for this hour of the morning. "Haul yourself out of it and get a move on. There's a shower unit attached to your room."

Kendler sat up, head throbbing like the interior of a bass drum. He stifled another groan, wishing he had not celebrated with the field team last night, or at least had used moderation. His gaze drifted around the circular room. Across from the bunk, he found a door. Stenciled in white above it on the flat gray wall was PERSONAL HYGIENE UNIT. "Got it, Val."

"Remember the water's rationed," the woman warned. "When you're through, meet me in the control room."

"Right, give me half an hour or so." Kendler smiled, recalling his first bout with the Retrieve shower. He had just worked up a thick lather that covered ninety percent of his body when the water played out. Panburn had sacrificed his shower allotment that night so the psiotic could rinse away the coat of suds.

"Good. I'll break out something that should resemble breakfast," the camp director replied.

"Go light. The mere mention of food has my stomach doing flip-flops."

"I warned you to beware of Rani's Prehistoric Jungle Joy Juice." Val Tarkio's amused chuckle died in mid-chuck when he switched off the intercom.

Kendler swung his legs over the edge of the bunk.

Or he tried to do so. The action took longer than he expected, and opened a whole new world of pain for him. Every muscle in his body throbbed in agonizing protest while he struggled to overcome inertia. Tautly drawn knots stiffly tied his calves and thighs. He groaned. It did nothing to soothe the series of kinks that ran down his spine from neck to coccyx.

You're getting too old to run a cross-country marathon with a dinosaur, he chided himself. It did not help either. His body still ached.

He attempted to push from the bunk. White fire lanced through his right arm. A string of jumbled profanities tore from his lips. He glanced down at his elbow, expecting to see flames licking at his flesh. Deep purple, fringed with angry red, the bruised joint appeared swollen to twice its normal size. He had momentarily forgotten about his brief encounter with Val's Cretaceous mammal yesterday. From the elbow's persistant pulsing, he knew he would not be able to forget it again for another day or five.

Whoever had first called an elbow a "funny bone" had a decidedly sadistic sense of humor. He winced while he gingerly tested the injury with a fingertip. *You're in one hell of a shape for a man who is about to return to his world as a conquering hero.*

By sheer stubbornness rather than stoic moral fiber, Kendler managed to stand and hobble into a shower that was not designed to accommodate his two-meter height. Feeling like an accordion that had seen better days, he skunched over and depressed the nozzle control. A warm torrent of water blasted from the shower head. Painfully, he turned within the stream, rinsing himself, then switched off the water.

From a niche built into the wall, he lifted a bottle of antiseptic soap and squirted a green puddle onto his chest. Limited to the use of one arm, he could manage no better. Sudsing a mound of lather there, he worked up, then down.

Kendler smiled. The soapy massage brought relief to his tight muscles, allowing his mind to wander back to the dream Val Tarkio had so rudely interrupted. His smile widened.

For others, such a dream would have been disturbing—the dead imposing themselves into the minds of the living. For Kendler, the dream of his father, mother, and sister sunbathing on Rochelle's Point, as they had done so often that summer before Kate Dunbar conned an eighteen-year-old boy into joining the Psi Corps, sent a glowing warmth through his pain-throbbing body.

The dreams were like a reunion. For an all too brief time, his family lived again. His father's deep, rich voice resounded while they discussed the possible bright futures open for his only son. He saw his mother's understanding smile and felt her comforting touch. He playfully parried his twin sister's verbal jibes.

After twelve years, his conscious memory had faded his family's images to featureless, ghostly quaverings he could no longer bring into focus. But in the dreams, they lived again. He could once more hold the love and warmth they had shared. The dreams were the homecoming he would never have. The dreams were all that was left to him—the Kavinites had seen to that.

Kendler clamped his eyes closed to hold back welling tears that were not born in the stinging soap covering his face. *Twelve years is supposed to make it easier.*

He slapped his good palm against the nozzle. A warm jet streamed from the shower head to rinse away the thick suds. *Twelve years doesn't change anything. A hundred years hasn't changed the Kavinites.*

Trying to divert the bitterness that seeped up from deep within him, Kendler recalled the Cretaceous forest outside the dome, its awesome magnificence. A maturing womb, preparing to conceive a wondrous child, Val had described it.

A child that will butcher its mother. The Holocaust of 2123 pushed into his mind, the Global Wars that had destroyed a planet and banished man from Earth until the conception of the Retrieve Program.

After the Holocaust, the remnants of humankind cloistered in the L-5, Lunar, and Martian colonies moved beyond the limits of the solar system, inhabiting the star worlds they discovered. While Man encountered an exotic variety of life forms, plant, animal, and mineral, there were no intelligent beings with which to share the galaxy's wonders. Despite the years of speculation, no alien, friendly or hostile, greeted Man.

Kendler frowned. Frustration, fear, cosmic loneliness— perhaps that was what divided mankind, separated it into two camps, the imperial Kavinites, who sought to establish a rigid central authority to govern human development, and the Lofgrinists, who maintained that planetary independence offered the diversity Man needed for continued existence. Kendler knew the histories, the scholarly expertise that attempted to define the great chasm that divided man into two factions. He did not know the answers; frustration, fear, and cosmic loneliness seemed as viable as the opinions of the experts.

Whatever the cause, the end result was the same—war. For a hundred years, the Kavinites and Lofgrinists did their utmost to blow one another from the galaxy. They almost succeeded. Humankind was wiped from the face of two hundred planets, Kendler pondered while he toweled himself dry, then stepped from the shower cubicle. When the Peace Accord of 2450 was finally signed, only fifty known colonized worlds remained and only ten of them retained any semblance of the civilization that had existed before the Century Conflagration. On the majority of the eighty worlds now making up the Kavinite Empire and the Lofgrin Alliance man was still in the Stone Age.

There were other colonized worlds, the ancient records gave them names, but they were lost, forgotten seeds planted among the stars and left untended. They sat waiting to be rediscovered, brought back into mankind's fold.

Or perhaps they have the common sense to keep their mouths shut and pray they aren't found again. Kendler slipped into a fresh pair of coveralls.

After a hundred years of official peace, the Kavinite Empire and the LofAl planets still battled. To be sure, it was now a political cold war, with each faction vying to sway newly colonized worlds and rediscovered planets into their camp. Though at times the political maneuvering grew hot.

Such was the case with Seker, a lost world that had found itself rediscovered by the Kavinites and Lofgrinists seventeen years ago. After being coaxed, cajoled, courted, and threatened by the two factions, Seker's inhabitants faced the decision of committing themselves to one of the political camps. Noe Kendler, who then headed Seker's Supreme Ministry, openly supported LofAl membership.

"The Lofgrin Alliance is a loose organization of independent worlds huddled together for mutual protection," Nils recalled his father explaining. "It is the lesser of two evils."

Twelve years ago, while Kate Dunbar wined and dined fifty prospective candidates to woo them into her Psi Corps, the Kendler home on Rochelle's Point exploded in what was later termed a "freak accident." The methane storage tank of the house's waste-conversion unit apparently developed an undetected leak. A spark from a faulty relay on the unit's pump ignited the escaping gas. The resulting explosion leveled the home. Its three occupants, Noe, Gwin, and their daughter Calyn, died.

Sabotage was suspected. But no hard evidence was uncovered to link the Kavinites with the waste unit's malfunction. The official "freak accident" conclusion to the investigation into the explosion came six months after the Kendler family died. The citizens of Seker accepted the pronouncement.

All except the sole survivor of the Kendler family—Nils Kendler.

The waste-conversion system had been Nils's responsibility. No methane had been leaking from the storage tank. He knew that better than all the investigators who had plodded through the ruins of the Kendler home. The morning of the explosion, he had run his weekly safety check on the unit. There had been no leakage; there had been no faulty relay.

After the "accident," Kendler contacted a Psi Corps representative stationed on Seker. A month later he found himself on Lanatia, administrative world to the LofAl planets. Four years later, four years of rigorous training, he received his field agent status. A year after the accident ruling, Seker entered the Lofgrin Alliance.

"Nils?" Val's voice came over the intercom. "Nils, are you still there?"

"Still here, Val," Kendler answered.

"I was beginning to think you'd drowned," she replied. "You have forty-five minutes until jump-up. I need ten of those to establish the temporal interface."

Forty-five minutes? Kendler felt a flush of chagrin. He had not slipped away like that in years. Yesterday had gotten to him more than he realized. His mental defenses were down, and the past welled up. It made no sense to dwell on Seker. Nothing he could do would change the past. Not even Retrieve could bring back what had been taken from him—what was past was past.

"Nils?"

"On my way to the control room," Kendler answered.

His legs and back painfully throbbing their protest, he ducked into a corridor leading to the camp's other domes. Following stenciled arrows on the walls, he meandered through the compact maze, eventually entering the control room. Val Tarkio sat in the center of a U-shaped universal console surrounded on three sides by banked panels of switches, buttons, meters, and monitors. Her eyes were glued to two screens filled with the images of his captured Cretaceous monarchs.

"Morning," Kendler called to the biologist. "Where's everyone else?"

"Morning?" Val glanced up, flashing him a pleasant smile. "It's two in the afternoon. The rest of the team have been in the forest for hours."

"Two in the afternoon?" Kendler stared at her in disbelief.

"You had a rough time of it yesterday . . . then topped it off with a considerable portion of Rani's home brew. We decided to let you sleep." Val motioned with a tilt of her head to a desk and chair across the room. "It's not much, but if your stomach can handle it . . ."

"Thanks for the use of a bunk and the extra sack time." Kendler eyed a plate and mug atop the desk. What appeared to be scrambled eggs and two protein wafers filled the plate. Steam rose from the mug. He took a deep breath; a rich aroma filled his nostrils. "Does that mug hold what I think it does?"

"Coffee, real coffee, one of the few luxuries Base One allows us. The rest is synthetic. Cheaper to jump down in dehydrated bulk." Val's gaze returned to the monitors. "No problem about last night. After your jungle romp, you needed a good night's sleep. Besides, I'm not going to jump up anyone still reeling under the effects of Rani's brew. Base One frowns on field teams' setting up distilleries."

Kendler smiled and looked back to the breakfast. On second glance, it appeared much more palatable. He hobbled across the room and carefully seated himself.

"You look like you're in a bad way." Val stared at him with concern.

"I wasn't in shape for a game of tag with your forest friends." Kendler took a tentative sip from the steaming mug and sighed. The coffee was tongue-scalding hot and strong, but good.

"Sure you didn't injure something other than the elbow?" Val asked. "Where do you hurt?"

"I hurt all over more than anyplace else." Kendler shrugged his shoulders. He winced as the kinks in his back tied themselves in double crochets.

The field base director shook her head. "Might have Base

40

One check you out, just in case. They've got a physician on staff."

"Will do that." Kendler shoveled a forkful of egg substitute into his mouth. Synthetic or not, it tasted like scrambled eggs; his stomach appreciated that.

Another few forkfuls and he cleaned the eggs from the plate. He lifted one of the protein wafers. No way of disguising the bland taste, but they washed down easily with the rich coffee. He settled back in the chair with a pleased sigh.

"There's more coffee, if you'd like some." Val pointed to a thermal container on a shelf hung on the wall behind her.

Trying to ignore the soreness of his calves and thighs, Kendler pushed from the desk and walked across the room to refill his mug. He took a sip, then glanced at the monitors the biologist studied so intently. While the small color screens lacked the impact of meeting the carnivores face to face, his *rex* and her suitor still appeared impressive.

"They really are monarchs, aren't they?" Kendler mused aloud. "Wonder how they'll accept being on display?"

"Feeling guilty about your part in their capture?" Val's eyes rolled to him.

"A bit," he said. The giant lizards were monstrously regal creatures. He had experienced the power contained in those gargantuan bodies, a primordial magnificence that defied description. It had to be lived as only a psiotic such as he could before it could be truly understood. To cage that magnificence seemed a sacrilege.

"Forget the guilt," Val said. "If it weren't for you, these two would be just two more extinct dinosaurs. But this king and queen will have a new era, a new world over which to reign."

Kendler looked at her, puzzled. Val smiled. "I haven't time to explain, but Beamin will. I'm sure he'll give you the ten-standard tour of Base One before he lets you off-planet. Right now, it's time to complete the temporal interface. If you don't intend to take that coffee with you, better drink it."

In tonsil-scalding gulps, Kendler did just that, sorry there was not enough time to savor it slowly. Under Val's direction, he climbed atop a circular platform in front of the biologist's desk, positioning himself at its center.

A buzzer sounded and a red light flashed on a panel before the woman.

"That's Beamin's warning signal." Val's hands busied themselves with a series of switches. "Two minutes before jump-up."

41

Val's fingers darted over the control panels. "This should take slightly longer than your jump-down ... about five minutes relative time. It will seem like an eternity to you. Counting the seconds makes it easier, keeps the mind occupied."

She depressed a blue panel. A glass cylinder descended from the dome's ceiling to surround Kendler. "Sixty seconds to jump." Her voice came from a speaker inset in the cylinder's wall. "Give our regards to the Base One crew."

"Will do." Kendler smiled weakly, telling himself he was not worried about the jump-up. It did not help. In the next five minutes he would travel sixty-five million years, back into his own time. "And say my farewells to the rest of the team."

Val interrupted the countdown at thirty seconds. "Nils, thank you."

He tilted his head to her. It was the best bow he could manage within the cylinder. The attempted gallant gesture was lost on the biologist. Val did not see him; her eyes and hands were on the console. When she ended the countdown, he saw her flip open a switch cover and depress a red panel.

Val Tarkio and the Retrieve dome vanished.

SIX

There were no physical tremors to indicate his jump, no nausea, no dizziness, no splitting headache or throbbing temples. Yet Kendler's breathing quickened and his heart echoed within his chest like a resounding gong pounded by three thousand out-of-beat hammers.

Colors rushed at him. He stood at the heart of a kaleidoscopic maelstrom that swirled and churned about him. He could only chance a guess at what each color represented—the rise and fall of a sea—a volcanic eruption—the birth of Man. Each flashed in a fraction of a second of his relative time, mere color bursts, physical events through which he moved far too fast to comprehend. An ice age could be lost in the blink of an eye.

Faster, the hues whirled about him like an engulfing color wheel. The shorter waves of the spectrum went first, the blues, the greens, blending into reds and yellows. Rather than exploding in a blinding white, the rushing swirl faded to a flat gray, featureless, unprepossessing.

One and two and three and four and five and six and . . . Kendler took Val's advice and counted the seconds to combat the sense of loss that suffused him. Earth's history passed before his eyes as no more than a gray wall, a nothingness.

In the future, when Retrieve fully established itself, perhaps jumpers could afford a more leisurely journey through time's corridors. Now expedience was the key. He was not a sightseer, but a necessary human tool that had been borrowed from the Psi Corps and was now being returned to Kate Dunbar as quickly as possible. He slipped through Earth's short life without touching it or being touched. Resigned, he released an overly held breath and closed his eyes.

One hundred ninety-five and one hundred ninety-six and . . .

A sledgehammer slammed into his gut and buried itself there. He groaned, doubling over. His eyes flew wide. An invisible hand slapped its open palm against his forehead. He wrenched upright. Another moan twisted from his lips.

The flat gray no longer surrounded him. Color erupted. Hues contorted and twisted, bent from their churning swirls by some unseen force.

It caught him. Like a man buffeted by tornadic winds, he felt it tear at him, trying to jerk him from his feet. His arms flailed the air in a desperate attempt to maintain equilibrium. It hammered at him from all directions simultaneously. He reeled under the ceaseless blows, thrown from one side to the other like a marionette in the hands of a madman.

If I'm thrown from the timestream?

Ignorant! Kendler was painfully aware of his total ignorance of the mechanics of time travel. No one had briefed him in more than the basics—step on the grid—we push this button—minutes later, you arrive.

Another tornado descended, plowing into the small of his back. He staggered to keep his feet beneath him, fighting not to fall . . . to fall and be ripped into the grotesquely twisting colors . . . to be thrown into an unknown instant of time . . . lost . . . alone?

The sledgehammer returned, and another.

Kendler's lips writhed. An endless scream tore from chest and throat. His spine buckled.

His eyes saw.

The force whipped him back and forth. He struggled against its overwhelming power, staggering. And . . .

. . . he saw.

He *saw!*

The hurricane of sensations gave way to reality. His eyes perceived the truth. He stood, unmoved, his body standing straight and steady.

The winds, the invisible hands, continued to pound, slamming and tearing at him—into his mind. The force bombarded his brain, jumbling his sensory perception, warping the fabric of reality.

The colors around him slowed. Yellows and reds flowed into blues. The striated spectrum returned, spinning madly.

He felt. *Psi!*

Strong, stronger than any mental emanations he had ever encountered . . . yet? He could not define the difference he sensed. He tried to open himself, to merge with the source. Nothing. It evaded him.

The invisible hand slipped about him, gently closing. The skull-splitting pain ceased abruptly, replaced by a calming cloud of tranquillity. The buffeting winds dissipated.

The blazing colors about him lost their violent churnings and slowed to elongated, continuous bands . . . slowed . . . slowed . . . slowed. The unseen fingers enwrapping him tightened to a firm but gentle fist, as though it tensed to pluck him from the timestream. Again Kendler opened his mind to the force.

Closer.

Where? Who?

The colors took shape. The psi force, if it was that, mounted. Kendler's mind spun while the disorienting emanations bombarded him in an unyielding torrent. An involuntary moan crept from his lips. Unconsciousness flowed up into his awareness, luring him toward darkness. He fought to maintain consciousness. He focused on the images that formed around him.

He glimpsed it—in mind or in eye? He could not be certain. For an instant, it was there, the desiccative smell of sand and flint invading his nostrils. The invisible fingers enclosing him trembled. The grasp slipped. The psi torrent weakened.

The hand released him. Kendler's whole being quaked. The presence fled him. The colors returned, swirling and spinning in a maelstrom's fury that blended into the gray nothingness of time's limbo.

The scene Kendler glimpsed remained etched in his mind. Clouds, thin and wispy, scurried across a blue sky—the sun, fiery as a devil's anvil, reigned over a desert barren of all but sand and rock. Dominating all, a pyramid, a sleek, four-sided structure that towered toward the sky, a titan spearhead meant for the heart of the sun.

SEVEN

Kendler could not shake the overwhelming sequence of events. They replayed over and over in his mind like a loop of spetape. Around him, the featureless gray speckled with blossoms of color, then streaks, then broad, slowly revolving bands. Abruptly the colors froze.

Once again, he stood within a glass cylinder. Beyond the transparent cage stood a room similar to Val Tarkio's control dome, only five times as large. Kendler's gaze ran over the scene, locating a blue-coveralled woman seated at the control console. Jon Beamin, Base One director, stood at the blonde's side. He glanced up from console to jump grid. A relieved expression spread across the man's face, erasing the worry lines that had furrowed his brow. He stepped across the room when the glass cylinder slid upward.

"Are you all right?" Beamin held out a hand to help Kendler from the grid.

"All in one piece." Kendler glanced at his arms and legs to reassure himself. "For a while I wasn't so sure I'd be able to say that."

"Jan picked up some type of power fluctuation on the monitors," Beamin said. "What happened?"

"Don't you know?" Kendler shot the man a you're-the-expert-not-me look.

Beamin shrugged his shoulders sheepishly. "Never seen anything like it. Every jump we've ever made has been a direct linear movement. With you, it was . . . I don't know . . . for a moment, for a full ten seconds, we lost you. It was as though you had stepped from the timestream. Of course that can't . . ."

Kendler felt weak, as the director's meaning penetrated his daze. His body's aches returned. His stomach did a queasy flip-flop. "I need to sit down a moment."

"The infirmary." Beamin pointed to a door on their left. "I'd like our physician to examine you . . . just in case."

Kendler offered no objection. Nor did he ask in case of what. Instead, he followed the Base One director into the infirmary. A woman with short-cropped red hair sat bent over a microscope. She looked up when they entered.

"Doc, I've got a patient for you." The woman slipped from her stool and walked to them while Beamin gave a thumbnail summary of the jump-up.

"No problem. Shouldn't take more than ten minutes," the physician said, then turned to Kendler. "Strip and hop on the examination table."

Kendler obliged and stretched out on his back atop the med unit, doing his best to ignore the cold surface that sent rippling gooseflesh over his body.

"Myra Rey," the doctor introduced herself while she positioned a scanner over his chest. "What did you experience during jump-up?"

"An invisible giant tried to play handball with me in the desert." Kendler winced when a stethoscopic probe descended from the scanner and pressed an icy stainless-steel face against his bare flesh. He then recounted everything that had occurred.

"It might be equipment failure," Beamin added when Kendler concluded, sounding unsure of the explanation. "Or a fluctuation in the energy cells."

"I don't think so." Kendler shook his head. "Mechanical malfunction doesn't explain the presence I sensed."

Beamin hesitated a moment, as though considering the psiotic's remark. "Perhaps, but you can't be certain it was psi emanations. The control monitors indicated you slipped from the timestream, warped to . . . somewhere. This fluctuation, or warp, could have affected you mentally, in any of numerous ways. You indicated you've never encountered psi forces as intense as the ones you experienced. Nor could you locate their source."

"I don't know." Kendler agreed with Beamin's agruments. The strength and lack of definition of what he had felt baffled him. There had been no singular source to the emanations; he had been bombarded from all sides. The invisible hand had closed around him, physical as well as mental. Yet Beamin's interpretation of the events left him unconvinced. "I just don't know."

"Perhaps both of you would be interested to hear that Mr. Kendler has nothing physiologically wrong with him," Dr. Rey interrupted. She handed Kendler the med unit's readout and motioned for him to rise. "That is, other than an over-abundance of lactic acid in his muscles and a nasty-looking but relatively minor injury to his right elbow."

While Kendler dressed, the physician opened a drawer and extracted a wide loop of transparent plastic. She slipped the loop over his head, then slung his right arm through it.

"Give the arm a couple of weeks' rest. Keep it in the sling for at least that long," she said. "There's some soft-tissue damage, but nothing that won't heal itself if you rest it."

Kendler nodded. The sling relieved the elbow's pulsing.

"I can't think of much you'll need the arm for during your flight back to Lanatia," the physician said.

"Lanatia flight?" Kendler looked at Beamin.

"It skipped my mind with the jump-up fluctuation," the Base One director said. "There's a freighter in orbit, waiting to return you to Lanatia. Kate Dunbar's orders. You're scheduled to shuttle up in three hours."

"Kate say anything else?" Kendler felt uneasy. His return cruiser was not due for four days. If Kate was returning him via freighter, it meant something new was breaking that involved him.

Beamin shook his head. "The communiqué simply said you were to return on the freighter *Gai Lung*."

Kendler did not expect anything else. That there was nothing only reinforced the disquieting feeling that nagged at him.

"I don't want to cut short your visit," Dr. Rey said, "but I do have tissue samples to classify and store in the deep freeze."

After apologizing for interrupting her work, Beamin motioned Kendler toward the infirmary's exit. Kendler asked, "Deep freeze?"

"Part of our reclamation of Earth's past. The tissue samples will be used to clone extinct life forms," Beamin said. "Under normal circumstances, cloning is more efficient. In the case of *Tyrannosaurus*, your services were needed, shall I say, for expediency's sake."

"Flash. Show." Beamin visibly winced at Kendler's comment.

"Perhaps," the Base One director acquiesced. "We need something big to titillate the public and win their approval for Retrieve. And we need it fast. As I mentioned, under normal conditions specimens are cloned and brought to maturity here at Base One. The process consumes more time, but the expenses are minimal compared to the energy expended in jumping up fully matured specimens."

"What about my specimens?" Kendler asked. "When will they be jumped up?"

Beamin glanced at a wall chronometer when they reentered the control room. He turned to the girl seated behind the console. "Everything on schedule for the Cretaceous jump-up?"

"The cargo will arrive in Section 10 in thirty minutes," the blonde replied.

"Care to see the arrival?" Beamin looked at Kendler. "In fact, there's ample time to give you a tour of the base before your shuttle departs. That is, if you're interested?"

Kendler replied with a nod and an appropriately enthusiastic smile. While his legs did not feel up to a guided tour, it would be better than spending three hours on his backside waiting for the shuttle.

"Good." Beamin beamed like a new father preparing to display a series of holographs of his first child. "We'll see Mother first. It's on the way to Section 10."

Kendler did not bother to ask what Mother was, knowing he would receive a full explanation soon enough. Instead, he followed Beamin down a corridor that led from the opposite end of the control room. They passed a series of administrative offices, then halted before an immense, unmarked, green-painted steeldoor.

"This was our original shuttle berth." The director placed his right thumb on a mini-vidcom screen beside the door. The screen came alive with a soft green glow as the thumb-lock identified his thumbprint. A previously unnoticed smaller door at the center of the larger slid open with a slight pneumatic wheeze. Beamin motioned Kendler inside.

The psiotic stopped when he stepped within the room beyond the steel door, awed by the sights that met his eyes. Mother proved to be more than a vacant shuttle berth. He glanced at the director. The man's beaming expression grew when he noticed his guest's unspoken reaction.

"Welcome to Earth's womb." Beamin was unable to conceal the pride in his voice.

The wombs of Earth would have been more accurate, Kendler decided as he once again surveyed the converted shuttle berth. Mother was just that, the wombs of new Earth. Lining the fifty-meter-long walls, filling them from floor to a twenty-meter-high ceiling, was a montage of equipment. Kendler was unfamiliar with the majority of the devices.

Beamin's arm swept over the scene. "These are the various incubators, embryonic units, and accelerated growth modules. At the moment, Mother is recreating the mid-Ordovician Period."

Kendler's gaze roved over the kilometers of stainless steel, glass, and plastic that interlocked in a complex maze to form Mother's belly. Twenty Retrieve members moved up and down the rows of equipment, monitoring the units Beamin identified. While the director walked with him down one line of Mother's mechanical wombs, Kendler read the neatly typed labels on each unit: *Hudsonaster narrawayi*, *Echinosphaerites aurantium*, *Malocystites emmonsi*, *Streptelasma rusticum*, and *Hesperorthis tricenaria*. All the species were totally unknown to him, extinct creatures from Earth's forgotten past. Here they were recalled to life, growing to maturity in closely guarded environments.

"The field teams gather samples, then jump them to Base One. In the case of the mid-Ordovician and earlier times, fertilized eggs and occasionally living specimens are transported because of their relative small size," Beamin explained. "However, for most time periods, the field teams take tissue and ovum samples. Within ten years, Mother, or other similar units, will be filled with clones of the larger life forms that once ruled this planet."

As they walked farther into the expanse of Mother's interior, Kendler glimmered a bit of what Val Tarkio had meant when she said his two monarchs would give new life to an extinct species. The realization assuaged some of the guilt he felt about the circus existence the carnosaurs would live once off-planet.

"Our basic objective is to reclaim Earth, to transform its

barren surface into a global park, each section representing a period of Earth's past," Beamin said.

Kendler glanced at the man, uncertain whether he heard him correctly. "An ambitious project."

"But one that can be accomplished, with public support." There was no trace of doubt in Beamin's voice.

They reached Mother's far wall. The director pressed his thumb to another lock. A door slid open. Heat, thick with souplike humidity, blasted Kendler's face when he stepped into the next compartment. The room he entered equaled Mother in size. However, the ceiling and walls were glass. Condensing moisture clouded the transparent panels and ran down the surfaces in glistening rivulets. Row upon row of tables neatly filled with flower pots lined the room.

"Our nursery," Beamin said from beside the psiotic. "Field teams supply the seeds and spores. We germinate them here, then transplant when the individual plant is established and hearty enough to survive on its own."

Kendler eyed the various rows of pots. The Base One hothouse held the oppressive heat and humidity of the Cretaceous forest.

"These are *Eospermatopteris* and *Protolepidodendron,* a fern and a primitive scale tree." Beamin pointed to the pots. "They will eventually be part of our Devonian forest."

The Earth reclaimed and transformed into a gigantic park. The immensity of the Retrieve Program slowly sank into Kendler's brain. Insane, impossible, mind-boggling; he found himself unable to comprehend the task to which the project was committed. He turned to the Base One director and shook his head dubiously.

Beamin smiled. "This way and I'll show you a sample of what we're doing."

Walking to the end of the hothouse, they exited the nursery. Kendler found himself standing outside the Base One complex. Earth, dead Earth, stretched as far as he could see, barren and lifeless. Overhead, he detected the shimmer of a force shield. Beyond the artificial barrier spread a sickly pale-blue sky.

"The shield is necessary. There's still an atmosphere, but it's too thin to support human life." Beamin led Kendler to a floater disc. The man took the controls when they stepped onto the metal platform. "One day, if Retrieve survives the politicians, the force field will come down and Man will breathe Earth's air once again."

The director depressed a single white button set atop the floater's guidelev. The platform vibrated roughly when its small motor caught, then settled to a smooth hum. Beamin eased the control stick back. The disc drifted upward to a height of ten meters and hovered there.

Kendler's hands tightened around the floater's support railing. He held no love for this type of open-air vehicle. The enclosed security of a lazily drifting airship or a darting heliocraft conformed to his idea of flying. Despite a floater's low altitude limitations, he remained unconvinced that standing atop a less-than-stable-feeling piece of metal was how Man was ever meant to fly.

"Section 10 is five kilometers east of the complex." Beamin pointed the direction with his free hand. "We'll drop in on the arrival of your Cretaceous friends, then take a quick fly over our other projects."

Kendler nodded, and the director edged the floater forward. The psiotic's hand squeezed around the metal railing as though he intended to wring it in his grasp. The rush of wind through his hair only increased Kendler's nervousness. He stared down, studying the terrain below in an attempt to take his mind from his distrust of the vehicle.

Other than a series of low-rising hills and a track-worn carrier route, the scenery they flew above offered little more than the desolation Kendler had first glimpsed when he stepped from the nursery. This was not the Earth that belonged to Val Tarkio and the other Retrieve field teams. This was the Earth his ancestors left for their children, a monument to man's intolerance for man. This was a dead planet, totally barren of plant or animal life, with an atmosphere that could no longer sustain the beings it had given birth to.

Beamin tapped his shoulder and pointed ahead. Kendler's gaze followed the man's finger. A small force shield shimmered the air within the larger field that protected all the surface area of Base One. Within it stood a Cretaceous forest.

"Section 10," Beamin announced. "At least its beginnings. At the moment, it's only two kilometers in diameter, but ten years from now . . ."

"How?" Kendler asked. "From what I saw in Mother and the nursery, I understood you were concentrating on earlier periods."

"We are." The Base One director slowed the floater until it hung in the air outside the force field. "When the decision was made to capture a *rex*, we also decided to jump up some of the king's habitat as well. The Cretaceous forest will be fully established years ahead of our timetable. However, dinosaurs won't walk through it for at least ten years. In the meanwhile, the forest will serve to house the two specimens you captured until they are shipped off-planet."

Inside the force field, a land carrier trundled before them, hauling a flatbed piled with what appeared to be raw flesh. It halted beside a jump grid. The flatbed tilted to one side and dumped the meat onto the ground.

"*Triceratops* made from recombinant DNA," Beamin explained while he glanced at his watch. "Your friends should be arriving any moment."

A blue glimmer rose around the jump grid as a force field came to life. The carrier turned and made a hasty retreat. One moment, the grid stood empty; the next instant, two roaring Cretaceous lovers poised atop it.

"My God!" Beamin's eyes widened and his jaw dropped several centimeters. "I didn't realize . . . they're magnificent!"

Kendler smiled to himself. Rani would be delighted when he learned of the director's reaction. Kendler admitted his own pride and pleasure in the man's awe.

Beamin turned to Kendler and shook his head with amazement. The psiotic grinned, watching the man's gaze return to the gigantic lizards. Beamin mumbled something that was lost on Kendler, who found himself engrossed in studying the carnosaurs.

The force field enclosing the grid flickered and died. The two carnivores cautiously stepped from the platform and waddled-walked toward the small mountain of raw meat. Their tongues darted into the air, sniffing. Their monstrous heads swiveled on their disproportionately slim necks to survey their new surroundings. Apparently assured they were in no danger, they dropped their blunt snouts to the offered fare. The Cretaceous monarchs dined on a world that had not felt their thundering strides for sixty-five million years.

Eventually Beamin dragged his attention from the tyrant king and queen. His palm pressed a blue panel attached to the support railing. A force shield crackled alive, canopying the floater. The disc rotated ninety degrees, then shot forward with a sudden jerk.

Kendler's hands once more clenched the rail. No longer did the wind rush through his hair. The field successfully eliminated that. Except for the floater's steady, vibrating hum, and the ground rushing beneath the craft in an indistinguishable brown-gray blur, he felt no sense of motion. Kendler breathed easier.

"Sorry about the speed," Beamin said. "We've quite a distance to cover until we reach our next project."

Fifteen minutes later, the floater skimmed over its destination. "The Precambrian sea," Beamin said as he eased the floater downward to hover above the breaking whitecaps. "Earth's true womb. Here every Terran life form had its beginnings."

Kendler listened, unable to follow the exotic names and time periods Beamin began to reel off in nonstop fashion. He did catch something about force shields being used to section the seas, thus maintaining each period's ecosystem.

"One of the spinoffs in creating the ecological balance in each section was a treasure in metals," the Base One director said. "The ocean's floor is a gold mine, literally. When our ancestors decided to turn their homeworld to ashes, they hadn't developed the technology necessary for mining the oceans. We, however, have that means in our hands. One of the reasons Retrieve has managed to stay alive for the past ten years."

Beamin hastened on, the floater barely missing the wind-whipped waves. The Cambrian, Ordovician, and Silurian seas passed beneath while the disc sailed toward a rocky beach.

"The true beginning of terrestrial life." Beamin waved an arm to the ground below. "Small plants with bractlike leaves that are related to ground pines. From these meager seeds, forests will grow."

Forests replanted by man. Kendler thought of the flower pots filling the nursery. The immensity of the Retrieve undertaking remained, but he now sensed that despite balking politicians, Beamin and men like him would eventually reclaim a world their ancestors had destroyed in angry stupidity.

"If we had time, I'd show you Earth's first air-breathing animals," the Base One director said. "Scorpions and millipeds are living amid that algae and fungi."

"Impressive," Kendler said, making no attempt to disguise his awe. "You've already done so much."

"It's a beginning." Beamin eased back on the guidelev,

lifting the floater back to a height of ten meters. "Just a beginning."

"A global zoo," Kendler said with a touch of cynicism.

"Certainly," Beamin replied. "The recreational value of a reclaimed Earth can't be overlooked. Though I prefer to think of it as a living museum. We hope it will spark a tourist trade that will make Retrieve financially independent. As well as providing a tourist park, we'll also furnish easily accessible material for scientific studies."

Beamin neatly maneuvered the floater in a 180-degree turn. He pushed the control stick forward to return them to the Base One complex.

"What about Man's development?" Kendler asked. "How do you intend to handle that?"

"Reconstruction of various cities and rural environments from the stages of Man's development," Beamin said. "For the greatest accuracy, we could separate each section by force fields as we've done with the ocean, then populate them with people jumped up from each period, or their clones. However, that doesn't seem practical. Men would readily grasp the fact they were being held captive."

Kendler got the distinct feeling that if some method existed to keep captives ignorant of their bars, Beamin would be willing to use time-hijacked men to inhabit the reconstructed civilizations.

"Of course, we could always use robots," the man continued. "However, I suspect once we've established everything, we'll have volunteers from all the LofAl planets willing to populate our cities and farms."

Kendler grinned, considering Beamin's comment as lifeless earth replaced water under the floater. He did not doubt the prediction would prove correct. In fact, he suspected volunteers would be willing to pay Retrieve for the opportunity to live in the reconstructed societies. The lure of something new and exotic was undeniable.

The floater slowed when the Retrieve complex came into sight. Beamin gently brought the disc to the ground beside the door to the nursery.

"What do you know about pyramids?" Kendler asked while the director switched off the floater.

"Your jump still troubling you?"

"Can't get the image of that pyramid sitting in the middle of the desert out of my mind," Kendler answered. "Can you hazard a guess at its time period?"

Beamin shook his head as they reentered the complex. "Sorry, I'm not much help in that area. My specialty is Earth prior to the advent of Man. I know several civilizations made architectural use of the pyramid. Beyond that, I'm not much use. I could check and see if anyone on my staff can help, if you'd like."

"No, I don't believe that's necessary. It's probably just me. The whole thing could have been a hallucination, as you said." Kendler did not believe that, but he would rather Kate Dunbar did any checking that had to be done. If there was something to the presence he felt, he did not want to call any further attention to the pyramid until the Psi Corps director received a full report.

Kendler's gaze traveled over the embryonic units and incubators when they entered Mother. Soon the sea would cradle the infant life that grew around him. Despite the fact that Earth would eventually be the galaxy's greatest tourist trap, the Retrieve Program and what they had accomplished touched an indefinable something within him. If one in a thousand of those who eventually walked Earth's surface again shared the feeling, the project would be worth the expenditures needed to make it a reality.

"Thirty minutes before the shuttle lifts off." Beamin's voice broke into the psiotic's thoughts. "Can I interest you in a quick drink . . . a toast to the successful completion of your mission?"

Kendler had started to decline when he noticed the effects of Rani's home brew had worn off. The aches and pains he had suffered earlier were mere dull throbs now. He grinned and nodded to the director. "I believe I'll take you up on that."

His right arm securely cradled in a suspensor field, Kendler endured the gees required for the shuttle to break free of Earth's gravational bonds with no more than a curse or two for the reawakened pain within his body.

From his position behind the craft's pilot, he glanced at the sphere he was leaving behind. Once he had read that one of Man's first space adventurers had described the world he saw from space as a blue marble. The marble's hue had faded during the centuries since the remark had been made. Eventually, if Retrieve received the continued life it sought, the color would deepen again. He tried to ignore the swelling of his chest. But he could not deny the sense of pride he felt for his part in Earth's reclamation.

In a slow turn, the shuttle's nose swung away from Earth.

Before Kendler loomed the freighter that would return him to Lanatia and the offices of Kate Dunbar. The Cretaceous forest and his foot race with *Tyrannosaurus rex* seemed eons from the five-kilometer length of the metal behemoth he approached.

EIGHT

The cradle collars released around the capsule. Kendler flinched and gritted his teeth against the metallic clang that reverberated through the interior. He cursed, feeling like a man lying within a hollow gong. The resounding din eventually faded from his inner ear and he focused his attention on the mini-panel attached to the capsule's curved wall thirty centimeters from the end of his nose.

The control display flashed its digital monitoring of the capsule's life-support system in a variety of amber and green lights. Kendler mumbled another string of expletives. *Control panel!* The misnomer increased his irritation with each blinking second.

The capsule held no controls, only the life-support system, and there was damn little he could do to affect its function. To be sure, the pressure switches beneath the fingertips of his right hand could increase and decrease the temperature, dim or brighten a single interior light, slightly enrich the oxygen content of the air, and, of course, dispose of the contents within the waste tubes attached to him fore and aft. Even these controls existed for their psychological value rather than need. He would be in chemo-sleep for 108 of the next 120 hours.

But actual controls that allowed him to direct the capsule's flight did not exist. For the penultimate leg of his return flight to Lanatia, Nils Kendler found himself strapped flat on his back within the claustrophobic interior of a dead flinger. A fact that had been carefully kept from him until three hours ago.

Dead flinger—the term held new meaning. Normally a flinger was used to transport a small cargo from freighters to a planetary destination when the cargo was considered too unimportant for the freighter to make the jump from tachyon space to normal space. The freighter made its delivery without delaying its flight to its final destination.

A bullet fired from tachyon space into the normal universe, Kendler thought. Should there be a miscalculation in the capsule's trajectory, or should a shuttle not be positioned to intercept the flinger when it entered the Lanatian System, the dead in the flinger would be one Nils Kendler.

"One minute to explusion," an anonymous voice came sharp and tinny from beside his head. "Would you like to hear the countdown?"

"Rather go blind." Kendler twisted to the speaker on his right. "A 'good luck' will be sufficient."

"Good luck," the tinny voice replied. "Thirty seconds and counting."

The speaker went dead with a harsh click. Only the sound of his own breathing floated within the capsule. Kendler cursed again, fully maligning Kate Dunbar's lineage. He also threw in a few well-chosen words for the tinny voice that gave him the thirty-second count. His mind slowly did a countdown of its own in a thirty and twenty-nine and twenty-eight and twenty-seven rhythm.

He tensed in anticipation of the instant he would be shot from the freighter's belly into normal space.

. . . and three and two and one.

The jarring explosion and the crushing gee-force he expected did not come. There was a whoosh, like the rush of a container within a pnuematic tube, and the slight sensation of acceleration when the flinger shot from the freighter. Moments later an uneasy nausea rolled through his stomach. The capsule jumped from the tachyon universe into the reality of normal space.

Kendler lifted his right hand and let his fingers run along the wall, reassuring himself with its solidness. The flinger and its personally precious cargo had made the transition successfully.

A prick, like the bite of an overly large insect, stung Kendler's left forearm. Something hissed, and a coolness invaded the psiotic's body. He glanced down to see a servo-hypodermic pull from his arm. He blinked, eyelids suddenly weighted. The injection drew him into four and a half days of chemo-sleep.

"Kendler . . . Kendler . . ." the voice insisted, dragging him up from the faceless void of oblivion. "Nils Kendler . . . this is Flinger Intercept Shuttle NR-7952. Kendler . . . Kendler . . ."

"Kendler . . . her . . ." His intended words lost themselves in an unintelligible string of garbled syllables. His tongue felt thick and swollen, refusing to conform to his mental commands.

"Kendler, this is Flinger Intercept Shuttle . . ."

"Kendler here." He succeeded in his second attempt to answer, though his voice sounded like a slow-motion caricature of itself.

". . . NR-7952 out of Lanatia . . ."

The voice from the speaker continued uninterrupted by his reply. Kendler tried a third time, remembering to depress the switch beneath his left thumb. "Kendler here."

"Kendler?" A tinny voice equaling the one from the freighter asked as though uncertain it had heard him.

"Kendler here," he repeated, gaining a bit more control over his tongue. He blinked several times in an attempt to push the drugged drowsiness away. "How far out are you?"

"Along your side. We've been trying to raise you for the past twelve hours," the voice answered. "Are you all right?"

Alongside? It took a few seconds for that to penetrate the drug haze blanketing his mind. He had slept the full five days of the flight. "A bit disoriented . . . They overdid it with the chemo-sleep. It'll take a few moments for me to shake this."

Kendler heard a sigh of relief in the voice when it came back on the speaker. "You had us worried. Give us ten minutes and we'll have you out of that coffin."

"Ten minutes," Kendler confirmed and released the switch under his thumb.

Now that the shuttle drifted alongside, ten minutes seemed like an eternity to endure within the cramped confines of the flinger. He took a deep breath. An effluvium of stale air assailed his nostrils.

An involuntary shudder crept up his spine. Apparently the capsule's life-support system was not designed to sustain him beyond the scheduled rendezvous. Had the shuttle not made the intercept . . .

He edged the possibility away. It made no sense to ponder might-have-beens. He heard the clang of lifelines attaching themselves to the flinger's exterior. A slight jar ran through the capsule when the lines tautened to haul him into the shuttle.

Kendler blinked several more times and yawned continuously in an effort to combat the residual effects of the chemosleep drugs still coursing through his veins. The straps across chest and legs inhibited any attempt to stretch. He did manage to lift his arms a few centimeters and flex them.

The flinger shuddered again. A louder clang resounded through the capsule, followed by the voice on the speaker. "Got you nestled in our belly. Soon as we pump some air into the bay, we'll have you out of there."

"Think I would breathe space to get out of this thing." Kendler heard the rush of air outside the capsule.

"Understand your impatience," the voice replied. "But I don't believe whoever is waiting for you planetside would. This intercept flight had Priority Red A stamped all over it. Relax, I've got a man on the way back now."

"I'm relaxed," Kendler answered, not liking the sound of Priority Red A. First the freighter, then the flinger, and now a priority intercept. Kate Dunbar wanted him home as quickly as possible. That spelled anything but a few leisurely days of rest and recreation.

Metal grated against the capsule's hull. The sealing collar released with a "phwack." Simultaneously, the straps binding his chest and legs opened and slid back. Kendler pushed up on his elbows. They felt watery, threatening to collapse beneath his weight. The flinger's hatch opened above his head.

"Easy. You've been out for five days. Your body isn't ready to operate on its own." A young man's face poked into the opening. He manuevered himself so that he straddled the hatch and reached down. "Ian Bishop, co-cap on this flight."

The young man's hands locked under Kendler's armpits and easily hauled him from the flinger's interior. Carefully, with Bishop's assistance, Kendler managed to lower himself to the bay's deck and stand there on legs that felt less than solid. He took one step, then another. Somewhat wobbly, but he retained his balance.

"Soon as you're situated up front, we'll begin the descent." Bishop moved ahead of him and opened the hatch to the shuttle's cabin.

Ducking, Kendler scooted into the cabin to be greeted by the source of the tinny voice that had awakened him—Captain Wanda Hedi.

"Strap in there." Her voice came smooth and soft compared to the crackling piece of tin he had heard in the flinger. She pointed to a contour couch behind the one Bishop settled into. "You'll find some tubes of soup and tea attached to the right arm."

"Anything more solid?" His stomach was very aware of the fact he had not eaten in five days.

"Liquids until we've landed," the flight captain answered. "Those are standard procedures for flinger passengers. You've got to accustom your stomach to digesting food again."

Kendler strapped himself into the couch. The prospect of soup and Lanatian tea was less than appetizing. Bishop and Hedi directed their attention to the shuttle's controls and the descent.

Kendler slipped the tube of soup from the side of the couch. He popped its top with a thumb, then held it for thirty seconds to allow its interior heating mechanism to warm the contents. Placing the tube to his mouth, he squeezed. The warm, bland taste of chicken broth flooded his taste buds. He swallowed.

Immediately, his stomach's rumblings were replaced by nauseous churnings. He stopped the next mouthful in midsqueeze, unsure whether he could keep the bland liquid down.

"There's a barf-spout on your right." Captain Wanda Hedi glanced at him over her shoulder.

Somewhat chagrined, Kendler lifted the funnel-mouthed tube and spit his half-mouthful into its intake. For several uncertain seconds, he held the tube until his stomach stopped its queasy turnings. Slipping the spout back into its niche, he cautiously squeezed another sip of soup and swallowed. His stomach rumbled when it received the fresh liquid, but the nausea had passed. He sipped again.

"Think you'll make it?" Hedi looked at him.

"As long as I take it slow and easy." Kendler smiled sheepishly, embarrassed by his near upheaval.

"You've got the time," the shuttle captain replied. "Twenty minutes before we've got clearance for the descent."

Kendler nodded and went back to nursing the tube of chicken broth. Ten minutes later, he polished off the soup and opened the tube of tea. The delicate Lanatian tea proved to be a perfect complement to the broth. His stomach accepted it without one rumble. Feeling far more satisfied than he had anticipated, he stuffed the second empty food tube into a disposal unit.

Hedi mumbled something to her co-cap. Hands floated over the control panels, fingers dipping and punching. The shuttle moved. The only sense of motion came from the stars that drifted across the heavens before them. A blue orb crept into their field of vision until it blotted out the blackness of space—Lanatia.

That early astronaut's description of Earth filtered through Kendler's thoughts. Surely Lanatia now appeared as Man's homeworld once had. White clouds swirled in fluffy banks across its blue surface. Here and there green and brown hues dappled the nine continents that floated like gargantuan islands on the planet's endless seas.

"Here we go," Hedi announced while she and Bishop worked the craft's controls.

A roar blasted from behind Kendler as the thrusters cut in for a five-second burn. The ship nosed down, falling toward Lanatia.

From day into night, the shuttle slid around the planet on its final orbit. Below, city lights, like smears of iridescent paint on black velvet, cut through the darkness.

Rockets growled again, slowing the descent. Dawn shattered the night; day filled the sky like a holographic display projected at ten times normal speed. Clouds blanketed the planet's surface. Here and there, through rips in the milky covering, Kendler glimpsed dark patches of terrain.

For a brief instant, the shuttle nosed upward as it skipped on the dense atmosphere. Then its nose came down at a forty-five-degree angle. The churning soup below took form, thunderheads that rose like an airborne mountain range.

Hedi banked the craft, its delta wings digging into the air and turning. The shuttle dived into the towering bank.

Lightning flashes, wind, and thunder reverberated within the cabin. Outside rain pelted the ship. Turbulence rocked the metallic bird as it hit air pocket after air pocket.

They shot free of the obscuring clouds. Sunlight bathed the naked earth below. A blue ribbon sliced through the green forest the craft shot over. *The Benfo River,* Kendler identified the major landmark. He scanned the horizon, locating the gleaming white towers of Port Antoan.

"One minute to touchdown," Hedi shouted above the rockets' roar.

The craft shook violently when the landing gear dropped from its belly. A broad gray band opened in the forest. The shuttle's nose dipped once again, gliding toward the landing field.

Abruptly, Hedi pulled back on the controls. The nose eased upward. Rubber screamed, biting into the tarmac. Braking rockets snarled to halt the ship's head-on rush toward a crash barrier at the end of the runway.

A landbound bird once again, the shuttle slowed to a crawl, swinging around to face a line of terminal buildings on the right. A ground crew stood waiting, their arms flailing the air with berthing directions. A tunnel corridor snaked out and attached itself to the shuttle when it stopped. Hedi's and Bishop's fingers danced over the controls one last time. The craft died, a nesting eagle.

"The hatch is back to your left." Hedi waved an arm to the opening portal.

Kendler climbed from his couch. He took a tentative step, then another. His legs felt much steadier after the light meal. Ducking through the hatch, Kendler moved slowly up the tunnel corridor, allowing his body to acclimate itself to the simple act of walking. By the time he entered the terminal, his strides were long and confident.

"Kendler, Nils Kendler?" A man's voice called.

A young man approached wearing the expression of a young puppy begging someone to throw a ball so that he could retrieve it. He stood out like a proverbial sore thumb—administrative assistant junior grade written all over him.

"I'm Van Eavy, Psi Corps, general assistant to Director Dunbar." He smiled an administrative assistant smile.

Kendler nodded, as much to hide his amusement as to acknowledge the introduction. Rumors abounded speculating on Kate Dunbar's habit of selecting her personal staff via interviews conducted on her office couch. While Kendler gave no credence to the gossip, the old woman definitely reveled in her shady reputation. She did her best to enhance the image by surrounding herself with a staff of young, handsome, virile-looking men.

But Kate Dunbar was no one's fool. The old warhorse would never allow anything as obvious as sexual preferences to compromise the smooth functioning of her corps.

Eavy reached into an interior pocket of a stylishly cut jacket and pulled out a leather folder, which he handed to Kendler. Flipping it open, the psiotic scanned the identification papers. All appeared in order.

"I've a skimmer outside," Eavy said. "Director Dunbar has made living arrangements for you at corps headquarters."

Corps headquarters—another indication Kendler's stay on-planet would be short.

"Luggage?" Eavy questioned.

"I'm wearing it." Kendler gestured to his flight coveralls.

"The skimmer's this way." Eavy gave Kendler's attire a rather distasteful once-over, then started toward an exit.

Within the skimmer, the young man punched their destination into the auto-console. The ground craft rose to hover a meter from the ground, then slid forward to lock onto a concourse guidance beam.

"You have an appointment with Director Dunbar at two o'clock," Eavy said with the air of a man announcing a royal audience. He glanced at his watch. "Three hours from now. Director Dunbar . . . uh . . . requested you be on time."

Kendler smiled inwardly. Eavy displayed all the signs of developing into a successful administrator—his diplomacy was showing. Kate Dunbar did not request, she demanded, normally with a long string of profanities for emphasis. She expected those demands to be met. A condition those under her usually fulfilled, not in fear, but with respect. Kate Dunbar stood in front, beside, or behind her psiotics, which-ever the situation required.

"Three hours from now, at two o'clock," Kendler repeated to assure Eavy he understood. He then settled into his seat and gazed outside as the skimmer entered Port Antoan.

Despite his years in the corps, Lanatia lacked any of the feelings associated with home. Seker remained his homeworld, distant both in the light-years that separated it from the capital of the Lofgrin Alliance and the time since he last walked the clean sands of Rochelle's Point. Lanatia was a stopover, a place to kill time between assignments. While he owned a small cabin tucked away in the forest beside Lake Varde, it was not home, only an isolated cubbyhole to climb into and lick the wounds of his latest merge, to give time for scars to form and protect his sanity.

The skimmer floated downward to settle on the ground, bringing Kendler from his wool-gathering. Outside rose the twin towers of the Psi Corps headquarters.

NINE

Kendler stepped from the shower. Five days of sleep-sweat washed away and his body tingling from the massage jets, he felt like a new man. Somewhere between the landing and now, the last of the chemo-sleep drugs had worn off and the grogginess had lifted from his brain, which added to his new exhilaration.

Moving before a mirror on the wall above a small sink, Kendler studied the face that looked at him. He could not describe it as a young face, despite the fact it had only seen thirty years. Crow's-feet already radiated from the corners of his pale-blue eyes, and "character lines" furrowed a broad forehead.

He perused several shelves of toiletry items tidily arranged for the convenience of Psi Corps guests. His attention was drawn to a straight razor and shaving cream set beside a canister of foam depilatory. The relative ease of applying a depilatory had never replaced the age-old custom of slicing away facial hair with a keenly honed edge. The majority of men within the LofAl preferred the razor.

With a shake of his head, Kendler selected the foam. To him there was something insane in the psychological makeup of a society in which fifty percent of the population began every day by placing a razor to its throat.

Studying himself in the mirror, he ran a hand over the bush sprouted over cheeks and chin. Thick and full, the beard neatly framed his face. Surprisingly, the jet of his facial hair was a shade or two deeper than the coal black of his slightly shaggy hair. *Not bad.* He admired the beard nature had provided during the long voyage to Lanatia. *It will need trimming to keep it shaped, and . . .*

He shook his head and pressed the canister's top to fill a palm with a lathery mound of depilatory. His eyes rolled back to the mirror; his hand rose to spread the foam over the black bush. His fingers paused.

Kate Dunbar won't like it, he mused, *but dammit, it looks good!*

Turning on the faucet, he washed the foam away, imagining the less than placid expression on Kate Dunbar's face when he walked into her office. If she screamed too loudly, it could always come off.

The change of clothes Eavy had mentioned hung in the room's single closet—flight coveralls. He sucked at his teeth. The coveralls were yet another indication that Dunbar had something scheduled for him.

Dressing, he walked to a servo-unit in the wall and punched up a breakfast of eggs, steak, toast, juice, and coffee. After a few cautious bites to be certain his stomach could handle the solid food, he waited for any telltale rumblings of impending nausea. His belly remained quiet; he eagerly wolfed down the meal.

The last bite cleaned from the tray, Kendler glanced at his watch—1:45. Any thoughts of leisurely settling back and letting the breakfast digest faded. He pushed from the chair.

At the end of the corridor outside the room, Kendler found a liftshaft. He stepped in and floated up to the hundredth floor, which formed Kate Dunbar's office.

A young male receptionist looked up from a stack of folders on his desk when Kendler exited the liftshaft. "Director Dunbar left orders for you to go right in when you arrived."

Kendler proceeded through a pair of dark-stained wooden doors marked in bold, gold letters—KATE DUNBAR, DIRECTOR PSI CORPS. The thick beard felt three times as bushy as it had a moment ago.

He surveyed the spacious office, locating the corps director hunched over a display screen on her three-sided desk. She looked up from the terminal, waved him to a chair, and returned to her computer search.

The beard feeling more conspicuous by the moment, Kendler seated himself and watched Kate's silver-haired head bob up and down while she scanned each informational flick of the screen.

"I ask for one bit of information and the morons in Registry send me progress reports on every freighter in the Alliance. I believe Registry goes out of their way to hire employees with the mental capacities of pissants." Her voice held a bit of gravel. Affected or legitimate, Kendler did not know, but it suited her. "By the way, Nils, I like the beard. I was going to suggest . . . ahhh, here's the Kendler special."

The woman's voice trailed off as she lost herself in the display again. Kendler grinned with nervous relief. So much for the beard. He stifled a chuckle that rose in his throat. "The Kendler special?"

"The freighter *Assel's Luck*." She swiveled around to face him. "It's carrying your Earth prizes. *Assel's Luck* will orbit Lanatia next week and the Alliance will get its first look at your overgrown lizards."

"Are they making the transit all right?" Had Kendler not known, he would have guessed Kate's age at seventy, rather than her actual hundred years. Her snow-white hair, bright-blue eyes, and diminutive size gave no indication of the punch she could deliver if the circumstances warranted it.

"No problems logged on the report." Kate opened a humidor on her desk, selected a carved meerschaum from a pipe rack beside it, and packed the bowl.

Her gesture did not go unnoticed. Kendler had given her the intricately carved pipe three years ago, an ancient relic of old Earth that had survived the centuries intact. The Psi Corps director lit the pipe, puffed deeply, and inhaled. The pungent odor of a latakia-laced blend drifted across the desk in a blue cloud. Kendler tilted his head to escape the frontal assault on his olfactory senses. The tobacco had the distinct odor of boiling coal tar.

Dunbar took another deep puff and exhaled slowly. She presently used her third set of cloned lungs, yet she persisted in what Kendler considered an abominable habit.

She smiled, apparently satisfied with whatever gratification she received from the pipe. She eyed Kendler thoughtfully. "Have you ever considered giving up the life of a field agent?"

Kendler's right eyebrow arched in an unspoken question.

Kate's smile grew with obvious amusement. "That beard gives you quite an intriguing appearance. I could always use another member on my personal staff."

"Salacious old woman." Kendler winked. "Bundling doesn't require that one be a staff member. Other arrangements could be made."

For a moment Kendler thought he might, *might,* have caught her off-guard. A tinge of flushed pink did seem to creep into her cheeks for an instant. Whatever he imagined was immediately masked when the woman grinned slyly and laughed.

"If I thought you were serious, I'd make those arrangements, Nils Kendler," she said. "Hell, I might anyway . . . call your bluff. See if you're more than just another pretty face."

She was attempting to turn the tables and back him in a corner. Kendler's only answer was a suggestive smile and the up-down movement of his pale-blue eyes as though he were sizing her up as a possible bundling mate for the evening.

Kate ignored the gesture by puffing on the meerschaum until she drew another cloud of smoke into her lungs. "I was going to suggest the beard as an aid on your next assignment."

"A beard isn't known for increasing psi abilities," he said.

"It might, however, allow you a certain freedom of movement." Her words came around the pipe's stem clamped between her teeth. "What do you know about the planet Morasha?"

The name held a familiar ring, but Kendler thought for a moment before he recalled where he had heard it. "A lost colony. Contact was reestablished within the past few years."

"Two years ago," Kate corrected. "Morasha was a Terran colony, though not settled by any Earth government, but by the Lukyans."

"Lukyans?" The term meant nothing to the psiotic.

"A religious sect that gained dubious popularity as humankind began to settle the planets of Sol System. Lukya is a mishmash of various old religions, rigidly structured. After the Global Wars and with the advent of a tachyon drive, the Lukyans immigrated en masse from a solitary Martian colony to Morasha," Kate said. "They sought to create a paradise where 'true believers' could live in a world of harmony. The best we've been able to piece together is that the Lukyans virtually isolated their planet from the rest of the inhabited

70

worlds prior to the Century Conflagration. The religious leaders feared contamination from societies outside their own."

"An attitude that has diminished since rediscovery?" Kendler asked.

"Enough to allow the Kavinites and the LofAl to establish diplomatic embassies in Ban-Dorit, Morasha's capital city." Kate glanced over her shoulder to the computer. "Gustaf, the Morasha visual."

The lights blinked off and blinds shuttered closed as the computer responded to the command. At the center of the darkened office a ball of striated reds and yellows appeared, a holographic projection. Two meters in diameter, it slowly revolved in the air a meter from the carpet.

"Morasha, a second-grade Terra-type planet orbiting a Sol-type star. Except for a desert equatorial belt and relatively small polar caps, Morasha's climate on its five continents is classified as temperate to tropical," Kate said.

The projection winked. Kendler smiled. The visual now hanging in the air was designed to produce the sensation of descending toward the planet. The footage had been shot during an actual shuttle descent and was not merely a computer interpretation. Faster he fell into the atmosphere, shooting through a sea of clouds.

"During the separation following the Century Conflagration, the Lukyans went through an extended period of regression. Many of the technological skills they had when the colony was established were lost," Kate continued the briefing. "Only in the past hundred years have they regrouped, and they are once more progressing. It's projected they'll undergo a technological revolution of their own within the next thirty to fifty years."

The holographic projection now revealed a makeshift shuttle port. A city rose beyond it in the distance.

"The toll of that regression was heavy," Kate said. "Superficial reconnaissance missions have located ruins of several cities on all five continents, but minimal human activity. Only on the continent of Uttal is there any extensive population. The largest city is Ban-Dorit. On the other continents, three human groups have been identified. All live in tribal conditions."

The projection now displayed a miniature city. Kendler perused the structure hanging before him. It was ancient beyond any city he had visited. Kendler was touched by the sense of viewing a world that time had left untouched.

"Why me?" he asked.

"Six months ago, Morasha began experiencing civil disruptions. It started as a rise in the crime rate within Ban-Dorit. Other cities soon reported similar increases in criminal activities," Dunbar said, puffing on her pipe. "Three months ago, the riots began—mass rioting with no apparent cause. Again it began in Ban-Dorit, then quickly spread to the other Lukyan cities."

Kate paused. Kendler heard her relighting the pipe.

"Gustaf, lights," she said to the computer. The lights immediately flashed on. The shuttered windows opened. The hologram dissolved. "Shortly after your departure from Earth, all hell broke loose on Morasha. A form of mass hysteria, as best we can determine. Periods of total insanity abruptly grip every man, woman, and child on-planet. Murder, rape, pillaging, burnings . . . you name it. One moment all is normal, the next, complete chaos."

Kate paused, her eyes on Kendler. She drew deeply on the pipe and exhaled in a sudden burst. "These periods of hysteria last from a minute to an hour in duration. Our embassy on Morasha is up against the wall. They've detected no pattern to the outbreaks. A week or a fraction of a second can go between the attacks. Nor have they found any physiological reason for the hysteria. They've run the gamut from solar radiation to dietary changes."

Kendler remained silent, trying to form a mental image of a society abruptly gone mad, then in the next moment returned to normal. He could not.

"The LofAl's top man on Morasha is Ambassador Stal Lore," Kate continued. "He feels the hysteria is somehow psi-induced. He's requested a team to investigate that possibility."

"And I'm that team?" Kendler looked at her doubtfully. No known psi power was capable of what she had described.

"Lore believes the Kavinites are behind the hysteria . . . though his staff has been unable to link their activities to the mass hysteria." Kate neatly sidestepped his question. "The present Morashan government in Ban-Dorit is leaning toward LofAl membership. However, they have received the full brunt of the populace's anger. The Morashans are demanding some solution to the outbreaks, and the government can't deliver. The situation is ripe for a Kavinite move to topple the present power structure and replace it with one of their own persuasion."

"When am I scheduled to leave?" Kendler remembered Stal Lore. They had worked together six years ago on Vire. Lore was a good, solid man, not given to paranoid flights of fantasy. Methodical in his approach, he would not call for help unless the situation warranted it.

"Departure's at seven this evening. Any further information you'll need on Morasha has already been fed into the cruiser's computer. You'll receive a full briefing en route. You'll also be sleep-fed the language." Kate pressed a vidcom on the desk. "Send in Caltha Renenet."

"Cruiser?" Kendler stared at her in disbelief. A military vessel would be like a red light to the Kavinites. "Am I going in the front door on this one?"

"You and your partner will arrive on-planet as members of a crew on shore leave."

"Partner?"

Before Kendler could press his objections, the double doors to the office swung inward. A young woman in muted-violet flight coveralls entered. A river of raven-black hair cascaded over her shoulders, framing a delicately oval face, and flowed downward to veil the curves of her breasts. Her dark, almond-shaped eyes briefly alighted on Kendler before moving to Kate Dunbar. A hint of a smile touched the corners of her mouth.

Small and fragile-looking, she reminded Kendler of some porcelain doll that must be carefully locked behind glass to protect its beauty. One touch and she would shatter. He could not deny her attractiveness, but there was a vulnerability to it rather than strength. He dismissed her as he turned back to the Psi Corps director. "I don't work with a . . ."

"Your partner for Morasha." Kate eyed him. "Caltha Renenet, twenty-eight, six years in the corps and one of the strongest, if not *the* strongest, receivers I've ever had."

"Kate . . . what are you doing?" Kendler glanced back to the young woman. She smiled at him. His confusion increased. He never worked with a partner. He was a loner. "A partner . . . it's . . . not my style. I'm a merger . . . I . . ."

"Nevertheless, Caltha will be your partner on this assignment." Kendler thought he detected a hint of amusement in Kate's expression. The possibility that his bewilderment amused her annoyed him.

"I don't think you understood. I don't need a partner for a

merge. It's a one-man operation." He scrambled to organize his thoughts. "While I'm sure Ms. Renenet's quite capable, she'll be in my way."

"Mr. Kendler!" His head jerked around to Caltha Renenet. The pleasant smile was gone, replaced by a stone mask. "Your talents as a merger are well known throughout the corps. But as you mentioned, you are a *merger*. Your abilities are limited to the faculty of entering another mind and controlling it. Your capabilities of receiving psi emanations are virtually negligible, no more than any nonpsiotic."

"Limited?" His annoyance twinged with anger. Her deliberate choice of words worked their way under his skin. "Every psiotic is *limited*, Ms. Renenet."

"Precisely, Mr. Kendler." She coolly stared at him. "We've no idea of what awaits us on Morasha. I believe you can grasp that fact. If this mass hysteria stems from a form of psi-induced insanity, the abilities of a trained receiver will be most expedient in locating the source of the problem."

Her condescending attitude and her patronizing tone grated within him like a steel rasp. Without a logical reason, she attacked. He took the defensive. "I'm not questioning your qualifications, or your training. I am *concerned* about a partner. I don't work that way. I don't—"

"She's right," Kate cut him off. "Where Morasha is concerned, time is of the utmost importance. If Caltha's talent can save a day or two, then she's worth whatever personal inconvenience you may find in working with a partner."

"I've never needed a receiver before," Kendler insisted. "I merge with enough minds and find the answers that are needed. In eight years, my methods have never failed. I—"

"Methods exist to block merge probes, Mr. Kendler, ways of locking information deep in the subconscious at the first indication of an attempted mind-merge." Caltha Renenet's tone moved over him like an evening breeze sweeping across a polar icecap.

"Nils, give it up," Kate said, apparently delighted by the exchange. "Caltha's abilities have proved themselves time and again. Last year she was responsible for locating the cruiser that went down on Palaula-3."

"I'm not questioning her abilities," he said for the third time. He was not. He recalled the Palaula-3 rescue. Hauling the cruiser crew from that methane giant had been nothing short of miraculous. That Caltha Renenet was the key psiotic on the mission was impressive. "I seriously doubt our ability to function as a team. It's simply not the way I work."

"It's a moot point," Kate said. "It *is* the way you'll work on this assignment—together as a *team.*"

He had more to say, but left the comments unspoken. He knew Kate's tone. Her face, firm and determined, only echoed the "closed decision" he heard in her voice. Like it or not, Caltha Renenet was his partner for Morasha. He nodded, resigned.

"Good," Caltha Renenet said. "I hope your display is not indicative of our relationship while on assignment."

Kendler held his tongue, hoping his icy stare conveyed his reply. It would be a subzero day in the pits of hell before Caltha Renenet and he had any type of "relationship."

She answered with a smile. He read triumph on the uplifted corners of her mouth and accepted her victory for round one. Round two would come; the next time he would not be taken off-guard.

"Will there be anything else?" Caltha turned to Kate. "I still have several matters to attend to before departure."

"The rest of the day is yours," Kate replied. "Just be on the shuttle at seven."

Caltha Renenet left without another glance at Kendler. *Limited.* Her comment repeated itself in his mind while he watched the door close behind her. The fragile beauty he had glimpsed moments ago disappeared, replaced by an image chiseled in granite. *Limited!*

"Quit your sulking, Nils. You're not handsome when you pout." Kate smiled with saccharine sweetness. "Psiotics! You're all prima donnas. Each of you has your optical nerves strung through your bowels. It gives you a shitty outlook on life."

"I love you, too." Kendler glared at his superior.

"This assignment isn't an adventure I've arranged for your personal pleasure. It's a job that needs doing, one to which I've assigned two of my most capable agents," Kate said. "Understand?"

He nodded. He understood, but he did not have to like it—or Caltha Renenet.

"Now," Kate continued, "I believe you've something to report pertaining to your jump-up from the Cretaceous Period."

Kendler's head jerked up. Kate Dunbar's intelligence network threaded its way everywhere. "Who was it? Beamin, the girl working the controls, or Dr. Rey? They're the only ones who know about the jump-up."

"Myra Rey," she replied. "She's a low-grade receiver who used to work on my staff before you joined us."

"Your personal staff?" Kendler raised an eyebrow. "I thought you preferred young men."

"Depends on what night it is," Kate said without batting an eye. "What about the jump?"

Kendler shook his head in amazement, then detailed all that had occurred on his return to Base One.

"Beamin might be correct. The disturbance could be anything," she commented when he concluded.

"Agreed. I've never experienced psi emanations like that, yet . . ." He paused, delving for the right words. "It tried to snatch me from the timestream. I had the distinct feeling it would have succeeded, but it misjudged my speed. The best it could do was show me the pyramid."

"Do you want this probed further?"

"I would have done it myself, if you hadn't yanked me back here," Kendler said. "As it was, I didn't want to draw any more attention to the incident until I talked with you."

Kate nodded her approval. "I'll assign one of my staff to compile a report on Earth's pyramids. It will be waiting when you return from Morasha."

"Good. Now, if there's nothing else, there are a few matters I'd like to see about before leaving." The first being a visit with Galt Lampbert to convince his old friend to pull Caltha Renenet's personel file. If he was stuck with a partner on this assignment, he wanted to know everything he could about her before departing Lanatia.

"Nothing else," Kate said.

Kendler rose and walked to the office's doors.

"Nils," the Psi Corps director called after him. He turned and looked at her. "I told Galt Lampbert to let you see Caltha's files. I think it's only fair. She's already read yours."

Kendler's eyes narrowed in angry disgust when he exited the room. It was well known Kate Dunbar had no psi abilities of her own. Sometimes he seriously doubted that fact.

TEN

Two weeks out of Lanatia, the LofAl cruiser *Kelso* broke from tachyon space and entered orbit around Morasha. Five hours later, Caltha Renenet and Nils Kendler, dressed in standard LofAl Navy uniforms, boarded one of three shuttles destined for on-planet shore leave.

According to Kate Dunbar's plans, which awaited them in the ship's computer, their anonymity would be protected by numbers. Flood Morasha's single spaceport with one hundred naval types and an extra two could slip in unnoticed.

If we're lucky, Kendler thought as the shuttle eased from its berth and began the descent. At the terminal, they would contact a native Morashan, one Ome Reve, the young son of Tolin Reve, High Minister of Morasha's governing planetary council, and presently the employee of the LofAl Diplomatic Service.

The mere thought of Ome Reve flashed five images of the youth in Kendler's mind. The mental pictures had been etched into his short-term memory, along with the Morashan tongue, during sleep-programming while aboard the *Kelso*.

He smiled, feeling a kinship with the young man. The Lofgrinists' methods of integrating themselves into the society of a rediscovered planet were well known to Kendler. On

Seker, his homeworld, he had been given similar employment by the Diplomatic Service. His father had approved the position with an ulterior motive. His son could spy on the Lofgrinists. The service fed their young employee information to return to his father and in turn strengthened the man's pro-LofAl stance.

Sometimes it works; sometimes it doesn't. That the balance of planets between Kavinites and Lofgrinists remained stable, despite the constant increase in newly colonized planets and rediscovered colonies, indicated both political ideologies were equally influential.

Kendler glanced at Caltha Renenet out of the corner of his eye. She sat beside him, staring out a porthole. The shuttle banked steeply to avoid a blue-black storm front. For an instant, the terrain below filled the porthole. He could discern no familar topographical landmark. Morasha remained an alien world.

He looked at Caltha once more. She sat oblivious to his presence. Despite the personnel profile he had read before departure, he knew nothing about the woman except for her long string of successful assignments over the past six years. As with all agents, her background prior to enlisting in the corps remained the private information of Kate Dunbar.

Kendler smiled wryly, recalling a LofAl Council investigation of the Psi Corps directed by an overexuberant freshman council member in search of a cause to hitch his star to.

"I don't give a rat's asshole if one of my agents committed multiple homicide prior to being selected for corps service." Kate Dunbar testified before the investigating committee. "If an individual has a psi talent we can use, we use it. If that person steps out of line while under my authority, he or she deals with me . . . as does anyone who inhibits the efficient operation of my agency."

There was no veiled threat in the last comment, but a statement of fact. Had the council's president made the same remark, he would have been torn apart in the media and ground to hamburger in the next election. But coming from Kate Dunbar, it was another matter.

The comment never made the news telecasts, undoubtedly silenced by the pulling of invisible strings attached to Kate's fingers.

As for the freshman council member, he never saw the end of his term. Prior to the completion of the inquiry, a scandalous kickback scheme involving copper mining on the Kaggs

Triad surfaced. The councilman was censured by his fellow legislators and yanked back to his homeworld after a hasty recall vote.

Were there invisible strings tied to Caltha Renenet? What raw wounds had been gouged or old scars reopened to maneuver her into the Psi Corps? There had to be reasons. The financial lures dangled before psiotics by industry were too enticing to be ignored. The corps could not compete on a monetary level. There were always other reasons, motives. He understood why he allowed Kate Dunbar to repeatedly place his head on the chopping block—a Seker family to which he had once belonged. But what about Caltha Renenet?

During the two weeks aboard the *Kelso*, their mutual antagonism had never relaxed. They had been unsuccessful in their attempt to break through the barriers that rose between them. No matter how cordially a meeting, conversation, or a simple morning salutation began, it ended in conflict. If he said a sphere was round, Caltha insisted it was flat. If she commented on the blue hues of tachyon space, he demanded they were red.

You lose, Kate, he resigned himself. *We might be landing on Morasha for the same purpose, but as a team . . . never.*

A jolting tremor quaked through the shuttle. Rubber bit into concrete. The final roar of the braking rockets jarred Kendler from his thoughts.

Outside, a scene he had first viewed floating in the middle of Kate Dunbar's office rushed by. Morasha's solitary spaceport was no more than two X runways. The terminal, a generous description, was a single, low-slung one-story steelfoam building. A tachyon beam communications tower jutted fifty meters into the air from its roof.

The craft swung around to taxi toward the building. Kendler glimpsed the naked-metal silver of another shuttle crouched at the far side of the terminal. The sleek, hawkish lines of the craft marked it as Kavinite. He compared the shuttle to the one in which he rode—a winged predator and a pregnant whale.

The two shuttles from the *Kelso* that had preceded them sat on the opposite end of the terminal, facing the Kavinite vessel. Grouped beneath their wings stood the passengers and crew, awaiting the arrival of the third craft.

The shuttle taxied to a halt beside its sisters. No tunnel corridor snaked out to mate against the craft's hull. The exit hatch opened and a ladder lowered to the ground. The crew unstrapped themselves and moved toward the exit.

"Morasha, Mr. Kendler," Caltha Renenet said from beside Kendler. "I suggest the sooner you extract yourself from the couch, the sooner we can begin our work."

Kendler did not bother to glance at his "partner." He flipped the catches to the restraining straps across his chest, rose, and walked toward the exit. Poking his head through the hatch, he took a deep breath. For an instant, he had the distinct sensation of drowning. The humidity was stifling. Eighty-five to ninety percent, he estimated. After the *Kelso's* controled environment, Morasha's atmosphere was like breathing an ocean.

A rain forest surrounded the port, reminding him of the prehistoric forest he had ventured into two months ago. The smell of decaying vegetation hung in the air, sweet and heavy. Above the roof of the terminal building, he glimpsed Ban-Dorit's unimpressive skyline.

On the concourse, Kendler joined the crew members waiting to enter the terminal. A few moments later, Caltha Renenet weaved through the crowd to his side. She sneezed. Her breathing came in labored wheezes. Apparently she had not been prepared for Morasha's overwhelming humidity any more than he had.

The crew formed two lines and filed into the terminal. After a cursory inspection by bored-looking customs officials, they moved into a large waiting room. An overhead loudspeaker cracked to life:

"The Ban-Dorit Spaceport is situated five kilometers from the city gates. There is a skimmer available to transport visitors to the city. However, the craft has a ten-passenger capacity. We must ask you to remain patient and endure this slight inconvenience. Every member of the *Kelso's* crew will be taken to Ban-Dorit's main gates as quickly as possible."

The speaker clicked off, then almost in afterthought, the voice came over it again. "For those considering the possibility of walking to Ban-Dorit, we advise against it. The jungle surrounding the terminal poses numerous dangers for those untrained to deal with its variety of virulent life forms . . . animal and vegetable."

The crew members mumbled among themselves, protesting the delay in their leave, but accepted the inevitable. Deriding the lack of adequate facilities on the backwater world, they lined themselves before the exit to await the skimmer.

"Ome," Caltha said as they took their place in line. She pronounced the name as two words—oh, me—making it sound as though she were disgusted.

Kendler glanced at his fellow psiotic. She shrugged her shoulders and frowned. He surveyed the terminal, sucked at his teeth, and shook his head.

No Ome Reve waited, despite Kate Dunbar's assurances the native Morashan would be there to escort them to the embassy.

"You heard the man." Kendler tilted his head toward the loudspeaker. "We've no alternative but to wait for the skimmer."

The fifth load of *Kelso* crew members disembarked outside the gates of the five-meter-high stone wall encircling Ban-Dorit. Kendler and Caltha Renenet paused beside the craft to study the faces of the two guards and various beggars stationed by the city's gates.

"Still no welcoming committee." Kendler moved with the crew through the gates. Brightly robed Morashans lined the street within, posed beside wooden carts of fresh vegetables, the virtues of which they exalted loudly to each passerby. "Any suggestions?"

"We locate the embassy and Ambassador Lore as ordered." The tone of Caltha's voice and her irate glance all but came out and said she blamed him for Ome Reve's absence. "I believe we are capable of locating the embassy without the assistance of a guide, Mr. Kendler."

"Perhaps." He ignored her sarcasm. "I think we should prolong our roles as star cruiser crew members a bit longer. If something's up, Lore will find a way to apprise us of the situation."

"There are at least one hundred and two people within Ban-Dorit dressed in naval uniforms," she said impatiently. "If something has happened to our contact, and the embassy has someone searching for us, it could take days before they found us. Anything can happen in a matter of days."

Which was the point Kendler had tried to make. He let her remarks pass. It was not worth arguing over. Instead, he continued after the cruiser's crew. Caltha trotted after him.

"What are you doing?" she demanded.

"My job," he replied brusquely, his patience wearing thin as it always did when he spoke to the woman.

"*Our* job is to make contact with Ambassador Lore before we proceed with the assignment," she insisted. "We have orders, a schedule to follow."

He refused to answer. Schedules were nice, if they fitted the situation. When Ome Reve had not met them at the terminal, the situation had changed. Now it was time to play it by ear.

"Mr. Kendler," Caltha persisted, "what do you intend to do?"

Kendler pointed to the eight crew members in front of them. "Follow them awhile."

"What will that prove?"

"Nothing," he said. "But if I know spacers, it will lead to Ban-Dorit's equivalent of a tavern. Unless Morasha has some sanctions against bars, the tavern will subscribe to the universal custom of all bars and have dark corners. And a dark corner, Ms. Renenet, will give me protection while I merge."

"Merge?" She glared at him.

"Taverns also provide an assortment of patrons from various walks of life," he explained. "If I probe enough, we'll eventually find someone who knows the way to the embassy. If anything is askew, the fewer questions we ask, the less we'll attract attention. It's the best I can come up with on short notice. Unless, that is, you're an ambulatory receiver?"

"You know damn well there aren't any ambulatory psiotics!" She mumbled something else, which he turned off.

"Shall we find that dark corner then?" To his surprise, the woman offered no objection. She could not argue the fact that all psiotics required immobility to focus their abilities. The dark corner of a bar would provide an accessible retreat away from the city's normal activities and the opportunity for them to probe passing minds. In this case, two minds would be better than one, or at least more expedient, he admitted.

His faith in the crew's ability to locate a flowing oasis amid alien terrain proved well founded. No more than fifty meters from Ban-Dorit's gates, without leaving the street they entered on, the crew was waylaid by a heavy-set woman. In a loud, enthusiastic voice, she proclaimed the potency of a local wine served within an establishment bearing the name the Soaring Swallow.

The crew lacked Caltha's and his in-flight language programming and were unfamilar with the Morashan tongue.

Resourcefully, the red-robed woman overcame the language barrier. Signaling the crew members to wait, she rushed into an open door to her left. She returned holding an earthen jar and cup.

The alcoholic fumes that rose from the chartreuse liquid she poured were all that was needed to get her message across. For good measure, she passed the cup around. The crew members required no further convincing. They followed her inside the Soaring Swallow.

"Ome." Caltha nudged Kendler's ribs and tilted her head toward a youth who leaned against the wall outside the tavern.

Standing at a meter and seventy-three centimeters with facial features that were hawkish and at the same time innocent, the youth matched Kendler's mental images. Ome's dark-brown eyes peered at them while he pushed a stray strand of equally dark-brown hair from his forehead. He gave no further sign of recognition. Then his eyes rolled toward the tavern's open door, signaling them to enter.

"Kavinites," he whispered when they passed. "Have a drink. I'll return for you later."

They followed his directions and found seats at a table neatly tucked in their sought-after dark corner. Moments later Ome entered. He stood at the door and stared about the dimly lit interior as though searching for something. Apparently not finding what he wanted, he turned and rushed from the Soaring Swallow.

Caltha started to rise. Kendler grabbed her wrist, keeping her in her chair. "Wait," he said under his breath.

Two men in gaudy native robes shoved from a table near the door. They hastened after the youth. Caltha looked at Kendler, questioning.

"The Kavinites," he said, then waved for the tavern's matron to bring two cups of the chartreuse wine.

"What about Reve?" Caltha asked.

"He told us to wait," Kendler replied. "I suggest we do that."

The Soaring Swallow's rotund tavernkeep brought the requested cups. The Morashan wine tasted every bit as potent as its aroma.

...some training had to...

...and natural alpha level ... was probably evoked in ... "The ... features break ... and change. The ... ... to ... beyond her normal ability.

ELEVEN

Caltha's eyes opened vacantly. They coursed over the room without seeing. Her eyelids blinked several times. Her body shuddered slightly. Despite having watched her transition back from alpha level awareness five times in the past hour, Kendler reached out and touched her shoulder.

"Are you all right?"

Life returned to her jet-black eyes. She glanced at Kendler as though unable to comprehend his question. An irritated expression flashed across the delicate features of her face. She nodded, her gaze darting to his hand. Immediately, he let his fingers slip away.

"Anything?" he asked.

"Nothing." Her head moved slowly from side to side. "Only stray, random thoughts . . . sexual fantasies, marital disputes, financial worries." Her voice trailed off.

Kendler edged what remained of her second cup of wine in front of her. "I think we'd better let it drop for a while. We're draining ourselves."

"We haven't got anything." He sensed an uncertain desperation in her voice. Her head hung down, chin against her chest. "The embassy . . . it's been three hours since Reve left. We've got to do something."

He studied her. Not since corps training had he worked with another person. Watching a psiotic delve a target was a frightening experience. The mental energy required to reach and sustain alpha level awareness was physically evident in Caltha's face. Her features were taut and strained. The irritable edge to her voice went beyond her normal antagonism for him.

"If necessary," he said, "we can ask for directions."

"No." She shook her head emphatically. "You were right earlier. We stand out like sore thumbs. The Kavinites are searching for us. We'd play into their hands."

"Any suggestions?" He tried, but could not disguise his lack of patience.

"You try again," she said firmly. "Then I'll try. We'll come up with something eventually."

Kendler turned away from her to hide his disgust and anger. His own five merges in the past hour were taking their toll. He could merge again, maybe another five times. *But there are limits*.

He surveyed the tavern. Ten patrons sat scattered at various tables. Only two of the *Kelso*'s crew remained. After a few drinks, the majority had left to explore the recreational opportunities Ban-Dorit offered. He wished he were with them.

"If we keep this up, one of us will collapse face down on the table from sheer exhaustion," he said. "What shape will we be in then?"

"We have to keep trying." She stubbornly refused to acknowledge their mental and physical drain. "You must try again. You *must*."

Her tone and expression were a plea. He glanced at her, again glimpsing desperation. He cursed inwardly when he found himself giving in to her against his better judgment. If he expected a sign of gratitude or even a look of relief, Caltha Renenet gave none.

Once more, Kendler's gaze traveled over the dimly lit tavern in search of a target. An old man entered from the street. Brushing dirt from a patchwork robe, he called out for a cup of wine. While the tavern matron filled the order, Kendler closed his eyes and opened to the newcomer.

Third day, Sarthetha will have the normal fare of stew on the hearth . . .

The Morashan's surface thoughts invaded Kendler's mind. He tasted the pleasant bite of the chartreuse wine washing a fine coat of dust from his tongue . . . the arthritic aches that worried the man's swollen joints . . . the tickle of a cough that crept up from chest to throat . . .

The psiotic caught himself and withdrew from the sensory input. Cautiously, he wove himself into the old Morashan's consciously focused thoughts. Nothing. The man knew nothing of the LofAl embassy. He held only the barest knowledge that men from the stars now dwelled within his city.

Kendler delved deeper. The barrier loomed before him. For the sixth time that day, he ran head-on into it. Like a black wall of seared nerve paths, it rose. The psiotic tested it, probing, prodding to penetrate. It held, sealing the old man's subconscious from him.

He withdrew.

"Well?" Caltha greeted him when his eyes opened.

"The same as before . . . nothing." He took a deep breath in an attempt to find some inward source of untapped energy. There was not one. "I hit the barrier again."

"The scar?" Caltha asked. "In every one of your targets?"

"There's an aura of madness, insanity. That's all I can discern. The rest is driven deep and sealed in the subconscious. I can't reach it." Kendler shrugged his shoulder helplessly. "With time, I think I might find a method of bringing it to the surface."

"We don't have time," she answered.

"Nor the strength."

"We must go on." Her voice held pained determination. "I'll take the next customer that walks in the door."

"Have it your way." He downed the remaining swallow in his cup and waved for another drink. "However, when you pass out, I'm leaving you here."

Her face hardened when she read the sincerity in his face. "I refuse to shirk my duty, Mr. Kendler. I won't give up."

"Crap! I didn't say give up, just rest." The woman was infuriating. *Duty?* Next she would be singing the LofAl anthem to him. "The embassy isn't located in this sector of the city. Someone here would know its location if it were. We'll give Reve another hour. If he doesn't show, then we'll play tourist and see what we can glean in another part in Ban-Dorit."

"Another hour? We should have met Ambassador Lore three hours ago."

"Lore's not going anywhere." His exasperation mounted.

Before Caltha could reply, her gaze was drawn to the

tavern's door. Kendler looked up. Ome Reve entered. A bundle wrapped in yellow paper was tucked under one arm. He glanced at them and shook his head.

The youth sat at a table and ordered wine. When the matron brought a cup, he leisurely drained its contents. Eventually, he rose and asked the woman if there were facilities available to relieve himself. She pointed to a door at the rear of the tavern. He thanked her and walked to the door.

"Follow me," he said when he passed Caltha and Kendler.

Waiting a few moments, they pushed from the table and moved through the rear door. The young Morashan waved them into an alley behind the tavern. He then tore open his bundle and produced two brightly striped robes.

"These will hide your uniforms." He handed each of them a robe.

Without comment, the two psiotics slipped the garments over their heads.

"I apologize for the delay." The youth smiled sheepishly. "We learned the Kavinites suspected the cruiser's purpose. They had agents at the terminal. It was too risky to make contact there. Before your arrival, there was no way to inform you of the change in plans. I was to meet you at Ban-Dorit's gates."

"Then you found two Kavinites on your tail," Kendler added, the situation clearer now.

Ome Reve nodded and grinned widely. "After making you comfortable in the Soaring Swallow, I led them on a shopping spree through our Grand Bazaar. For an hour they watched me squeeze vegetables and thump melons. I then returned to the embassy with an armload of fresh produce. There I informed Ambassador Lore of the situation, waited until my shadows decided I had nothing to offer them and gave up their vigil outside the embassy. I returned as quickly as possible."

"We were afraid something had happened." Caltha finished tying a sash around her waist.

"The Kavinites underestimate us Morashans." The youth chuckled with self-pleasure. "Now we must go. Ambassador Lore is anxious to talk with you."

Kendler waved the youth to lead the way. Ome moved down the alley onto a busy street. Suntanned Morashans, all clothed in brightly colored robes, moved around them. None gave the threesome more than a passing glance. With their dark hair and robes, the two psiotics blended in with the crowd.

Kendler's impression of Ban-Dorit via Kate Dunbar's holographic projection had been wrong. The city was not old. The sense of antiquity came not from the age of the structures around him, but from the ancient architecture and building methods.

Mud brick, handmade from all indications, provided the main construction material for the buildings Kendler saw. The bricks were covered in a yellow-white stuccolike plaster. Few of the structures rose higher than three stories.

The streets, if the narrow passages they traversed could be described as streets rather than corridors through the maze of buildings, were laid in cut and mortared stone. The need for paved streets eluded Kendler until they were caught in a brief tropical downpour. The rains in this tropical climate were a daily occurrence. The streets would have been a constant mire if left unpaved.

At one point, they passed several buildings constructed of duroplast panels. Ome explained that the structures formed Morasha's governmental complex. The panels apparently were relics from Man's first days on the planet. Kendler suspected the buildings had at one time sheltered the original colonists. Though centuries old, the complex stood as the most modern structures within Ban-Dorit.

Weaving through a maze of interconnecting corridor-streets, Ome brought them into a wide avenue that flowed with Morashans. The youth glanced at his two wards, eyeing Caltha particularly. Concern lined his brow.

Kendler looked at his fellow psiotic. Clatha's exhaustion from their hour of probing was more than apparent. Their walk had only made matters worse.

Ome's lips parted to speak. Kendler shook his head, silencing him before he uttered a sound. Caltha was operating on sheer determination. It would serve her right to pass out on her feet, but it was something they could ill afford at the moment.

"How much farther to the embassy?" he asked their guide.

"A kilometer," Ome replied. "I have made our walk farther than needed. I felt it best to avoid the main thoroughfares. Kavinites, you understand."

"Understood." Kendler nodded. "But the day has been long. I need to take a breather for a few minutes."

Relief swept across Caltha's face, but she said nothing.

"There is a public garden with benches." Ome motioned ahead. "It's a short distance farther. There is a fountain with cool water, if you are thirsty."

Kendler waved the young man to continue. Ome did, slowly. Caltha's obvious exhaustion said she could not be pushed. Kendler searched around for any place they could rest.

The street was far busier than the smaller walkways Ome had led them through. People scurried here and there on either side of the avenue. The center of the street was reserved for a slow procession of hand-drawn carts and an occasional wagon pulled by a massive bovine animal Kendler could not identify.

Something about the Morashans bothered him. It took Kendler several moments to put his finger on it. It was the way they carried themselves. While their strides were brisk, their heads hung downward, eyes lowered, never rising to meet the people they passed.

The black scar, the realization edged into his mind. *Do they all carry it?*

He pushed the migrant thought away. He could probe the scar later, when he had more time. Now he needed to find a place to rest before Caltha, or he himself for that matter, collapsed.

Shops lined both sides of the street. Ome apparently was leading them through Ban-Dorit's equivalent of a business district. Pottery stores, metalsmiths, cloth merchants were all neatly labeled by brilliantly hued signs hung above their doors or open windows.

More noticeable were the shops that lay vacant. Door and display windows stood securely boarded shut. Others had been gutted by fire. Another reminder of the black scar, but no place to rest.

Kendler glanced at Caltha. Determination once more furrowed her forehead.

Eyes on the back of my neck! He sensed them drilling into his flesh. Someone stared at him.

Irrationally, the psiotic stopped. He pivoted around, ready to confront the owner of that stare. No one was there. His fist bunched, knuckles straining white.

"Mr. Kendler!" Caltha's voice, an octave above its normal vocal range, sliced into his brain like a sharp razor. "What the hell are you doing?"

He swirled on her. Hate burned on her face, twisting its

89

beauty into a grotesque mask. His arms tensed. He caught himself before he slammed a fist into her mouth.

Eyes, all around, staring at me. They surrounded him, pressing in.

Someone screamed.

Kendler jerked around. A man ran down the street, ripping at the robe he wore. A woman wailed in terror. The psiotic could not find her, nor the eyes.

"Our Creator!" Ome's voice came as a low rumble that rose to a shrieking plea. "It comes. *It comes!*"

"You sniveling son of a bitch." Caltha inexplicably turned on the youth. Her palm whipped out, brutally slapping his hairless cheek.

Darkness, not that which comes from the absence of light, but darkness that seethes in the repressed crevices of the soul, seeped upward, boiling in Kendler's brain. *No!* A piteous whimper gurgled in his throat. *It comes from outside.*

He tried to grasp it. Easily, it evaded his mental snare, defied definition. Inward, ever inward it pressed, a foreboding darkness.

Screams erupted around him. They invaded his ears, drilling to the center of his mind. Among them, he heard his own voice chorusing the horror that enveloped him.

Death!

Demons pushed their way through cracks in the cobble stone street. Like creatures spawned in half-remembered nightmares, they leaped into the air on leathery wings. They swirled around his head, screeching profanities.

Hallucinations.

His brain rejected logic. The demons were real, solid forms whose swarming horde darkened the sky. Their claws raked out. Bladelike talons pierced his skull, skewering deep. Spewing fountains of molten lava erupted.

Death comes to Morasha. I . . . I am death . . . I wield the flaming blade!

He gazed into the face of the demons beating the air above him. He summoned them to him. "My minions. Gather! We reap our harvest!"

A river of blood rushed through the street, eddying around his ankles. Fire licked at the buildings about him, a rightful tribute to death. And he was death's living arm.

No!

The flames fluttered, dying.

They must continue, must sear the city. He willed them to flare, to kiss the heavens with their fiery breath.

No! The voice within him screamed its rage again. Or did it come from without?

He trembled: fear knotted his gut. His body shuddered as tremor after tremor quaked through his every cell. He felt it, heard it, his body ripping apart. He screamed while the rent grew, splitting him into two entities. He stood facing a man who wore his face. The man laughed at him with maniacal glee while he stood weeping.

Unreal!

The mirror-image Nils Kendler blurred, transformed into a leather-winged demon.

My mind . . . use my mind.

He reached within himself, seeking a solidity to anchor himself to and contain his sanity. He withdrew from the blood-washed street and plunged his consciousness into itself. He blotted out his sensory input and sank into his mind, letting it close around him like the petals of a wounded flower.

The invader remained.

It is an invader! The joy of that realization surrounded him in a veil of sanity. It was not him. The horrors that flooded him, the dark desires, were not him, but an invader!

Kendler pulled deeper within the core of rationality that dwelled at the center of his mind. He retreated until the invader churned without. It thrust, jabbed, stabbed. It threw itself against the mental barricade of sanity he raised about him. The walls held, remained inviolate.

Steadying himself, he expanded outward until he once more commanded his own senses. He opened his eyes, and whimpered. The nightmare persisted, no illusion.

Total chaos reigned on the Ban-Dorit avenue. Across the street, two men rolled on the ground. Each clawed at the other's face, fingers raking at eyes. A woman cried out in terror. Kendler turned to find the source of the cry beating her fists against the door of a shop. The door did not open.

Like a man lost in a dream, he stood and watched a purple-robed man rush behind the woman. His arm rose and fell, slamming into the back of the woman's neck. She crumpled at her attacker's feet. The man bent to rip open her robe and expose the vulnerable nakedness of her body. Kneeling between her spread thighs, he hoisted his robe about his waist. His sex jutted, rigid and angry. He fell atop the unconscious woman to sate himself.

Down the street two men danced wildly before a flaming building. Others carried torches, laughing while they tossed them into open windows of shops.

Kendler reeled, his mind numbed by the images transmitted by his eyes. The purple-robed assailant lifted himself from his victim. He staggered backward and sank to his knees in the middle of the street. Burying his head in hands, he wept.

Three men rushed him, brandishing wooden clubs. Blows rained. The kneeling man jerked, writhed, twitched, then lay still. His head was no more than a jellied mass of red. His attackers turned on one another.

Kendler closed his eyes and held them tightly shut in the vain hope of erasing the nightmare visions. This was why he had traveled to Morasha—to face this and find its source.

The foreboding darkness, the sense of death, tore around his mind. It railed against him, attempting to breach his mental barrier. *Psi?* He did not want to ponder it or its origins. The battle he fought drained more than mental energies. His body ached. Knotting cramps worked through every muscle. It would be so easy to relax, to let the walls crumble and surrender himself to the raging torrent. So easy.

No! He rebuffed the mental bombardment. He refused to give in to the darkness—could not give in. A scream ripped into his thoughts. *Caltha!*

His eyes flew open and he pivoted in the direction of the distressed cry. His fellow psiotic stood against the wall of a shop beset by two Morashans. Her robe, what was left of it, clung to her in ragged strips. The naval uniform beneath was ripped from neck to waist. Her attackers' objective was obvious. Yet, other than torn clothing, Caltha appeared uninjured.

A situation one of the men meant to remedy. His hand ducked into his robe to yank free a curved knife.

Before the Morashan could take a step, Kendler moved. In a smooth chop, the psiotic slammed a hammer-balled fist atop the assailant's wrist. The blade fell from a limply dangling hand and careened over the stone-paved street.

While the man blinked, trying to comprehend what had occurred, Kendler drove home a clean strike to his solar plexus. The Morashan groaned, air driven from lungs. He tumbled to the ground and rolled about clutching his gut.

The first attacker temporarily out of commission, Kendler turned to the remaining man. The Morashan now held Caltha pinned against the wall.

Kendler stepped behind the man and slapped an open palm atop his right kidney. Theoretically, the blow should have sent a shock wave through the man's innards powerful enough to rupture the unprotected organ.

The only result was a pained howl and Caltha's release. The Morashan whirled around. Kendler backstepped to avoid the thick arms that swung wide to seize him.

An old-fashioned haymaker that connected solidly with the assailant's jaw succeeded where martial-arts training failed. The man went down like a felled tree. Kendler pivoted back to face a new attack from his first opponent. The man was gone.

A blur at the corner of his eye drew the psiotic's attention. Caltha rushed him, brandishing her former attacker's knife.

Standing his ground before the charging woman, Kendler waited until the last moment. The blade lashed toward his abdomen. He sidestepped the keenly honed sliver of steel. Caltha's arm wrenched back for another try. His left arm snaked out, hand clamping firmly around her small wrist.

He shouted into her snarled face to jar her free of the force controlling her mind and body. The diminutive woman answered with a hand flung at his face, fingernails outstretched like talons of an attacking feline.

In a redirecting block, he sent her hand flailing over her head. Not waiting for a renewed attack, he followed through with a direct jab to her delicately shaped chin—a blow that he guiltily admitted enjoying. Caltha crumpled to the cobblestones.

To his left, Kendler located a vacant shop. Not bothering to try the lock, he lashed out with his right foot. The door cracked, splintered, then swung inward. A hasty glance within to assure himself the building was empty, and he returned to his unconscious "partner." He lifted her, surprised at her weight. She felt like a sleeping child in his arms.

Within the abandoned shop, he carefully laid her on the floor. Her jaw would ache when she woke, but a bruised chin was a far cry from a slit throat. Pulling off his robe, he spread it over her half-naked body.

Outside once more, Kendler found the last member of the threesome. Ome stood across the street shouting obscenities into the flames that licked from the windows of a burning building.

Before another Morashan could waylay him, the psiotic darted across the broad avenue. He grabbed the youth's shoulder and yanked him around.

This time, Kendler was prepared for the screaming attack that came. Easily he dodged a blow intended for his face. He then applied a twice-proved method for overcoming the madness that gripped Morasha. He connected an uppercut to Ome's jaw. The young man went out like a light.

Grabbing the youth's wrists, he dragged Ome back across the street and deposited him beside Caltha on the floor of the vacant shop. Kendler then slammed the door closed and braced his back against it, hoping his weight would keep out any berserker who had noticed his entry.

His head swirled. The darkness still clawed at him. He closed his eyes and focused all his energy against the presence.

Outside, the screams and cries of a city gone mad echoed in his ears.

TWELVE

It passed with the same abruptness with which it had come. One instant the ripping maelstrom ate at the walls of Kendler's psyche like a corrosive acid. The next moment, nothing.

As though a brace had been jerked from beneath him, his body went limp. Legs, liquid and fluid, gave way. He slid to the floor and sat there, back against the door. He tried to pick himself up and attend his unconscious companions. Not even a finger moved. The will and strength to move abandoned him. He was drained, mentally and physically.

With a great effort, he rolled his eyes back to Caltha and Ome. If he had possessed the strength, he would have shaken his head. The two lay side by side like children wrapped in sleep's protection, neither disturbed by the violence that had invaded their minds moments ago. Irony touched the weak smile that crept to the corners of Kendler's mouth.

Sleep. The possibility tempted him. *I could use a year or three of oblivion.* Of their own volition, his leaden eyelids drooped. They twitched in a feeble effort to fight against his gentle downward drift.

"Nils . . . Nils . . . Nils . . ." Caltha's voice intruded like the constant drip of a leaky faucet. He tried to ignore her. He had earned the right to rest, if only for a few short minutes. The voice groaned louder, terrified. "Nils . . . Nils . . ."

His eyes slitted open before sleep sealed them. Caltha no longer lay peacefully on the floor. Her robe-draped body twisted and wrenched violently.

"No! Nils, Nils." Desperation permeated her cries. "Nooooo!"

Kendler forced himself to move, scooting over the floor to her side. Perspiration beaded her forehead. Her hands lay to either side of her head, balled in clenched fists. Her head jerked spasmodically from side to side.

"Caltha," he whispered. "It's all right. It's over."

The psiotic did not respond. Her lips writhed as though forming unvoiced curses. For some nightmare tormentor, or for him? Kendler wondered.

Gently, he nudged her shoulder. Still no response. He shook her lightly to break the haunting dream. "Everything is all right. It's over now."

Her eyes flew open, wide and horrified. A piteous moan quavered over her trembling lips. Her terrified eyes darted about, finally alighting on him.

"Nils," she muttered, unsure, disbelieving, "you're . . ."

He smiled down at her. "A bit ragged for the wear, but still here."

"God! Oh my God! It was real." Her eyes clamped tightly closed. She shuddered.

"Shhhh." His hand returned to her shoulder in comfort. "It's over. It's passed."

"The men . . the knife . . . it wasn't a dream." She looked up at him, her expression a plea for him to tell her she was wrong.

"The men are gone now," he assured her.

"I tried to kill you, Nils." Her head rolled away from him. "I wanted to slit your throat. I would have . . ."

"No damage done. We both survived. " Compassion suffused through him. Something he had thought he would never feel for Caltha Renenet. "You might have some trouble chewing for the next few days. When you came at me with the knife, there wasn't time enough to be gentle."

Her fingers tentatively tested her jaw. She winced. Her head twisted back to Kendler. The fright, the need of comfort, he had seen a second ago were gone. In their place blazed familiar antagonism. Her gaze turned to Ome, still unconscious beside her.

"Did you also have to strike the boy, Mr. Kendler?" Her indignant tone returned, as did the "Mr. Kendler."

"Easier than letting him hurt someone, or worse, getting himself killed." He sounded apologetic in spite of himself.

Kendler sank to sit cross-legged on the floor. Caltha glared at him with contempt. All the barriers rose between them again. Kate Dunbar would never comprehend how wrong she had been when in a flash of administrative genius she had arranged this partnership.

If he managed to survive this assignment with his sanity intact and without strangling Caltha Renenet somewhere along the way, he would make damn sure the Psi Corps director heard every detail of her blunder. If she decided to draw and quarter him for insubordination, it would be worth it to have had his say.

Caltha looked at Ome once more. Her hand reached toward him.

"What are you going to do?" Kendler asked.

"Wake him. We do have a job to do," she said, challenging him.

"Let him sleep it off," Kendler said. "We both need to rest. The whole city is recovering from the attack. It's probably total confusion outside that door."

"All the more reason to move now," Caltha replied. "We can take advantage of the confusion to conceal our movements."

He disliked admitting she was right as much as he disliked the prospect of moving again. But he reluctantly nodded for her to wake the Morashan youth.

One firm shake and Ome's eyes fluttered open. He wiped at his face and grinned widely when he saw his companions. The grin abruptly faded. "What happened? What are we doing here?"

"Don't you remember?" Kendler glanced sternly at Caltha, who appeared as if she were about to recount the attack.

"No." Ome shook his head and looked at Kendler for some hint to his bewildering predicament. A sense of horror crept into his face. "*Nayati!* It happened again."

Kendler nodded, recognizing *Nayati* as the Morashan term for the mass hysteria.

The youth closed his eyes and lowered his head. A tremble visibly ran through his body.

"What do you remember of the *Nayati*?" Kendler asked.

"Nothing," Ome answered. "I felt its madness touching me, I think I cried out. Then . . . nothing."

"Are you sure?" Caltha asked. "Can't you remember anything else?"

"No," the boy repeated. "Nothing."

Before Caltha could question further, Kendler cut in. "Ome, I think we should get to the embassy. Are you ready to continue?"

The youth nodded and pushed to his feet. Caltha sat up. The draping robe fell to her waist, revealing her bare breasts. Ome's gaze immediately moved to the exposed flesh. His eyes widened with youthful surprise and delight—an expression that transformed to terror in the next instant.

"Did . . . did . . . I do that?" he stammered and swallowed several times.

"No, these are a very natural development for a woman." She smiled gently at the youth while she casually lifted the robe to cover herself. Neither her voice nor her action hinted at the slightest trace of embarrassment. She acted so natural, as though having her body unexpectedly exposed to two men was an everyday experience. "However, I think you should procure me another robe before we continue."

Obvious relief erased the tension from Ome's face. He smiled. "It shouldn't take long, half an hour at the most."

With that, the young Morashan turned and hastily left the abandoned shop. Kendler studied his fellow psiotic, surprised by what he had just glimpsed of the woman's personality.

"What are you staring at, Mr. Kendler?" Caltha turned back to him.

Kendler smiled. "You."

Indignant lines bunched around her tightly drawn mouth and an eyebrow deigned to rise. "I'd think you'd have seen enough of me already. One cheap thrill is all you get."

Nothing I haven't seen before slipped into his mind. He let the retort slide by, refusing to be maneuvered into another verbal fencing match. "You may cultivate one hard exterior, Caltha Renenet. But what you just did for that boy was nice, damn nice, even human. While he might not be able to thank you, I can . . . thank you. You handled an awkward situation in Class triple-A style."

"I did nothing," she insisted.

"Ome was so damn frightened that he had attacked you during the *Nayati*. Something I don't believe he could walk around with in his head. The Lukya religion is still a stern master. The way you concealed your embarrassment and put him at ease . . ." Kendler caught himself. His voice rose in volume and pitch. What had started as a compliment edged toward argument. He could combat the insanity of the Morashan *Nayati*, but could not cope with Caltha Renenet.

"Forget it," he finally said. "Forget I opened my mouth."

He pushed from the floor and walked to the door. He felt weaker than he wanted to admit, but he had to do something to vent his frustration.

Opening the door a few centimeters, he peered out. The confusion he imagined was nothing compared to the scene outside. People crowded the street, rushing in every direction, fleeing from the inescapable invader that might descend on them in the next moment.

Amid the chaos, some rationality reigned. A few Morashans had formed an ineffectual bucket brigade to fight the fires still blazing across the avenue. Others knelt beside those lying wounded in the street, administering what aid they could. The dead were left where they had fallen, no longer needing the attention of the living, the survivors.

"Ni—Mr. Kendler," Caltha said behind him. "I'm afraid I misunderstood what you were trying to say. I read something else into your words. I hope . . ."

He switched her off. It was the only way he could deal with his "partner"—ignore her.

"How is it?" she asked when he closed the door.

"Ugly." He sucked in a deep breath.

"Will it impede getting to the embassy?"

"I don't think we should even consider going to the embassy," he replied.

"What?" She stared at him incredulously. "We have orders to meet with Ambassador Lore."

"We were directed to meet with the ambassador, given a schedule for arrival on Morasha, but *not* orders," Kendler said. "I've never known Kate Dunbar to quibble about the route her agents take, as long as they reach their destinations . . . within her expectations."

He could see the wheels turning in her brain, ready to refute him. Not waiting for her reply, he continued, *"Nayati* is bigger than Kate led us to believe. We need time to examine it from all angles. An attempt to meet with Ambassador Lore will endanger our success in doing that. If Ome is right and the Kavinites suspect our being on-planet, the embassy will be under constant surveillance. The aftermath of the *Nayati* is exactly what we need to lose ourselves in Ban-Dorit. If he's cleared, Ome will act as our go-between with Lore."

Caltha offered no comment, which bothered him more than a cutting retort.

"It's the only way to retain our mobility in the city," Kendler added. "If we're tagged at the embassy, we'll have Kavinite shadows every time we step outside."

"We need to see the results of Lore's own investigations," Caltha finally said. "I don't want to duplicate his efforts. There's no need walking into dead ends."

He could have argued the point, but did not. What one person discerned as a dead end might prove an open avenue through the eyes of another. Lore was thorough. Kendler had learned that on Vire. For the moment, he was willing to accept the ambassador's dead ends. "Lore can send us his findings through an intermediary. We'll pass on our progress the same way. It's not as efficient as face-to-face contact, but better than Kavinites on our heels."

Keeping the robe pressed to her chest, Caltha leaned forward and hugged her knees. She pursed her lips, then took a deep breath. Her head tilted forward slightly.

"You're right," she said, obviously pained to admit he could be correct about anything. "What about quarters in Ban-Dorit?"

"Ome can help us there," Kendler replied.

"We will be endangering the boy if he's selected as our intermediary."

Kendler nodded. "I think we should leave that decision to Ome and Lore."

The door to the shop swung inward. Ome's head poked through the opening. Seeing them, he smiled and walked into the room to hand Caltha a blue flowered robe. Still clutching Kendler's robe to her chest, she stood. She asked the two men to avert their eyes, then walked to the back of the room.

"A garment shop had been broken into down the street," Ome told Kendler. "Its merchandise was strewn in the street. The owner was dead. He lay in the doorway, throat slit."

"It's over now." Kendler detected guilt and shame in the youth's face. He wanted to say something to assure him the *Nayati* was not his fault. But all the words that came to mind seemed trite and weak.

Ome looked at the older man. "But when will it come again?"

Kendler's only answer was awkward silence. To his relief, Caltha joined them, handing him his robe.

"Ready." She smiled, displaying the new robe. If possible, the blue hue of the material enhanced her beauty. She turned to Ome. "We can't guarantee the *Nayati* will not strike again. However, the sooner we begin our work, the sooner we will find its source."

"It is a short way to the embassy," Ome said.

"Not the embassy, but a hotel." Kendler offered no explanation of their change in plans.

"Hotel?" Ome questioned the alien word that had slipped into Kendler's speech. After several attempts to understand what they wanted, the youth grinned widely. "A *topwe*."

"Yes," Kendler replied. Sleep-learning was not foolproof. *Topwe* had not been a word fed to them by the *Kelso's* computer. But on hearing it, its logic was clear. *Topwe* meant a house with rented rooms.

Ome told them of a *topwe* run by a distant cousin in a respectable section of the city not far from where they stood. "My cousin provides two meals a day. She is an excellent cook. My father says her first three husbands died of obesity because they could not refrain from gluttony at her table."

None too certain of the recommendation, Kendler accepted Ome's offer to lead them to his cousin's home. Then he gave the youth a cover story. Caltha and he were sister and brother whose family had died and whose home had burned in the *Nayati*.

"We should be on our way," the youth said. "Evening comes. While Ban-Dorit is a peaceful city, the *Nayati* provides temptations too great for many of our citizens to resist. The many shops that have been broken into will attract looters. There are those who take advantage of the dead and wounded on the streets. They will not hesitate to create another *Nayati* victim if they feel they can gain a purse."

They followed Ome outside. To Kendler's surprise, Caltha pressed close to his side, her eyes wide in horror. While she had conscious memories of the *Nayati*, they had not prepared her for what met her eyes.

The scene repeated itself on each new avenue they crossed—burned-out homes and shops, the dead lying where they had fallen, the Morashans who could walk tending those who could not.

They passed several children wandering alone, crying for their parents. Other carried bundles under their arms and clutched the hands of younger children as they moved through the city. Their eyes were blank, their faces expressionless. Kendler shuddered, unable to evade speculation on what had happened to their parents and what would happen to them.

"We will be at my cousin's in a few minutes," Ome assured them while they moved down a street of fire-gutted homes. Smoke curled from the charred ruins.

Kendler glanced at their guide. Did his cousin's house still stand?

Two more turns and they entered a narrow corridor-street that appeared relatively unscathed by the *Nayati*. Relief washed over the young Morashan's face. He apparently had shared Kendler's concern for his cousin's home.

"My cousin's." Ome stopped before a bright-blue-painted wooden door. He knocked, but no one answered. Kendler noted his worry. The youth knocked harder, his knuckles sounding like a clapper striking a wooden bell.

Footsteps came from within. The door opened and a rotund woman, face drawn and haggard, stared at them as though accustoming her eyes to the night's darkness. A smile slowly spread on her lips.

"Ome!" Her arms flew wide and surrounded the youth. She squeezed him in a crushing hug. "I thought you had forgotten your cousin Suletu."

The greeting was overjoyous, a flood of relief celebrating their survival of the *Nayati* once again. After enduring his cousin's hugs and a sloppy kiss on the cheek, Ome turned to his wards.

"Suletu, I have brought two old friends who are in need of your help." The youth then repeated the story Kendler had given him with enough melodramatic embellishments to bring tears to the eyes of a jaded holodrama writer.

Suletu shook her head sadly when Ome completed the tale. Her gaze moved back and forth between Kendler and Caltha. "Yours is not an unusual story these days. Ban-Dorit's avenues are walked by an army of the homeless. That I could offer some aid to ease your suffering! Yet I cannot. Nor do I believe you'll find any *topwe* within the city that can. Our doors overflow with those who have lost their homes. I have but one room left vacant, not the two you require."

"We'll take it," Kendler said, too weary to wander Ban-Dorit's streets in search of other accommodations.

Caltha's eyes shot to him. He could almost feel the venom in her gaze, but she said nothing.

"The room is on the second floor facing the street." Suletu smiled widely and stepped back to allow them to enter. "I know this is not a good time, but I am afraid I must speak of money. I must ask for a night's payment in advance."

Automatically, Kendler reached between the folds of his robe to delve into the pockets of the uniform beneath. His fingers touched LofAl standard chits. To use them here would give their identities away. His shoulder slumped. "I'm afraid we left in such a hurry that I forgot my pouch."

Suletu's jaw tightened. Before she could question his lack of funds, Ome produced three coins and spread them in her palm. She smiled, her doubt assuaged. "Ome, there is meat, bread, and wine in my kitchen. Gather it and bring it upstairs for your friends. I will show them to their room."

Upstairs, Suletu opened the door to a room and motioned them inside. While it could not compare with the luxury of Lanatia hotels, the room was clean and large and did have a glass-paned window overlooking the street below. The furniture, all handcrafted wood from its appearance, was massive. A long table stood along one wall. Atop it were an oil lamp, two cups, a bowl, and two water pitchers. One pitcher for drinking, Suletu explained, the other for washing.

A standing closet, a chest of drawers, a single chair, and what appeared to be a desk were the room's only other furnishings. The lack of a bed was obvious. Kendler's gaze fell on a hammock slung in the room's far corner. He remembered his sleep lessons aboard the *Kelso*. Night on Morasha often brought visitors into Ban-Dorit, jungle denizens of the insect and reptilian variety.

Kendler caught Caltha watching him peruse the hammock. A disgusted expression shadowed her face. Renewed irritation crept back into him.

Without a doubt, his "partner" thought he had ulterior motives when he accepted the single room. The possibility of lovemaking in that awkward and painful-looking rope web was ludicrous. He seriously doubted his ability to *sleep* in the hammock.

"There is another hammock stored in the top drawer," Suletu said. "Also blankets."

She walked to the chest and opened the drawer. "I breakfast with the rising of the sun and sup when it sets. For those who miss meals, I usually leave something out in the kitchen. There is a common sitting room below, and on the roof there is space to spread prayer mats."

Ome entered balancing a tray of sliced meat, half a loaf of dark bread, and a jar of wine in his arms. He edged the pitchers and bowl on the table aside with an elbow and managed to deposit his load without spilling anything.

"Is there anything else you'll need?" Suletu asked. Kendler shook his head, as did Caltha. "Bring the cups and tray down to breakfast. May your sleep be undisturbed and your dreams the color of the rainbow."

With that, she left the three alone. If Caltha had any complaints about the sleeping arrangements, she kept them to herself, which suited Kendler. He was too tired to argue over imagined sexual overtures.

Ome suggested Caltha take the room's only chair. She refused and simply sank to the floor, using a wall to support her back. The youth then tore the bread into three pieces and filled the cups with wine. Piling one piece of the bread with meat slices, he picked up a cup and took the meal to Caltha.

"Are the *Nayati* always as violent as the one today?" She accepted the food.

"There have been worse." The boy seemed reluctant to discuss the topic. "There have been lesser *Nayati*."

Kendler had no wish to unduly distress the youth, but questions needed answering. "What was it like when the *Nayati* began?"

"As it was foretold in the *Mansur*." Ome brought Kendler his portion of the meal. "The sacred prophecies written by the most venerable Tahir-Valin."

"Prophecies?" Caltha asked around a mouthful of the makeshift sandwich.

"Tahir-Valin was among the first faithful to walk on Morasha. The Creator blessed him with the gift to view the future. With his holy eyes, he saw the collapse of the Lukya discipline and the loss of our ancestors' vast knowledge. He saw Morashan warring with Morashan until they were no better than animals crawling in the dirt." Ome lowered himself to the floor with the remaining bread and meat. "He called this time *Nayati*, the great wrestling."

Prescience existed, Kendler knew, but it remained the least understood and controllable of the psi abilities. Tahir-Valin apparently had been a latent psiotic.

Downing his first bite with a swig of wine, Ome continued to recount the similarities of the holy man's writings and Morashan history. "The Lukya discipline once split in a thousand factions, each proclaiming they walked the true path.

Each cult sought to impose its will on others. Fighting erupted."

Kendler listened to the youth. Morasha's regression was an all too familar story shared by many of the planets lost during the Century Conflagration. Bit by bit, interior strife chipped away a young society's unstable foundation. The religious fanaticism of the colonists only fanned the flames. Not long enough on their new world to survive a major conflict without great losses, they began to regress.

"The *Yamarka*, who founded Ban-Dorit, sought to salvage the world they saw crumbling about them," Ome said. "Their mission, as it is to this day, was to preserve all knowledge and reeducate the peoples of Morasha when the *Nayati* passed and Man entered *Adain*, the new age of light."

Ome told them of the *Yamarka* monks who traveled the land seeking peace. The majority never returned to their brothers in the early years of their pilgrimages. Yet they persisted, slowly sowing the seeds of peace.

"The *Wunand* sect also survived the wars in great number. Of all who follow the Lukya discipline, their beliefs border on what many call insanity." Ome paused for another swallow of wine. "The *Wunand* refused to lay down their arms and vowed to rid Morasha of all but those who proclaimed their ways of worshiping the Creator."

The Morasha holy war continued. While many died, the heaviest losses were the schools and *Yamarka* monasteries, and with them the carefully preserved knowledge.

"Fifty years *Yamarka* and *Wunand* warred, until, at last, they sat in peace," Ome said. "It was said to be the end of *Nayati*, the madness of Morasha. But war is not madness, it is stupidity. Only now have we learned the true meaning of *Nayati*, the true darkness of insanity."

Kendler maneuvered back to his original question. "You said the *Nayati* began as Tahir-Valin prophesied?"

Ome swallowed the mouthful of meat he chewed. "Tahir-Valin called it an indescribable anger that is not rooted in the rational."

He paused to drain his cup in a determined gulp, then sucked in a deep breath. "It began just as that, an irritation that grew for no reason. Tempers flared, lifelong friends no longer tolerated one another, families lost their stability. The irritation spread, growing into a seething anger."

"Followed by a period of increased crime rate?" Caltha asked.

"At first that was what our leaders believed, merely a time of increased criminal activity. Our prisons overflowed with those who awaited trial. Now that *Nayati* is realized, the prisons are empty. Those beset by insanity are not criminals and all of Morasha knows insanity."

The youth pulled the wine jar from the table. Caltha and Kendler refused a second portion. Ome poured himself another cup. "This is what the *Mansur* predicted. We live *Nayati*, the destruction of our people."

The youth's gaze moved from Kendler to Caltha, then back, as though he expected some small word of encouragement, something that would allow him to cling to hope that he was wrong. Neither psiotic said anything. An uncomfortably heavy silence blanketed the room until Caltha held out her cup for a refill.

Ome responded without hesitation. Whether she had tried or not, Kendler recognized the sympathetic link she had established with the boy. Without a doubt her physical attractiveness and Ome's youth accounted in part for the link. If the young Morashan was selected as their intermediary to Ambassador Lore, it would make things easier.

"This afternoon," Kendler pressed, delving for answers to something that had bothered him all afternoon, "you remembered nothing about the *Nayati*. Has anything returned yet?"

Ome lowered his eyes and shook his head as if shamed by the inability to recall the events. "I remember sensing the *Nayati* descending around me, then waking on the floor of the shop. Nothing more."

Caltha's face tightened with puzzlement. Kendler signaled her off the subject. There was no need to probe deeper. She gave him a go-to-hell look, but held her curiosity.

"The Lukya religion . . ." Caltha asked. "Have there been any major changes in its structure since the coming of *Nayati*?"

"For the majority of my people, worship remains true to the *Yamarka* teachings," Ome said. "But a large number of *Wunand* cults have seen a revival, especially here within Ban-Dorit."

"What type of cults?" Caltha continued.

"They preach doom, teaching their followers to prepare for the end of our world," the youth replied. "Within Ban-Dorit's walls, there are at least twenty such groups."

The pessimistic view of Morasha's future was easy enough to comprehend after experiencing a *Nayati*. Kendler was surprised such cults did not dominate the Lukya religion.

"And you, Ome," Caltha asked, "are you a follower of these doomsday beliefs?"

"I am *Yamarka*," the youth answered. "I believe in Tahir-Valin's prophecies. But we of Morasha have misinterpreted them in the past. Perhaps we do so again."

Kendler washed down the last of his meal with the remaining sips of his wine. Ome's optimism was sincere. He grasped for any hope, no matter how seemingly thin, to sustain his belief that Morasha did not face its end.

The youth rose from the floor and stretched his legs. "I must return to the embassy. Ambassador Lore has been awaiting our arrival for hours. I'm certain he fears something happened to us during the *Nayati*."

"Wait a moment longer." Kendler extracted a wafer recorder from the breast pocket of his service uniform. "I want you to deliver a message to Lore."

Deciding Ome might have picked up LofAl standard at the embassy, Kendler dictated in native Lanatian. He apprised the ambassador of their change in plan and the need for anonymity. He then passed the recorder to Caltha.

The woman quickly added a request for reports on Lore's investigation into the *Nayati*. She clicked off the recorder, then flickered it on again to footnote her request with instructions to reimburse Ome for their night's rent in the *topwe* and to send funds to cover their expenses for at least two weeks. She handed the recorder to Ome to deliver it directly into the ambassador's hands. The youth nodded and left.

"Don't you think you were overly secretive with the boy?" Caltha stretched her legs and rubbed them.

"Until Lore gives Ome clearance, the boy doesn't need to know what we're considering." Kendler followed her example and stretched his own legs. He pointed to the hammock. "Want that one or the spare?"

"This one," she said. "I don't have the strength to hang the other."

Kendler groaned to himself, doubting his own ability to rise and retrieve the other hammock from the drawer. For a moment, he considered spreading blankets on the wooden floor in a pallet. The possibility of stretching out rather than dangling in a rope web was most attractive. Then he remembered the jungle's insects and reptiles and their nightly habit of venturing into Ban-Dorit. He pushed from the floor and walked to the chest.

"What are we considering, Mr. Kendler?" Caltha asked.

"Nils!" Kendler yanked the webbed hammock from the drawer. "After two weeks of 'Mr. Kendler,' I don't think I can live with it much longer. The name is Nils. There's nothing that says we have to like the situation. But we can make it easier on one another . . . Caltha."

She nodded hesitantly, apparently too tired to argue. "That still doesn't answer my question . . . Nils."

Kendler slipped one end of the web over a hook inset in the wall. "I don't know. What did you make of the *Nayati?*"

"I've never experienced anything like it. I was totally possessed by the sheer strength of the emanations. I struggled against it, but it controlled me," she said.

"Psi?" He glanced at her.

"Definitely," she replied. "What produced a force that powerful, I won't hazard a guess." She paused and took a deep breath. "How did *you* manage to fight it off?"

Kendler sensed her disgust with her inability to cope with the *Nayati,* while he had retained control. Was that the root of their antagonism? Was she competing with him? Or was it vice versa?

Hooking the other end of the hammock on the opposite wall, he recounted all that had occurred during the *Nayati,* detailing how he had drawn within himself to ward off the overwhelming psi emanations. "I suppose I recognized it doing to me what I've done with my merge targets. Luck, most of all."

"I don't need to be patronized. . . ." Her voice trailed away and she glanced at the ceiling. She tried, he thought. It would take time for the barriers to come down, if they ever did. "I'll try your method if we face another attack."

"What do you know about psitronics?" Kendler hung his arms over the hammock and tentatively tested it with his weight. It held.

"Not much." Caltha rose to walk across the room. She took a blanket from the chest. "Any attempts to artificially amplify psi emanations have been total failures."

"That's the extent of what I know." Kendler watched her spread the blanket into the hammock. "However, Kate Dunbar manages to get healthy appropriations for psitronic research each year despite the failures. The Kavinites also spend tremendous amounts on similar research."

"You think they've had a breakthrough?" Caltha turned to him.

"It's a possibility. Or they might have established a union."

"Union?" Her tone was as doubtful as his thoughts. Finding psiotics capable of combining their talents was rare. "What I felt would have equaled at least a hundred minds in union."

Kendler admitted the unlikelihood of union. It would be impossible for the Kavinites to smuggle on-planet the number of psiotics necessary to produce what he felt this afternoon without Lore's getting wind of their movements. "It could be one mind, something we've never encountered before?"

"A genetically altered brain?" Caltha climbed into her hammock and stretched out with a sigh. She chuckled with amusement.

Kendler smiled. "I think we'd better concentrate on psitronics."

"Agreed," she answered.

The possibility of facing such a device frightened Kendler. According to their computer briefing on the *Kelso*, the *Nayati* attacks were growing stronger. Today he had barely maintained control of himself. By all indications, if a psitronic mechanism was involved, the Kavinites had yet to use it at full force.

"Nils"—Caltha almost said the name naturally, though her tone still held a formal edge—"why were you so insistent about not questioning Ome on his lack of memory about the *Nayati*? It seems important. Why should we recall every detail of the attack and Ome remember absolutely nothing?"

"The black scar," Kendler replied.

"The scar?"

He nodded. "Unless I've misread what I've found in Morashan minds, every man, woman, and child bears that mental scar. It's the only way they can deal with their actions during *Nayati*."

He saw her eyes widen through the hammock's webbing. "The Lukya religion! Even the *Yamarka* teaching is rigid and demanding. The Morashans can't accept the atrocities they commit while gripped by the *Nayati*, and so they bury their actions deep within the subconscious."

"Followers of truth could never admit to such actions," Kendler agreed. "To accept the horrors that dwell in their souls would drive them over the edge."

Kendler walked to the table and blew out the room's single oil-burning lamp. He gave his eyes a moment to accustom themselves to the darkness before returning to the hammock. His anticipated problems in mounting the awkward-appearing web proved unfounded. He managed to climb in on his first try. To his surprise the hammock was far from uncomfortable.

"What about the doomsday cults Ome mentioned?" Caltha asked in the darkness.

"They seem a reasonable reaction in a fanatical society," Kendler replied.

"They also seem to be an area ripe for Kavinite exploitation," Caltha said.

"Create enough furor to topple the present leadership, then slip in a government that's pro-Kavinite." It would be an obvious ploy on Morasha, where religion overrode logic. Yet the idea bothered Kendler. If there were twenty such cults in Ban-Dorit, as Ome had indicated, the Kavinites' efforts might be too diluted to be effective. "What about the possibility of the Kavinites being behind all the cults?"

Caltha did not answer. The soft sound of her gentle breathing floated across the room. Kendler smiled. His fellow psiotic found no difficulty adjusting to sleeping in a webbed sling. He pulled a blanket over his shoulders and snuggled down. Actually, he admitted, the hammock was relaxing. His slightest movement set it to gently swaying in a lulling fashion.

He closed his eyes and concentrated on the doomsday cults. If the Kavinites were involved in all of them, that indicated a larger Kavinite intelligence network on Morasha than Kate Dunbar realized. It would also mean a greater danger to her "team." If the Kavinites did have psiotics on-planet, it would not take them long to discover their Lofgrinist opponents.

"Paul . . . Paul . . ." Caltha's soft breathing was broken by a whimper. "Paul, it will be all right . . . Paul . . ."

She sobbed.

"Caltha, Caltha," Kendler whisper-called to her. "Caltha, are you all right?"

The sobs subsided and the gentle rhythmic breathing returned. She slept again, her nightmare passed. Kendler closed his eyes again. *Paul*, he repeated to himself, wondering what man disturbed her sleep.

He did not ponder it for long. At least on one point concerning the hammock, he was quite wrong. It was easy to sleep in.

THIRTEEN

Nils Kendler dreamed of Rochelle's Point. Spread-eagled on the face of a soar-kite a half kilometer above the turquoise sea, he floated. Below, the people on the white beach appeared no larger than spike-armored sand crabs. He barely made out their movements when they lifted their hands to shield their eyes against the sun. Occasionally, one of the watchers waved an arm to the modern Icarus sailing Seker's warm summer breezes.

A hand roughly rocked Kendler's shoulder. The peaceful scene winked out. The demanding hand persisted in shaking him.

He opened his eyes to find Caltha Renenet swaying at his side. *No, I'm swaying.* Or at least the hammock was, rocked by his rude awakening.

Caltha smiled at him, displaying a bit too much relish. She apparently was one of those people who derived a certain pleasure from interrupting the sleep of others. At least that smile indicated she enjoyed jarring him from his dreams.

"Go away, Calyn." He moaned and attempted to roll to his side. The hammock's sway grew. "A growing boy needs his rest."

"Suletu just knocked on the door." Caltha chuckled. "Come

on, growing boy. Ome's downstairs waiting on us. It's almost noon."

Kendler groaned again. His lower back ached sharply. He cursed the hammock, then realized the pain stemmed from an overly full bladder. "Did Suletu mention a toilet in her tour of the house? Or does Morasha have indoor plumbing yet?"

"At the opposite end of the hall," Caltha answered. "There's also a shower. You'll have to use one of the towels hung on the wall to dry yourself. Morasha doesn't have blowers."

"It would be impossible to ever be dry in this humidity." He managed to swing his legs out of the hammock and let gravity extract him from the web. Outside he found the bathroom, completely inlaid with white and green arabesque tiles. Fifteen minutes later, he returned to the room humming a song whose words and title he could no longer remember.

"Feel better?" Caltha smiled. It took Kendler off-guard, but he made no comment, afraid her good mood would evaporate.

"Slept like a rock," he said. "I remember closing my eyes and that's about all until you woke me."

"Who is Calyn?" She asked while he slipped into his Morashan robe.

He made no attempt to conceal his surprise. "A girl I once knew on my homeworld. Where did you hear of her?"

"You called me Calyn when I woke you." A strange little expression worried her face.

"A slip of the tongue." He shrugged his shoulders and smiled sheepishly. "I was dreaming about Seker."

Caltha turned to her hammock, pulled the blanket from it, and folded it. "Was she your lover?"

"No, afraid Kate Dunbar doesn't leave me much time for lovers." He chuckled while he took her blanket and deposited it along with his in the chest. "Seker still has social taboos when it comes to incest. Population is too small to allow sibling mate-bonding. Calyn was my sister."

"Was?"

He briefly recounted his family's death. "Calyn and I were closer than most lovers. She was a merger, too. Better at it than I am. Kate would have given both her arms to enlist Calyn."

"The Kavinites were responsible for killing your family?" Something he could not define flashed in her dark eyes.

"They were *suspected*." The barrage of personal questions

112

was completely out of character for her. In their two weeks together, she had barely tolerated his existence, let alone shown interest in it. "Nothing was ever proved."

She nodded solemnly as though he was sharing some intimate secret, a confidence that would remain secure with her. The reaction was puzzling.

"Since we're dredging up old memories," he said, "who's Paul?"

Caltha's eyes shot up to stare at him. "What do you know about Paul?"

"Nothing." He felt the barrier rise between them once again. "You called out to him last night."

"Oh." Relief softened her face.

"A lover?"

She grinned and shook her head, her long black hair undulating in captivating waves. "Lanatia has no taboo against incest, and I do love Paul more than any other male in my life. However, Paul's only seven years old, and he's my son."

"Son?" She could have knocked him over with the proverbial feather. "I thought the corps had a rule about married field agents, or any strong emotional attachments for that matter."

"My husband is dead," she replied. "He was an ensign just out of the naval academy, assigned to the *Roscoe Turner*."

She needed to say no more. Only a man locked away in a cryogenic chamber the past ten years would not know of the *Turner* Crisis. The Kavinites and LofAl had not come so close to open warfare since the Century Conflagration.

The *Roscoe Turner* had been on a standard reconnaissance mission to the Faber System when it mysteriously exploded. All the cruiser's crew were killed. The ship's flight records also were annihilated. That a Kavinite cruiser was also within the Faber System pointed to a military confrontation.

However, the Kavinites produced spetapes of the *Roscoe Turner*'s distress calls and a flight log that showed an attempt to aid the cruiser. After a lengthy inquiry, the LofAl Council accept the dubious evidence to avoid a declaration of war.

"Like your family, my husband died at the hands of the Kavinites," she said. "Though nothing was ever proved."

Kendler now understood that expression he had seen on her face. They shared a common bond, no matter how tenuous. The Psi Corps offered the outlet they needed to stand against those who had stolen loved ones from them.

Revenge? Perhaps once, Kendler told himself, *at the beginning.* But no longer. He could never extract from the Kavinites what they had taken from him.

But Caltha, had she realized that? Or was she still seeking an impossible retribution? He could not tell. Maybe he was groping for a reason to explain the animosity that existed between them.

"We've kept Ome waiting long enough," Caltha said, apparently unwilling to dwell on her past further.

In the common sitting room downstairs, the young Morashan sat talking with his cousin. Filling a small table between them was a pot of tea and a tray of honey-dripping pastries. After a brief exchange, Suletu excused herself, leaving the three alone.

"It took very little convincing to have my cousin prepare a light repast," Ome said, pulling another chair beside the table. "After missing breakfast, I knew you would be hungry."

The pastries looked anything but light. One bite confirmed their richness. The deceptively thin layers of crisp dough, nuts, and honey settled into Kendler's stomach like bricks, but the psiotic found he was unable to help himself. The taste was exquisite. He gobbled down three before washing their sweetness away with a cup of strongly brewed tea.

"Ambassador Lore asked that I give these to you." Ome withdrew a black leather pouch from inside his robe and placed it on the table.

Caltha lifted it, opened a single flap, and emptied the contents onto the table. Coins ticked against the wood, the Morashan currency they had requested.

"The ambassador is generous," Ome commented while he eyed the money. "Most within Ban-Dorit could support a family for a year with that amount."

Kendler smiled. Lore's tidy sum also included enough to grease a few palms if it should prove necessary during their investigation. He watched Caltha delve into the pouch and come out with four wafer recorders.

She held them up to display the numeral sequence printed on their faces. She then placed the recorder numbered one on the table and activated it with her thumb. Ambassador Lore's voice whispered from its mini-speaker:

"Welcome to Morasha. I understand from Ome that you

received your first taste of *Nayati* and survived. If I placed faith in omens, I would say it bodes well for your ultimate success on this assignment.

"First, let me assure you that Ome Reve has my full clearance and is well qualified as an intermediary during your investigation. He has orders to serve you in any capacity he can."

Silently, occasionally sipping tea, the three listened to the first recorder's message. After a brief warning about the *Nayati*'s increasing violence, Lore postulated what he viewed as possible sources of the attacks. He added nothing to what Caltha and Kendler had decided the night before.

"Shall we go to the next recorder?" Caltha asked when the first clicked off.

"Ready if you are." Kendler glanced at Ome, who nodded.

The following three tapes recounted all of Lore's investigations, including the possibility of drugs, hypnosis, and mental conditioning. All had led to dead ends. The tapes ended with a request that they maintain close contact with the embassy and a usual well-wishing for a hasty remedy to the situation.

"Doesn't narrow things down, does it?" Kendler tapped his fingers on the table.

Caltha shook her head. "I think we should begin with the cults."

Kendler picked up one of the recorders and quickly dictated a brief message of their intentions. He handed it to Ome for delivery to Lore later that day.

"Then you do not believe the insanity we experience on Morasha is the *Nayati* prophesied by Tahir-Valin?" The youth studied them carefully.

It suddenly occurred to Kendler that Ome was hearing all this for the first time. He apologized for keeping him in the dark.

"It is understandable." Ome seemed unoffended by their secrecy. "I might have been a Kavinite spy."

Kendler had not worried about that, but rather what the boy might tell his father. Apparently it did not matter to Lore if the Morashan leader learned every detail of the investigation. As it was, it would probably give the man something to hold to while the pressures against his government mounted.

Caltha told Ome of their plans to begin the investigation with the doomsday cults, and that they believed the *Nayati* to be a psi-induced phenomenon.

The youth sat thinking for a moment when she concluded.

"There will be no difficulty in taking you to the various cults. People come and go freely. The temples are open to all. But I don't understand this 'psi' you mentioned."

Caltha quickly explained. Ome's gaze moved between the two off-worlders. "You read minds?"

"Sort of." Caltha smiled.

"Can you read mine now?" he asked, obviously distressed by the possibility. Kendler thought he noted a slight reddening of the boy's dark cheeks.

Caltha shook her head and explained the need for a psiotic to remain immobile while he sought alpha level awareness. Ome smiled with relief. "It is good. It wouldn't be wise for one to have access to another's thoughts all the time."

Neither Caltha nor Kendler mentioned the methods that existed to short-circuit psi probes, or at least reroute them. Believing they might probe his mind unexpectedly would help keep the young Morashan honest.

"Who of these doom criers has the largest following?" Caltha divided the coins and pushed half to Kendler.

"Atla-Eron," Ome replied without a pause. "Locating him might be a problem. Shortly after the first *Nayati*, Atla-Eron was responsible for inciting a riot outside my father's house. A warrant was issued for his arrest, but the city guard has been unable to find him. He appears from out of nowhere, preaches doom, and then disappears before he can be detained."

"Most definitely the type of character we need to meet." Caltha glanced at Kendler. "Do you think you can locate him?"

"I am not certain," Ome said. "Rumors abound about where Atla-Eron will next appear. Most of the time, he does not appear. But I will attempt to find him for you."

"Meanwhile, we'll take a look at the other cults," Kendler said.

"We will begin at the Temple of Four Flames," the young Morashan replied. "There the priest, Danladi-Zeke, draws large crowds, though nothing compared to those of Atla-Eron."

"The Temple of Four Flames sounds as likely a place to begin as any." Caltha stood. "Shall we go?"

Kendler and Ome rose and moved toward the door. The youth grinned mischievously and winked at Kendler. "I would like to read the mind of Danladi-Zeke. It is said he has thirty wives. He must carry many interesting memories in his ancient head."

Kendler smiled while the Morashan led them into Ban-Dorit's streets.

Outside, except for the burned-out shells of destroyed buildings, no signs remained of last evening's violence. Like the black scars they carried in their minds, the Morashans also held a resiliency that sought normalcy in the face of the madness gripping their world.

FOURTEEN

Kendler slowly withdrew from the consciousness of the priest Sipatu-An. With the same cautious ease, he allowed himself to accept the input of his own senses.

Smell came first, the odor of closely packed bodies, squeezed tightly together so that he could taste their mutual warmth. Then the musky dampness of the ancient temple crept into his nostrils.

The tactile sense opened next. He felt Sipatu-An's followers pressed around him. Caltha's arm looped around his waist for support, firmly held him upright and kept him from collapsing amid the *Wunand* service.

"Nils," her voice whispered softly in his ear.

He stifled the weary moan that rose from his chest and slowly allowed his will to seep back into his body's muscles. He tested his strength, flexing fingers, toes, legs, and arms, making sure he could support himself before reestablishing total command of his body. The firmness of Caltha's arm did not ease.

He smiled to himself. The first day they had attempted this, he had sprawled face down on the dirt floor of the Temple of the Bright Path. As it was, his lack of control was mistaken for religious fervor, a charismatic display of deep conviction for the teachings of the priest Zorya-Mikk. To demonstrate that their own beliefs were greater than a mere member of the flock, many of Zorya-Mikk's acolytes went so far as to throw themselves into the dirt and writhe about.

Someday he would see the humor of the situation. Now he nursed a still slightly swollen and very sore nose.

"Nils," Caltha whispered again. "Is everything all right?"

He nodded, opening his eyes. Caltha appeared relieved. He felt the tension flow from her arm, though it remained at his waist, just in case.

One result of their week-long delving of Ban-Dorit's doomsday cults had been a lessening of their mutual antagonism. He was not sure what had brought about the change. Perhaps it was the fact that they now focused their energies on the investigation rather than each other. Or perhaps the reason lay in the necessity of placing one's body in the trust of another while attaining alpha level awareness.

Whatever, Kendler found himself grateful for the fellow psiotic at his side. Despite his vehement protest, he now had a certain security and comfort in working with Caltha, something he never experienced while on his own.

Normals knew of the dangers to which psiotics exposed themselves. But a true comprehension of the physical, mental, and emotional strain lay beyond their experience. He hated to admit it, but Kate Dunbar had been right. Caltha and he could aid one another if danger presented itself.

"Are you sure you can make it on your own?" Caltha's gaze moved over his face, seeking the betraying signs of exhaustion. During the past week they had pushed themselves beyond the normal limits of their abilities. Two more *Nayati* and the resulting horrors unleashed on this vulnerable planet drove them like an obsession.

"I'll make it," he assured her.

Caltha slipped her arm from around him. A pleasing warm glow remained where she had held him. He savored the lingering feeling, disappointed when it eventually faded.

He saw her still studying him out of the corner of his eye. He recognized the concern on her face. He felt it every time she emerged from alpha awareness. The effects of their seven-day probe of Lukyan doomsday cults were physically evident on her face. Shadowy circles ringed beneath weary-looking eyes. The same circles he had seen on his own face while he trimmed his beard that morning.

"Anything?" she asked.

Before he could answer, Sipatu-An concluded his sermon. The crowd sitting cross-legged on the temple floor broke into wild cheering. The priest held out his arms, signaling them to rise. They stood, their feet stomping in rhythm to their clapping hands. With Caltha's aid, Kendler managed to stand. There his charade ended. No strength remained to cheer or applaud the priest of oblivion.

Minutes passed before the din died and acolytes stepped through the flock of true believers to station themselves on each side of the temple's lofty doors. Each clutched a wicker basket before him, in what apparently was the galaxy's universal religious symbol.

While Sipatu-An's followers filed from the temple, the two psiotics stepped into line and exited to avoid drawing attention to themselves. Each dropped a copper coin into one of the baskets when they passed the acolytes, a magnanimous donation rather than a critical review of Sipatu-An's teachings.

Outside, Kendler stumbled when they started down the forty steps leading to the street below. His descent would have been far quicker and painful had Caltha not caught his arm and tugged him upright.

"Are you certain you're all right?" There was an edge to her voice; whether it stemmed from concern or weariness he could not discern.

"No," he answered. "I'm not sure of anything. My head is swirling in fifty directions at once."

Securely locking an arm about his waist, she helped him down the eternity of stairs and into a public garden spread at the foot of the temple. She did not bother searching for a bench, but guided him to the trunk of a towering shade tree. He gratefully sank to the ground, resting his back against the dark bole.

Caltha walked to a nearby fountain and filled a small cup she carried strapped to her belt in Morashan fashion. Returning, she handed him the water. Kendler took one small swallow, enough to wet mouth and throat. His head continued to spin and his stomach now threatened to heave up what remained of his lunch.

"It's time to call it a day." Caltha settled beside him. "We'll rest here awhile before we return to Suletu's."

She pulled a handkerchief from inside her robe, dipped it into the cup, and bathed his face. Not having the strength to vocalize his objections to the attention, Kendler closed his eyes. The water felt cool and soothing. He sighed and sucked in a breath to steady himself.

Caltha's fragrance surrounded him. He smiled. He had been too long within the sterile, antiseptic environment of Lanatia and LofAl embassies on various planets. Their deodorant showers, air-conditioning units, artificial perfumes, and body oils were designed to eliminate unpleasant odors. The trouble was, they also eliminated pleasant ones. He had forgotten what another human being smelled like. At that moment, Caltha Renenet smelled very warm, very human, and very feminine.

"Feel better?"

He looked at her and smiled. "The spinning's subsiding. I'll be okay in another few minutes."

"No rush," she said. "We don't have to meet Ome for two more hours. You've been pushing yourself."

He chuckled. "I'm not the only one. I seem to remember someone collapsing into her hammock last night without bothering to eat dinner."

"We're both pushing ourselves," she admitted. A slight touch of pink blushed her cheeks at the mention of her exhaustion.

"What we need is a vacation." He took another sip of water. "Or at least a couple of days off. Remind me to report Kate Dunbar to the Labor Relations Ministry when we return to Lanatia."

"A vacation . . . that would be nice." Her voice held a dreamy quality. She stared at the leafy boughs overhead. Abruptly her face hardened. "But we can't. The *Nayati* are coming more frequently. Ambassador Lore feels the present government can't last more than another two weeks unless the situation changes drastically."

Kendler tried to ignore the desperation she expressed. He could not. He labored under the same pressure. The whole planet was coming apart at the seams and they had not been able to do a thing to stop it.

In their week on Morasha, they had infiltrated fifteen of the doomsday cults and at least ten times that number of minds. Even Ome's anticipations about the exotic pleasures of the *Wunand* priest Danladi-Zeke and his numerous wives had fallen flat on its face. Danladi-Zeke, while he did have the rumored thirty wives, proved to be sexually impotent. The wives were all show. The seventy children he was rumored to have sired came not from his loins, but from the sexual prowess of acolytes, each sufficiently drugged so that he would not remember his venture into the priest's harem the next morning. Danladi-Zeke himself often watched his wives cavorting with their procured lovers—out of mere curiosity. The priest was as sexually dead as a slab of granite.

"I gather we struck out with Sipatu-An," Caltha said in a statement rather than a question.

"Right," Kendler verified. "Ever get the feeling we might be approaching this from the wrong angle?"

A muscle twitched along her jaw, and her lips pursed in disgust. "I don't know. After a week's work, I thought we'd have something. All we've got is a big, blank zero. I'd say let's try something else, but I don't know what."

"We could probe the Kavinites," he suggested.

Caltha did not bother to answer. They had discussed a direct approach after their first series of failures. Odds were that if the Kavinites were responsible for the *Nayati*, only a key individual within their embassy would know of the clandestine activity. To make contact with one Kavinite would alert the others to their psiotic shadows—unless they eliminated the person they contacted. They had discussed that possibility also. More than one unexplained death would effect the same results. Either way, one Caltha Renenet and one Nils Kendler would not be long for this world, or any other.

The fact remained, if they did not get some results soon, they were faced with a mental assault on the Kavinite embassy.

"There's nothing else we can do today." Kendler lifted himself from the ground and held out a hand to Caltha. "Let's head back for Suletu's."

She grasped his wrist and pulled to her feet. "It's so damn frustrating."

"Forget it. There's no use pushing when we're tired. We'll come up with something sooner or later." He did his best to sound confident and received a doubtful glance from his companion for the effort. He did not blame her. He did not believe it either, not at the rate they were going.

Outside the park, they turned down a street that once had been lined with prospering shops. It now appeared to have been the spearhead of a major military offensive. The two shops untouched by flames were boarded closed, a gruesome reminder of the *Nayati*'s increasing violence.

Whether the Kavinites overthrew the present government

no longer seemed of any importance to Kendler. If the *Nayati* continued for two more weeks, there would be no Morasha for either the Kavinites or LofAl to claim.

He studied the Morashans they passed. He understood their down-hung heads and eyes that refused to meet those who approached. While he could never wipe away the black scar each carried, he could help them forget the hell that consumed their world. That is, if he could find the source of the *Nayati*.

If—there was always that "if." It appeared larger now than it had a week ago.

Halfway to Suletu's, Kendler stopped and rested again. Caltha offered no objections. They sat on what remained of a wall that had once formed a storefront. Neither talked, nor did they gaze at the street scene around them. Ban-Dorit stood as a constant reminder of their failure. They could not face it. The Morashan city was the black scar they bore.

Ten minutes later, they stood and continued to Suletu's *topwe*. Ome waited for them in the common room, talking with his cousin. Excitement flashed on the youth's face when he saw them. He contained it until Suletu at last left the room to begin the evening meal.

When the clatter of pans and wooden bowls came from the kitchen, Ome leaned to the two psiotics. "I have good news. I have located Atla-Eron. I have seen him with my own eyes."

The youth beamed, obviously expecting praise for his achievement. The name meant nothing to Kendler, nor to Caltha, from her expression. Ome's wide grin drooped to an equally blank expression. "Atla-Eron, the prophet you asked me to find."

It hit Kendler. The man they had discussed when they had first begun their search of the doom cults, the man wanted by Ban-Dorit authorities for inciting a riot. "You saw him?"

"In the Den of the Holy Thief." Ome's grin returned. "I was there for my noon meal. The whole tavern was full, as it is at mealtimes."

Even in his short time on Morasha, Kendler had heard of the tavern. Its well-publicized dancing girls drew constant crowds, and there were rumors of less than legal business transactions in its back rooms.

"I had just received a bowl of soup when the doors to the tavern flew open." The youth's eyes widened and his arms gesticulated in the air to emphasize the tale. "There, haloed by the light, stood Atla-Eron."

Sensing the drama of the moment, Ome paused, his gaze shifting between Caltha and Kendler. "For what seemed like hours, he stood there, letting every head turn to him. Then he cried out, 'Sinners, desecrators of the sacred way! You perch on your hindquarters reveling in lascivious ways while the world rots at its core. You allow those who rule you to lead you by the nose to slaughter. Prepare your souls for the pits of hell and an eternity of demonic awareness!'"

Again the youth paused. Kendler could see Ome was not embellishing Atla-Eron's words, but quoting them verbatim.

"His eyes burned with the fire of the sun when he spoke," Ome continued. "He was like a man with the presence of the Creator about him. None could take his gaze from him."

"Was that all he said?" Caltha asked.

"Again he spoke: 'The way to eternal salvation is not sealed against you. Time remains to redeem your twisted souls and once again walk the Golden Way. Tonight when the moon kisses the tip of Isal, stand in its shadow and I will show you the way to salvation. Fail to heed my words, and you surely shall be damned.'"

Ome took a deep breath. "Then he stepped back and the doors slammed closed. I swear by all I hold holy, his hands never touched the knobs."

An easy parlor trick, Kendler mused, performed with micro-thin monofilament wire, or with less sophisticated electromagnets. Atla-Eron's entrance and condemnation of the tavern's patrons had all the earmarks of a Kavinite ruse. For the first time in a week, the psiotic felt elation shoot through him.

"I followed him," Ome said. "He walked down an alley beside the tavern. When I reached it, he was gone. He wasn't out of my sight for more than a second or two. Even running, which he wasn't, he couldn't have reached the end of the alley. It was as though he vanished into air . . . or carried a cloak of invisibility."

The disappearing act was harder to explain, but Kendler would have laid odds that a convenient doorway within the alley provided Atla-Eron an easy exit route. In his awe of the self-proclaimed prophet, Ome had simply overlooked the obvious. There were more technical explanations for the disappearance, but quite often the simplest approach proved the most effective.

"The Den of the Holy Thief wasn't Atla-Eron's only visit today," Ome said. "The city buzzes with reports of him appearing at the Temple of Lost Children, the Grand Bazaar, the House of the Martyred Monk, the Wall of the Widows, and even before the steps of the Planetary Ministry."

Caltha shared Kendler's excitement. He could see the expectation that erased the fatigue from her face. It was right; he could feel it. This was the break they had been looking for. Unless he was light-years off course, they would find Kavinites standing behind Atla-Eron, pulling his strings and making him dance to their tune.

"You mentioned something about the moon kissing Isal," Caltha said. "Does that mean anything?"

"When the moon kisses the tip of Isal, stand in its shadow," Ome answered. "It is where Atla-Eron has called all to meet him this night."

Isal meant something to the youth, but Kendler found no Isal within the short-term memory imprinted in his brain while aboard the *Kelso*. "I'm afraid that means nothing to us, Ome. What is Isal?"

The youth turned to Kendler, looking as though he had suddenly encountered a mental midget. "The Pyramid of Isal, of course. It is the most holy of all places on Morasha. In its shadow, Atla-Eron will speak to his followers this night."

Kendler did a mental double take. Kate Dunbar's supplied Morashan memory was lacking. He had no knowledge of any pyramids on-planet, let alone one that was revered above all holy shrines on this world.

For a moment, the memory of the Earth pyramid he had glimpsed during his Retrieve jump-up fluttered in his mind. He pushed the image away. More important was the Morashan Pyramid of Isal. If there was a location designed to evoke a larger religious impact on the planet's population, Kate Dunbar had also forgotten to supply that information.

"Where is Isal?" Kendler asked, his spirits lifting higher by the moment.

"Outside Ban-Dorit's walls," Ome replied. "It stands on the shore of Lake Baai, no more than four kilometers from the city's east gate."

Why hadn't he seen the structure during their landing? Why hadn't it been mentioned before? Why had Kate Dunbar let something like this slip by their memory conditioning? Kendler sucked sharply at his teeth in frustration. It did not matter, he told himself. They knew about Isal now, and it was up to them to find Atla-Eron.

"I didn't know Morashans built pyramids as religious

shrines." From Caltha's expression, the void in their programmed memories irritated her as much as it did Kendler. "When was it constructed?"

"It is a gift from heaven left by those who walked Morasha before Man," Ome said. "It is a symbol of life, that Morasha is the paradise Man has sought since the Creator banished him from the Holy Garden."

"Those who walked Morasha before Man?" Caltha frowned. "Aliens?"

"Star dwellers," Ome replied. "Those who prepared this world for the coming of Lukya."

"Is there any proof that the structure is of alien origin?" Kendler pressed.

"It is written in the sacred scriptures," Ome said. "It is all the proof any Morashan needs."

Kendler turned his head to hide his amusement. The holy word was the holy word, and only infidels and blasphemers would question its truth. While the possibility of discovering an alien artifact intrigued the psiotic, he put little faith in that possibility. Man was alone in the universe. The origin of the Pyramid of Isal probably lay buried in Morasha's early history when the first colonists constructed it for reasons now lost along with the technology that once belonged to this world.

"Can you take us to Isal tonight?" Caltha asked.

The youth looked at her with uncertainty. "It will be dangerous. Atla-Eron's followers are fanatics."

"It's what we want," Kendler assured him. "We must feel his mind to determine if he truly is a prophet, or an agent of the Kavinites."

Ome sat silently for a moment, then solemnly nodded his head. "I will take you to Isal."

FIFTEEN

A few hours of sleep and Suletu's evening meal of stew, heavy with large chunks of meat and vegetables, some identifiable, others not, made Kendler feel almost human.

Even with his elation about the resurfaced Atla-Eron, he dreaded the journey to the Pyramid of Isal. Caltha and he were rapidly approaching mental collapse. Yet if the doom crier went underground again, he might not reemerge until he could walk over the ashes of the present government. Fatigue or not, the psiotics had no choice but to walk the four kilometers to Isal.

Finishing their dinner, Caltha and Kendler excused themselves from the table surrounded by Suletu's boarders. They returned to their room to await Ome, who had gone to the embassy to apprise Ambassador Lore of their plans. Outside the room's window, the Morashan sun bled red in a brilliant array of hues while it settled toward the horizon.

"I'll make contact tonight," Caltha said as they stood at the window, watching passersby below.

"It's still my work day," Kendler said, reminding her of their agreement to use their abilities on alternate days as a measure to conserve their energies. "Atla-Eron is mine."

Caltha stared at him defiantly. "Certainly not. Your day ended at the temple. You haven't the strength to merge."

Kendler bristled inwardly. The Caltha who stood before him smacked of the Caltha Renenet he had first met in Kate Dunbar's office. The same Caltha Renenet who had not surfaced during the past week. His inexplicable antagonism for the woman rose, something he thought lay buried.

"There's no need for you to assume the role of a gallant gentleman," Caltha continued. "This isn't a casual evening out, but the possible key—"

"To hell with being gallant!" He realized that was exactly what he was being. He sincerely worried about Caltha's fatigue and mental strain. "I'll make contact."

She glared at him, exasperation hardening her face. Yet she controlled herself. "We'll flip for it."

Caltha slipped a silver Morashan coin from her pouch. She held it out to display the minted head of some long-dead *Yamarka* priest on one side and what appeared to be a pigeon on the other.

"Heads," Kendler said, reluctantly giving in to the determination reflected in her dark eyes.

She thumbed the coin into the air, caught it when it fell, and slapped it atop her left wrist. She glanced up at Kendler for a moment, then pulled her hand from the coin.

Heads.

Caltha mumbled something under her breath. Kendler felt a shifting in the pit of his stomach. Despite his outward display, he wished Caltha had won the toss. She was right. She was better prepared for contact with Atla-Eron. Only his stubbornness and pride stood in the way of his admitting it.

A knock came at the door, and Ome announced himself. Kendler looked at his partner. "Are you ready?"

"I think we might need these." She lifted two woven straw prayer mats from the floor and handed him one. "And our pistols."

Kendler retrieved two small handguns from beneath the blankets in the chest of drawers and gave one to Caltha. He tucked his own under his robe. It was a compact twenty-burst energy weapon, quite capable of performing the task it was designed for—to kill at short range.

"Sure you won't give me a shot at Atla-Eron?" Caltha asked while she opened the door for Ome.

Kendler shook his head, again allowing his pride to color his judgment.

Morasha's tropical night hung like a thick, damp blanket around them while the threesome moved through the gas-lit streets of Ban-Dorit. At least some of the streets retained their lighting; others were victims of the *Nayati*. Only when they approached the city's east gate did they encounter heavier-than-normal pedestrian traffic. Atla-Eron's followers gathered for the summoned procession to the base of the holy Pyramid of Isal.

Outside Ban-Dorit's protective walls, a night breeze moved through the rain forest to slightly cool the air. The threesome took their places among the others making the holy trek.

"They are bold," Ome whispered. "The Pyramid of Isal gives them courage. They would never be so open within Ban-Dorit."

If Kendler had detected awe in the youth's voice when he had described Atla-Eron's bold entry into the Den of the Holy Thief that afternoon, now he only heard contempt. Ome apparently had visited his family during the past few hours. Kendler could easily imagine the boy's father reminding him of Atla-Eron's opposition to Morasha's government, and Ome's own precarious position should the government topple.

Survival won over religious awe. It was natural. The Creator of the universe had instilled survival in all the creatures Kendler had touched minds with. The purpose of life was life. Man's higher goals were only society programming its expectation into the brains of its members.

The rain forest's darkness threatened to swallow them as they moved down the narrow jungle road. Kendler was grateful for the pilgrims who carried torches or candles to light the way. *We should have thought of torches*, he thought with the crisp focus of hindsight.

Here and there he caught the glint of metal in the hands of many of Atla-Eron's followers. It took a few squinting stares before he recognized the objects they carried. When he did, the heavy feel of the weapon hidden within his robe added to his sense of security. The doom crier's faithful had armed themselves with long machete-style knives and ancient explosive-projectile rifles.

Kendler's gaze moved back to the forest, remembering that "virulent life forms" warning they had received at Ban-Dorit's shuttle port. The jungle stood like a black-on-black wall against the night. Shadows shifted under the passing torches, conjuring images of predators poised to spring on the line of pilgrims. His fingers drifted to the hardness of the pistol, even more grateful for the protection it provided.

"Soon the forest will open," Ome said. "Isal stands in a large clearing. No trees grow within a kilometer of its base."

Kendler felt Caltha's eyes on him. She studied him carefully, trying to find the telltale signs of exhaustion. To his surprise, he no longer felt fatigued. The closer they approached Isal, the more his elation grew. After a week's failure, even the glimmer of success renewed his strength.

The moon pushed above the horizon and crept toward its zenith when they entered the clearing. Isal towered before them, an artificial mountain that pierced the night.

"It's enormous," Caltha whispered. "So massive."

Awesome, Kendler thought, unable to pull his gaze from the structure.

Black against the night, Isal stood in silhouette to the moonlit waters of Lake Baai. Standing in its shadow, Kendler felt dwarfed by it. The structure rose one hundred forty seven meters into the air. Each side of the four-sided pyramid was two hundred thirty meters in length. The base covered an area of five hundred twenty nine ares.

Kendler sensed the undefined power that radiated from all ancient things. He perceived and understood the Morashans' reverence for the structure. Not only in size, but spiritually, it dwarfed him, forcing him to accept his own mortality. The spark of life he carried within him would last but one hundred fifty years. Isal had stood before his birth, possibly before Man first set foot on the planet. Isal would stand an eternity after the life spark known as Nils Kendler was forgotten.

"The moon will soon reach Isal's peak," Ome said. "Do you wish to move closer?"

Kendler looked down the sloping terrain that led to the Pyramid of Isal and the lake beyond. In the moonlight, he saw the crowd of followers who pressed close to the structure's broad base. He roughly estimated three thousand had answered Atla-Eron's call.

"There's no need to stand at Atla-Eron's feet," Caltha answered. "However, we must be able to see him to make contact."

"If we remain at the edge of the crowd, there should be no difficulty in seeing him," Ome replied as he started down the slope.

Kendler attempted to relax and clear his mind for his forthcoming merge. He tried to limit his sensory input to the bare essentials required to walk down the hill. He could not.

The crowd yawned before him, a splitting chasm. It stood like a single entity, a mass mind that imposed its way into his brain. He sensed the fear of *Nayati* oozing like sweat from the Morashans, and under that, something dark, violent.

"They're ready to explode," Caltha said to him, apparently feeling that unfocused violence. "If Atla-Eron commands them to storm Ban-Dorit's walls, they will."

Atla-Eron would not be given the opportunity to incite his followers, Kendler thought. The moment the doom prophet came into sight, the psiotic planned to make his merge. Kavinite puppet or not, Kendler would not allow the man's tongue to form the syllables that would unite the mob into an army.

"The moon tops Isal." Ome's head craned toward the sky.

The pale silver orb rose above the pyramid's apex. A hush of amazement rushed through the throng of pilgrims. Kendler's attention was drawn back to Isal. A figure in glowing robes that flashed through the hues of the spectrum floated three meters up the west face of the Pyramid of Isal.

"The bastard's on a mini-floater!" Kendler cursed aloud in Lanatian while the crowd around him praised the Creator for the miracle they witnessed. The prophet's levitation left no doubt in the psiotic's mind that the Kavinites were behind Atla-Eron's activities.

"Glow-thread," Caltha commented on the prophet's dazzling attire. "My mother had a gown made from it when I was a child. Our Kavinite friends are twenty years behind the styles."

Simple gimmicks hidden by the night—cheap tricks—but damn effective, Kendler thought. Tricks the Kavinites aimed to play upon superstitious minds.

The crowd's hushed awe gave way to open cries of rejoicing. "Atla-Eron, Atla-Eron," the mob's single voice called to the prophet. The mutual voice shattered the night's silence like reverberating thunder.

"I'm going to go for him." Kendler stepped beside Caltha. "Can you hold me?"

"With Ome's help." She pointed for the youth to take Kendler's waist.

"This might take longer than usual," Kendler said. "If Atla-Eron's up to what he appears to be, I intend to turn it right back into his face."

"Find the source of the *Nayati* first," Caltha urged. "Don't endanger the assignment to divert a riot. Ban-Dorit can live through another riot. Morasha won't survive the *Nayati*."

"I'll kill both birds with one stone." He surged with newfound confidence. For the first time since they had arrived on Morasha, he *knew* what they faced. "With luck, Atla-Eron, Kavinite, and *Nayati* will be considered vile profanities by the morning."

"Still . . . be careful." Genuine concern tightened Caltha's jaw.

Kendler wanted to say something flippant to assure her he could handle the situation. No snappy quip popped into mind. Instead, he squeezed her hand. "Ready?"

"Ready." She slipped her arms about his waist as though giving him a playful hug.

Ome stood behind Kendler, his hands braced to each side of the psiotic's hips. Kendler leaned into the youth, locking his knees. Under normal circumstances, their awkward position would have drawn arched eyebrows. But all eyes were riveted to the prophet floating above the heads of his followers.

Kendler closed his eyes. One after another, he eliminated the input of his senses, isolating his mind within himself. He rose toward alpha level awareness, riding the streams of unfocused psi forces within his brain. He drew them to him, forming a stabilized sphere.

He reached out toward Isal, toward the man who hovered in the air before the pyramid's face. The crowd, its mass mind, pushed into his awareness. He barricaded himself against the undesired intruder and homed in on Atla-Eron.

Nothing.

Shock jarred his confidence. He refused to accept what his mind found.

Desperately, he probed again, delving the void filling Atla-Eron's head. Again, he tried to establish the merge, to complete the mental bonds that would link him to the false prophet. *Nothing!*

With raging resignation, he accepted the impossibility of himself, or any psiotic, ever merging with Atla-Eron. He flowed back into his own body. His eyes blinked open.

Caltha stared at him, her lips parted in disbelief. "What's wrong? You weren't gone thirty seconds."

"A blank! Atla-Eron's a blank." Kendler stood under his own power. "The Kavinites were prepared for us from the very start."

Caltha's expression was a denial of his pronouncement.

She refused to accept that the prophet was completely devoid of any psi channels—a blank. He did not blame her. Blanks existed, but they were a freak of nature, the result of a mutated gene that affected one in a billion of any given species, Man included.

"Hold me," she demanded. "You've passed your limits. You're exhausted.

Before Kendler could reply, Caltha was in his arms, her body limp as she pushed her mind toward alpha awareness. Seconds later, her eyes fluttered open, narrowing with uncontained rage.

"Those son of bitches! Those bastards," she cursed. "They don't give a damn whether we know they're behind Atla-Eron or not. With his mind closed to us, they've successfully hidden the source of the *Nayati*!"

Kendler shared her frustration. A successful conclusion to their assignment lay at their fingertips, yet it was light-years away. Knowing the Kavinites' methods, Atla-Eron was their only man on-planet who knew the secret of the *Nayati*. And that mind would never unlock its secret. Kendler had to admire their ingenuity.

"They've stopped us," Caltha continued. "We've reached a dead end."

"Not quite," Kendler replied, glancing at the prophet, who still floated above his followers' cheers. "They've thrown us a new twist. All we have to do is stick close to Atla-Eron. Sooner or later, he'll lead us to the source of the *Nayati*." *The sooner the better*, he thought.

A note of dissonance fringed the thundering praise that rose for Atla-Eron.

"What's that?" Caltha glanced from side to side to locate the rumbling disharmony.

"The Ban-Dorit city guard!" Ome pointed to a line of uniformed men descending toward the pyramid from the direction of the city. "They've come for Atla-Eron!"

Another line of armed guardsmen stepped from the forest to their left. To the south, yet another group of men emerged from the jungle.

Atla-Eron's bold call for his followers to assemble had reached more ears than those of his faithful. Kendler realized the guardsmen had probably been positioned about the pyramid for hours, waiting to close their trap. They now did so, successfully. With Lake Baai on the east and the three ranks of guardsmen on the other sides, they had boxed in the false prophet and his faithful.

The guardsmen had also managed to trap three unknown allies. Kendler surveyed their situation. Standing as they were on the west fringe of the crowd, they would find themselves on the front lines should a confrontation erupt.

"Back!" He grabbed his companions' arms. "Move toward Isal."

Neither objected, but fell back, weaving through the crowd. The cheering faded. The advancing guardsmen replaced the hovering Atla-Eron as the center of attention. For the few seconds needed for the situation to sink into their minds, the throng lost its voice. When they found it again, fear and anger rumbled from their throats, rising to taunting jeers of rage flung at the approaching guardsmen.

Cheering broke out to Kendler's left. Barely discernible above the multitude of heads, Kendler glimpsed a man dart from the throng. He ran toward the guardsmen to the west. For a split second, moonlight flashed from a long knife he swirled over his head. Then the view was obscured as the threesome sank deeper among Atla-Eron's followers.

The chorus of cheers mounted as more members of the crowd saw the man's lone attack. Kendler could feel their voices firing the zealot's passion, forcing his legs to pump furiously, filling him with strength beyond his natural ability.

The single report of a rifle cracked. For a heavy moment, the crowd fell silent. Kendler did not need to see the reason for their sudden quiet. Somewhere before the still-advancing line of guardsmen a lone man lay sprawled in the shadow of Isal, his foolhardy attack stopped by a single bullet from an overanxious guardsman.

The throng found its voice again, louder, meaner. Atla-Eron's faithful moved, pressing toward the guardsmen who surrounded them. Their cries demanded blood in return for the blood of their slain brother.

Kendler glanced over his shoulder. Atla-Eron still rode above the masses on his night-concealed floater. He stood unmoved, offering no encouragement to the crowd. The situation itself would spark the confrontation he had come to ignite.

A cry, high-pitched and ear-piercing, rose from behind the psiotic. There was no fear in the wailing sound. It was a call of defiance, a battle cry. Louder it grew as new lips added to its volume. The anger would not be contained. The Morashans pushed forward in strong determined strides.

Kendler, Caltha, and Ome found themselves pressed forward, caught by the human tide.

Rifle shots roared. Nearer, a volley of shots replied. Screams of pain and terror lanced into the now constant battle cry, only to be drowned by a deafening demand for blood. Atla-Eron's followers ran now, charging. The psiotics and their guide were swept along by the mad wave that rushed forward to vent its rage on the guardsmen.

Kendler struggled wildly against the current of humanity. He threw out an arm, locking his hand on Caltha's shoulder. He pulled her to him before she was washed away and swallowed by the bodies that swarmed about them.

"Ome!" she cried up into his face.

Kendler sighted the youth. He reached out. Too late. The boy was swept beyond his grasp.

Rifles cracked around them in a staccato rhythm. The guardsmen's fire was returned by those in the charging mob who carried arms.

Darkness! Kendler sensed a blackness deeper than the night seep into his mind, the foreboding darkness that had touched him three times during his week on Morasha. *Death! Nayati* descended.

Caltha shuddered, her body pressed against his. Her eyes rolled up, wide and terrified.

"Fight it!" he called over the screams. "Fight it!"

Nayati reigned. Insanity gripped the mob around them. No longer were the guardsmen the focus of Atla-Eron's followers' attention. They turned on one another, lost in the frenzy that possessed their minds.

Drawing within himself until the overwhelming presence was squeezed from his consciousness, Kendler then pushed outward to control mind and body.

His action came none too soon. A man brandishing the charred stub of a burned-out torch rushed him. Releasing Caltha, Kendler reacted rather than thought. He stepped into the attack. His left arm flew up to block the downward swing of the man's club, while his right drove into the Morashan's Adam's apple. Dropping the makeshift weapon, the man reeled back, both hands clutched to his throat.

Kendler turned to Caltha. She was gone. Frantically, his head twisted, searching for his fellow psiotic. Less than five meters to his left, he found her beset by a Morashan at least three times her size.

Not waiting to determine if Caltha had once more been able to combat the effects of the *Nayati*, Kendler picked up the fallen club, raised it, and rushed behind the man.

Caltha had no need of his assistance. The diminutive woman firmly buried her knee in her assailant's groin. He doubled over, howling in surprised pain. A deftly executed chop to the man's seventh vertebra left him unconscious at Caltha's feet. She turned and smiled at Kendler. He dropped the upraised club and smiled. Once again, she had managed to ward off the *Nayati*.

"Ome?" Her smile disappeared. "Do you see him?"

Kendler surveyed the chaos around them. Ome was nowhere in sight. He did not want to ponder what the young Morashan faced at the moment. Nor did he like their own position.

Taking Caltha's hand, he tugged her after him. Despite the dangers of the rain forest, at the present it was a far safer environment than the one surrounding them.

A dark-robed Morashan clutching a blooded long knife stepped before them. A wide grin split his bearded face. The knife rose.

Kendler's hand shot into his robe. Before he could free the pistol nestled there, two Morashan women jumped the man from behind. They dragged him to the ground, their clawlike fingers raking into his face.

Caltha pulled him now, once again working toward the jungle. They dodged the centers of violence they could and fought off attackers when faced with no other alternative, both preferring hand-to-hand combat to their energy weapons, which would have given their identities away. Eventually, they broke free of the *Nayati*-held mob and ran for the rain forest.

When they reached the trees, Kendler turned back. Below, the *Nayati* had transformed the clearing into a battlefield that spread out like some ancient painting depicting the fate awaiting sinners in the bowels of hell. The dead and dying lay strewn on the ground. The standing warred among themselves like blood-lusting berserkers.

The movement of light drew Kendler's attention to Atla-Eron. The false prophet, a blank, completely devoid of any psi ability, thus immune to the effect of the *Nayati*, floated gently toward the ground.

"Nils!" Caltha tugged at his arm. "The fighting is moving this way. Someone will see us. We've got to go deeper into the forest."

But Kendler watched Atla-Eron, who now walked along the base of Isal. The man's robes winked out. For an instant, the psiotic's brain said one thing—that Atla-Eron had disappeared into thin air—but his eyes saw another—the prophet had vanished into the pyramid's solid stone base.

"Nils!" Caltha shouted, pulling at his arm.

He turned and followed her into the forest. A hundred meters from the clearing's edge, they found a dense clump of bushes and sank behind them. For a moment, they stared at one another, then moved together, clinging to each other.

It stopped. The *Nayati* passed as always, with the same suddenness with which it had begun.

Slowly, Kendler and Caltha separated, their eyes locked together, neither speaking, as though uncertain it was over and they had once more survived the psi-induced hysteria.

Overhead, thunder rumbled, nature's thunder. The padding of raindrops striking the leafy canopy over them drifted through the forest's sudden stillness. Kendler leaned toward Caltha, his lips lightly brushing hers. She trembled. Or was it him?

Easing back a few centimeters, he studied her studying him. The trace of a smile moved over her mouth. When he leaned down to her again, she met him, her mouth covering his. Her arms opened to him. Tightly, they held each other, unaware of the rain that fell, bathing them in its coolness.

SIXTEEN

Guns in hand, walking in a general northwesterly direction, Caltha and Kendler made their way back to the Ban-Dorit road without encountering either dangerous beast or plant. *Beginner's luck,* Kendler reflected while he tucked the pistol beneath his robe. He would not want to attempt the jungle flight again without a native guide.

A shudder worked up his spine. The vision of Ome being swept away by the surging crowd flashed in his mind's eye. He would not hazard a guess at the youth's odds of living through the *Nayati.*

Tattered groups of survivors, Atla-Eron's followers and guardsmen alike, already limped along the road toward the city. Neither group had any fight left in them. They had faced the *Nayati* and both were losers.

In the morning, Kendler was certain philosophical and religious differences would flare anew. But for now, they were defeated, crushed to insignificance by the squelching fist of an invisible foe.

Ahead, above the dark tops of the jungle trees, an orange glow lit the night. The *Nayati* once again had extracted its toll within Ban-Dorit. New fires blazed through the city. Kendler felt Caltha's hand tighten around his. Her gaze focused on the fires' glow. Pain, fear, weariness lined the delicate features of her face.

He eased an arm around her shoulder and hugged her close. She offered no protest but clung to him. The warmth of her body suffused through the rain-drenched folds of their robes. The irrational antagonism that had separated them for weeks seemed eons in the past, melted and washed away in one kiss. He drew her closer.

The effects of the *Nayati* surrounded them when they passed through the city's gate. Kendler hung his head and stared at the stone pavement to avoid having to face the suffering and destruction left in the wake of the latest onslaught of insanity. He felt like a Morashan who avoided the eyes of his fellow citizens. Their shame and guilt now weighted his shoulders and he bore their burden equally. Their torment was now his.

His reason for being on-planet no longer was simply a Psi Corps assignment. It rose to a personal level, one he could not ignore. He had to break the Kavinites' hold on Morasha, not for Kate Dunbar, not for the LofAl, but to help these people piece their shattered lives together again.

Altruistic, aren't you? he chided himself, and admitted he was. That the Morashans might find peace again was important. Just as important was the thought that the genetic accident that had placed psi abilities in his head would mean something other than another tool to maintain the balance between Kavinite and Lofgrinist philosophies.

The *Nayati* had become his Morashan *Tyrannosaurus rex,* with a reverse twist. To Kendler, they represented the most formidable tests of his abilities he had ever encountered— two tests on the opposite end of the evolutionary scale. *Rex,* Earth's mightiest predator, pitted his brute instincts and physical strength against the psiotic.

The *Nayati* was mental—a man-generated force pitted against his own mental abilities. He faced a psi force that randomly sought to destroy a whole world. It had no pattern, no purpose but destruction. That the Kavinites with their false prophet Atla-Eron were behind the *Nayati* was of no consequence. It was the force he fought. He would overcome it—he had to.

They found Suletu sitting cross-legged outside her home, head buried in her hands, trembling as she wept. Caltha moved to her side and quieted the woman enough for her to explain that two of her boarders were dead in the common sitting room.

"The *Nayati*," she sobbed. "They killed themselves."

Leaving Caltha with the older woman, Kendler entered the house. The common room looked as though a tornado had ripped through it. At the center of the shambled room, sprawled on the floor, lay Suletu's boarders. Kendler knelt beside the bodies.

They had died in the *Nayati*. But they had not killed one another. Dark gashes opened each man's throat from ear to ear. Blood pooled about their heads on the floor. Kendler glanced around. A meter to his left, he found the murder weapon, a blood-smeared kitchen knife.

The black scar, he thought when he rose and walked upstairs to get two blankets in which to wrap the bodies. He did not need a vivid imagination to picture what had occurred during the *Nayati*. The two boarders had been sitting in the common room when the madness struck, and Suletu had been in her kitchen.

The two men had fought. One had knocked the other unconscious, or perhaps they had succeeded in rendering each other unconscious. Enter Suletu, knife in hand, mind controlled by the *Nayati*. Two neat slashes with the knife and the men died, never cognizant of what had happened or of their murderess's identity. Two more victims of the insanity that had razed a world.

No. Kendler shook his head. Suletu was no murderess, but yet another victim. He whispered a prayer of gratitude to the Morashan Creator who provided an ever-deepening black scar to protect the gentle woman's sanity.

Blankets in hand, the psiotic returned to the sitting room. Bundling the two bodies, he dragged them outside and laid them beside the front of the home. In the morning, Ban-Dorit guardsmen would gather them with the other victims of the *Nayati*.

"You can go back inside now," he said, turning to Suletu.

The rotund woman looked at him, then the bundled bodies. Relief eased her fear-streaked face. She nodded, and Caltha helped her back into the house. Suletu stopped at the door to the sitting room. "I must get my soap and brushes and clean," she said aloud to herself.

"It can wait until morning." Kendler rested a hand on her shoulder. "You should get some rest."

"No," Suletu said firmly. "I must clean this away. It must not stain my house."

She walked toward the kitchen, letting Kendler's hand slip from her. Caltha called after her, "May I help?"

The woman turned back and shook her head. "You go to your room. Leave this to me. It is my house and I must clean it."

Caltha started to reply, but Suletu walked into the kitchen.

"That poor woman." Tears welled in Caltha's eyes. "Her world has collapsed atop her and all she can think of is cleaning."

"Shhhh. Tears won't help." Kendler eased her to him and held her close. He stroked the damp strands of her long jet hair and kissed her forehead. "She does what all Morashans do after *Nayati*. She picks up what's left and puts it back together as best she can. She erases whatever traces of the *Nayati* remain so they won't be there to haunt her when a new day comes."

Caltha's gaze rolled up to him. "I know . . . it's just that it all seems so useless. Tonight was the worse. All those people killed and we couldn't do anything to stop it. And Ome . . . my God, what about Ome?"

He hugged her to him. Fighting back the tears that flooded his eyes at the thought of what had happened to the youth, he eased her toward the stairs. "Don't count Ome out. The boy can take care of himself."

His words sounded flat, but they seemed to provide some comfort to Caltha. "Tonight did give us something. We know for certain that the Kavinites have to be behind Atla-Eron."

"But we don't have proof," she muttered. "Proof . . . like what was never found when they destroyed the *Roscoe Turner* . . . or when they killed your family. We need proof."

Kendler helped her to the chair when they entered their room. "But we know the Kavinites were responsible for Atla-Eron's miracles—the mini-floater and the glow thread. Now all we have to do is find our false prophet again. He'll lead us to the source of the *Nayati*."

"And where do we find him?" Caltha accepted a cup of water Kendler poured her. "In all the confusion, he could have used the floater to skip to Morasha's far side."

"I think we can find Atla-Eron whenever we want." He sank to the floor beside her.

Caltha looked down at him. "Where?"

"Think," Kendler said. "Did you feel anything different about tonight's *Nayati*?"

"No . . ." Caltha stopped. Her eyes widened. "The Pyramid of Isal. The *Nayati* seemed to emanate from Isal."

"Are you sure?"

"No." She paused. "I was trying to fight off its effects, not give into it and seek the source."

"Same here," Kendler replied. "But I sensed the same thing. Plus I saw Atla-Eron escape. He walked into the base of the pyramid."

"Nils, are you certain?" Her disbelief was evident. "Could you have been hallucinating?"

"When the *Nayati* strikes, I'm not certain of anything," he said. "It's hard enough to hold onto sanity, let alone function. But I swear I saw Atla-Eron walk into Isal."

A light, almost questioning rap came at the door.

Kendler's head jerked toward the sound. "Suletu?"

"It's me," Ome's familiar voice answered from outside.

Caltha jumped up, opened the door, and held the youth in a crushing hug before Kendler could untangle his crossed legs and stand. The boy blushed at the unexpected display of affection.

"We thought that . . ." She gave him another joyous squeeze, then stepped back to wipe the tears from her eyes.

Kendler walked beside her and grasped Ome's shoulder. He would have hugged the youth too, but sensed the male-to-male affection would have been more than Ome's strict religious background could tolerate.

Caltha slipped an arm around Kendler's waist and hugged herself to his side. "He's all right."

"No more than a scratch or two." Ome grinned and brushed aside the tangled hair covering his forehead. A large purple knot pushed from his brow. Atop it, a shallow cut about three centimeters long oozed a slow trickle of blood. "Which is better than can be said for the three hundred who lie dead in Isal's shadow."

Caltha scurried him across the room and into the chair. "I'll get something to clean the wound."

Kendler offered his aid. "Pour some water and I'll get a cloth from the bathroom." Caltha nodded, and he got two towels.

"Are you sure about the three hundred dead?" He handed Caltha the towels. She dipped the end of one in a cup of water.

"Yes." Ome winced when she touched the wound. "I have been helping the guardsmen load the bodies into carts. At least five hundred more were wounded."

"You're lucky whoever did this didn't split your skull," Caltha said. "It needs a bandage." She paused a moment, then looked at Kendler. "My torn uniform blouse. I placed it in the second drawer."

Kendler found the blouse and tossed it to her. Tearing off a wide strip of the white fabric, she tied it about the youth's head. "That should help until you can get some real medical attention. It needs doctoring before it becomes infected."

"Such bother about so small a scratch." Ome smiled, reveling in the attention. "One would think I was dying."

Caltha lightly kissed his cheek. Kendler smiled. The scene was reminiscent of Suletu's greeting their first day on Morasha. He was not the only psiotic who had allowed this backward planet to personally involve him.

Ome's gaze returned to Kendler. "I remember this time."

"What?" He was not sure what the youth meant.

"The *Nayati*," Ome answered. "I remember it."

"How?" Caltha stared at him doubtfully.

"You talked about drawing within yourself to fight the madness," Ome said. "When I felt it descending, I drew within myself. The *Nayati* did not control me, but I could not control myself either. I could only stand there, watching the chaos. That is when the guardsman struck me with his rifle. I don't remember anything after that, except coming to. The guardsman was dead . . . a bullet through his head."

Kendler listened, believing, yet uncertain. Ome's fending off the *Nayati* indicated that he held latent psi abilities neither Caltha nor he had detected. He made a mental note for Kate Dunbar. Immediately, he erased it. He refused to be responsible for introducing anyone to the Psi Corps director.

"Did our journey to Isal accomplish anything?" Ome asked hopefully.

Kendler gave the youth a thumbnail sketch of their encounter with Atla-Eron's "blank" mind. Reading the disappointment on the youth's face, he then described how the Kavinites had provided the false prophet's apparent miracles. Though he admitted having no easy solution to Atla-Eron's disappearance into the solid base of the pyramid.

"There is no entrance into Isal," Ome said with firm conviction. "The *Yamarka* priests have searched for years to find a way into the pyramid and unlock its secrets."

Kendler stopped himself before he explained the centuries of technological advances that separated the priests and the Kavinites. "I saw him enter Isal. There must be something, a lock that opens a concealed passage . . . something."

"Then we must find the passage," Ome said.

"In the morning." Kendler glanced to Caltha, who nodded her agreement. "We'll return to Isal in the morning, after we've rested."

"No, tonight," Ome demanded. "We must find the passage and expose this prophet who mocks my people and their beliefs."

Kendler shook his head. "We're tired and need sleep. The pyramid will be there in the morning. If a passage exists, we'll find it then."

"No." Ome grew adamant. "We must go tonight."

"Ome?" Caltha's face displayed puzzlement over his reaction. "What's wrong with you?"

"Nothing is wrong with me, except that I forget you're not Morashan," the youth replied. "I feel that we are friends and that we share common feelings as friends do. But I have forgotten that you are off-worlders."

"What has that got to do with anything?" The boy's stubbornness annoyed Kendler. "We are friends. We came to Morasha to help you and your people."

"No, you are off-worlders," Ome persisted. "You can never understand what it means to be Morashan. Isal will stand in the morning light, but will Ban-Dorit? Will any Morashan? You will aid us, but only in your own time, when it suits your off-worlder purposes. Meanwhile, all my people may die in a *Nayati* this night. If you will not help, then I will find Atla-Eron and end his reign of terror this night."

Without waiting for an answer, Ome stood and yanked the bandage from his head. He threw it at Caltha's feet, then stormed from the room. The door slammed behind him.

Kendler stood in the middle of the room and stared at the door. He felt small. Personal involvement with Morasha and its people? He did not have the first inkling of what personal attachment to this planet meant.

Ome was right. Kendler was an off-worlder. His job, assignment, mission was to save the Morashans from the Kavinites and their psi-induced madness. If he failed, what did he lose? Nothing! Kate Dunbar would chew him up one side and down the other, but that had happened before. Morasha would be chalked up as an aborted political maneuver,

144

a tactical mistake to be balanced in a future confrontation. His world and life would remain intact.

Only Ome and the other Morashans would lose. Either the *Nayati* would destroy their planet, or the survivors would find themselves under Kavinite rule, a mere mark in the cosmic ledger in which the tabulations of conquest are recorded.

"Nils," Caltha called to him, her voice low and subdued. She turned, her expression mirroring the disgust he felt with himself. "I'm going after Ome . . . to help him if I can."

"I know." He sighed. "Want company?"

Walking before him, she rose on her tiptoes and tenderly kissed his lips. She then took his hand and squeezed it. "We'll have to hurry if we want to catch him."

"Yeah," he replied, none too sure of what they were committing themselves to. "We don't want that hot-headed Morashan finding Atla-Eron by himself."

He let a hand creep to the weapon concealed beneath his robe. He followed Caltha out the door, hoping they would have no need for the pistol.

SEVENTEEN

Three hours from the first light of dawn, an exhausted Caltha Renenet, Ome Reve, and Nils Kendler stood before the mountainous base of the Pyramid of Isal. The west face of the monument held a frosty sheen beneath the light of Morasha's single moon.

Kendler craned his head back, staring toward the pointed apex of the structure. Several meters above his head, he could see the smooth limestone veneer that covered the pyramid. The veneer had been chipped away around the base to expose the monstrous blocks of limestone from which Isal was built. The damage was the work of *Yamarka* priests searching for an entrance, Kendler speculated.

"The moon will be down in another half hour," Caltha said from beside him. "We should have brought some light with us."

Kendler did not answer. The walk to Isal, the damp breeze that blew off Lake Baai, the fact that he had not eaten in eight hours, had not slept in twenty-four, and mere fatigue made him think twice about what they were doing. Ome's heartfelt speech had been emotional and stirring. Caltha and he had let the youth's words play on their frustration and guilt. They had been correct in wanting to wait for morning. They should be sleeping, resting exhausted minds and bodies.

But now that we're here . . .

"Light will be no problem." Ome stooped to pick up a half-burned torch from the ground. "There are plenty of these around. Atla-Eron's followers dropped them during the *Nayati*."

Fantastic! Now we're going after Kavinites like cavemen driving a saber-toothed cat out of a cave with torch in hand! Kendler looked at his companions, toying with the idea of suggesting they sleep a few hours before beginning the search.

One glance at their exuberance and the migrant thought slipped away. Caltha and Ome wore the expressions of two adolescents on a scavenger hunt, rather than adults seeking the source of a psi-induced hysteria that had brought a planet to its knees.

"Where did Atla-Eron vanish?" Caltha's voice drew him from his thoughts.

"Just below where he floated," Kendler answered. "At the middle of the west base."

He ignored Ome's dubious glance. If the youth did not believe him, why were they at Isal? He knew the answer. When one's world is crumbling, a man grasps at anything—even fairy tales about false prophets walking through walls.

Ome slapped an open palm against one of the stone blocks that rose three and a half meters from the ground. The solid pop seemed to refute the possibility of stepping through the stone. Caltha reached out, her fingertips testing the solid wall.

"There has to be an entrance hidden along the base," Kendler said. "Perhaps a pressure-activated door of some sort. I suggest we start about five blocks to our left and work ten to the right. If we don't find anything, we'll cover another five to each side of these ten. That should cover the area where I saw Atla-Eron pull his disappearing act."

"If we don't find anything?" Caltha asked.

"We start again." Kendler shrugged his shoulders. "There has to be something here . . . somewhere."

Caltha eyed one of the limestone blocks from bottom to top. "If there is a device that activates a locking mechanism, it might be concealed along the upper edge of one of these blocks. Atla-Eron could have used it as he descended on his floater."

Even on his toes, with arms outstretched, Kendler could

not reach the upper limits of the blocks. The height posed a definite problem. "Any ideas how we reach up there?"

"Care to lend me a pair of broad shoulders?" She smiled coyly.

He bit his lower lip to hold back a retort about her walking all over him. Resigned to what appeared the only practical solution to the problem, he walked five blocks to the left and squatted. Caltha climbed atop his shoulders. He stifled a weary moan when he pushed upward. Despite her diminutive size, she felt like a ton of bricks. The comparison brought an ironic smile to his lips.

As a team, they worked their way along three of the stone blocks. Caltha's hands explored the upper reaches, Kendler the middle zone, and Ome everything from waist level down. Centimeter by centimeter, their fingers crept along the limestone face. Only when Caltha's feet felt as though they were biting into his collar bones did Kendler call for a rest break.

"I was never cut out for the life of a ladder." He carefully lowered his fellow psiotic to the ground, then sank to his haunches, rubbing his shoulders.

"Let me do that." Caltha's fingers firmly kneaded the back of his neck when she sat on the ground behind him.

"There is no time to rest." Impatiently, Ome stood over them. "The moon will be down in another ten minutes. If we have to work by torchlight, it will take twice as long."

If we wait until dawn, we'll have sunlight, Kendler mused, but said nothing. Instead, he closed his eyes and lost himself in the soothing feel of Caltha's massaging hands working the kinks from his shoulders.

"I will not waste time." Ome turned away from the two.

Kendler looked up to see the youth continue patting his palms against the stone. The psiotic closed his eyes again, sighing while Caltha's muscles untied a series of kinks. "Does he ever stop?"

"Did you ever stop when you were eighteen?" She chuckled. "You're letting your age show."

"If I'm old before my time, blame it on Kate Dunbar," Kendler replied.

"Time we got back to it." She stopped massaging.

"Up against the wall." He once more squatted to allow her on his shoulders. "Steady?"

"Steady," Caltha confirmed when she stepped atop her human ladder.

Using his leg muscles rather than his back, Kendler slowly

stood. He made no attempt to conceal his groan this time. He was tired, cold, and hungry.

"Aaeeiiii!" A startled cry tore from Ome's lips.

Kendler jerked around. Balance lost, Caltha cried out. Kendler reached up to steady her. His arms missed their target as his brain rejected the image his eyes sent to it—Ome stood two blocks away, his right arm embedded to the elbow in the base of Isal.

A heavy thud came from behind the psiotic. Kendler turned. Caltha sat sprawled on her backside, staring up at him in disgust. Before she could comment, he pointed to the young Morashan.

Ome slowly extracted his arm from the stone. In awed silence, he turned the arm over in the moonlight, studying it. Then, fingers extended toward the stone, he once more pushed his hand into the solid block.

"What the . . ." Caltha rose from the ground, brushing dirt and grass from her bruised pride.

"Atla-Eron's magic!" Ome called to them. They hastened to his side. "I've found the entrance."

Again the youth withdrew his hand and shoved it back into the stone.

"A projection!" Kendler felt like a fool. The use of a holographic projection of stone to hide the passage was an obvious ploy. "They must have a generator hidden within the pyramid to supply power to the projectors."

Sliding his own hand into the projected image, Kendler found the smooth-hewn surface he sought. He moved his arm around the opening in the stone concealed by the projection. A circle, a meter and a half in diameter. "They used an energy beam to slice into the rock. Plenty of room for a phony prophet to disappear into."

Ome looked at him, bewilderment on his young face.

"Caltha will explain it," Kendler said. "But there's no magic, only more Kavinite tricks."

Kendler poked his head into the disguised hole. The interior darkness was a shock, even for eyes accustomed to the night. He waited a moment, letting his eyes adjust. A faint glow was barely discernible in the distance. He pulled back.

"There's a passageway." Kendler turned to his companions. "I need a torch."

Ome scrambled away to return with one of the discarded torches and handed it to the psiotic. Slipping his pistol from his robe, Kendler aimed the needle-nosed weapon at the

149

rag-wrapped stick. He squeezed the trigger. A thin green lance of light spat from the gun. The oil-soaked rags burst into flame.

"What do you think you're doing?" Caltha stepped before the projection.

"Going inside." Kendler eased her away from the concealed passageway.

"Not without us." Caltha took a defiant stance, her eyes narrowed and her nostrils flared.

"I'm also pulling rank," Kendler said. "Senior corps member. One of us has to remain outside to tell the authorities what we've found in case . . . I'm not going to argue. I'm going in alone."

"Nils, I'm not going to wait here while you go inside and get yourself ki—"

"That's exactly what you're going to do." He felt like a Grade A son of a bitch pulling rank, but there really was no time to argue. Ome might have tripped an alarm system the moment he stuck his hand through the projection. "Only you're not going to wait here. Both of you are going to hide in the forest. If our Kavinite friends decide they don't appreciate uninvited visitors, you'll have to tell Lore what we've found. He'll make the necessary arrangements with the local authorities to deal with Atla-Eron."

Caltha did not answer. She stood glaring at him, making no attempt to mask her rage.

"If I'm not out of here in an hour, I want you to go to Lore. Understand?" Caltha still did not reply or move. He repeated in a firm voice, "Understand?"

"Understood, *Mr. Kendler*." Her voice seethed with contempt and anger.

"Good. Now get back to the trees and take cover," Kendler ordered them. Without a word the two started toward the jungle's edge.

Abruptly, Caltha wheeled around and faced him. "Nils Kendler, you're a stubborn bastard . . . but be careful, or you'll deprive me of the pleasure of kicking you in the cubes the next time I see you."

He grinned and kissed the air in her direction. "I love you, too. I have no intention of being anything but careful. Now get to the trees."

She turned from him again, and with Ome at her side trotted toward the rain forest. He watched them cover half the distance to safety, then glanced back at the holographic projection.

Torch held before him, Kendler slipped through the image and squatted within a perfectly circular hewn tunnel cut through the block's three-meter thickness. His hand tightened around the butt of the pistol.

In a waddling duck walk, Kendler inched his way through the limestone block. Beyond opened a rectangular corridor. No energy beam had sliced this passage in the stone. The corridor had been built during Isal's construction. The pyramid's limestone blocks formed floor, ceiling, and walls. The corridor was small; two meters high, a meter wide, he estimated.

A power line lay along one wall. It ran to three projectors mounted just inside the corridor. He smiled. Locating the power source posed no difficulties. All he had to do was follow the line.

Holding the torch before him, Kendler peered down the dark passage. The faint glow was still visible in the distance. He sucked in a deep breath to steady himself, then moved toward it.

Three quarters of the way down the thirty-four-meter corridor, Kendler made out a sharp angular turn at the end of the passage. He hastened forward. A suspensor globe clung to the ceiling beyond the dogleg. Past the globe, the passage slanted upward at a twenty-six-degree angle. The corridor opened to a two-meter width with a ceiling eight meters high. At ten-meter intervals suspensor globes hovered on the slanted ceiling. Kendler gazed upward, estimating the corridor's length at one hundred fifty meters. At the top of the incline he saw another juncture.

He tossed the torch aside and moved up the steeply slanted corridor. The floor betrayed no signs of use. A fine layer of dust covered the floor. It appeared as though it had not been disturbed in centuries.

For a moment, the dust threw him. Then Kendler remembered Atla-Eron's floater. He cursed the man and the ease with which he had glided up the incline. For the psiotic, it was a matter of one step at a time. He placed each foot solidly on the limestone floor before lifting the other, fearing he would lose his equilibrium and go sliding back to the bottom of the passage if he moved faster.

Kendler estimated fifteen minutes passed before he reached a small landing at the head of the ascending corridor. To his right opened another globe-lit passage. To his left stood another corridor, as dark as the entrance to the Pyramid of Isal.

He peered down the unlighted passageway for the few meters the suspensor globes behind him cut the darkness. He saw little. Like all the corridors within Isal, the limestone blocks lined floor, walls, and ceiling. He could find no ornamentation, statues or painting, normally associated with religious monuments, adorning the passage. Whether constructed by early Lukyan colonists or Ome's alleged aliens, the builders had put no faith in interior decorators. The psiotic could not even find a trace of graffiti marring the walls' clean surfaces.

Kendler turned and started down the lighted passage.

"That will be good right there." A woman's voice came from behind him. "Freeze and drop the gun. Don't try anything stupid. You've got three pistols aimed at your back."

Kendler did as the voice suggested. He froze and let his gun drop to the floor.

"Now, turn around, slowly," the woman commanded.

He did. A slimly built brunette stood between two dark-bearded men in Morashan robes. All three trained snub-nosed pistols at his stomach. Whether they were Morashan natives he could not tell, but the guns were definitely Kavinite design.

"Search him, Bakin." The woman waved one of her companions to Kendler.

"Arms against the wall and spread them," the man ordered and again Kendler complied. Satisfied he carried no concealed weapons, Bakin grabbed the neck of Kendler's robe and jerked the psiotic upright.

"Let's go." The woman motioned Kendler forward with the nose of her gun down the now lighted corridor he had turned away from seconds ago. "Atla-Eron would like a word with you."

"Is that his real name, or does he just use it on stage?" Kendler smiled at his captors.

His answer came as a sharp jab in the ribs from Bakin's gun, then an equally hard shove from the man behind him. Kendler stumbled down the passageway in front of the threesome.

They had covered twenty-five meters when the corridor did a ninety-degree turn to open into a small granite-ceilinged room. Again the walls were unadorned. Two cots were set flush against the right wall. A thin man with a dark Morashan beard sat on one of the cots. His eyes rose slowly and moved over Kendler. Atop a locker at the foot of the cot was a neatly folded glow-thread robe. Beside the garment, leaning against the wall, was a mini-floater.

Kendler had located his false prophet, although the circumstances were not those he had hoped for.

Atla-Eron nodded. The two men gripped the psiotic's arms and threw him against the opposite wall, pinning him there. He heard the cot squeak as Atla-Eron rose and walked behind him.

The flat of a palm slammed into the back of Kendler's head. His face smacked into the wall. His nose gave way with a nerve-grating crunch. A warm trickle oozed from his nostrils and over his upper lip. The saline taste of blood filled his mouth.

"We have no time for games. I will ask a question. If I do not receive the correct answer, Cerise will find a way to convince you to cooperate with us," Atla-Eron said. "Cerise, give our visitor a demonstration."

The woman's steps approached. Bakin stared at Kendler, a smile visible beneath his thick beard. Pain lanced through Kendler's lower back as the woman's fist drove into his left kidney. He groaned. Bakin's smile grew to a grin.

"Cerise calls that her three-centimeter punch," Atla-Eron said. "Why, I am uncertain, but it is quite effective."

Kendler recognized the terminology from his martial-arts training. Cerise's blow had been thrown from three centimeters with the weight and force of her twisting torso behind it. The strike was deadly if used by an expert practitioner. That he still lived told him that Cerise had only given him a "demonstration" as Atla-Eron ordered, or else the woman was less than expert. He hoped for the latter.

"We shall begin with a simple question," Atla-Eron continued. "What is your name?"

"Harem Reve," Kendler answered in Morashan.

"He's lying," Cerise said. "He was carrying this."

Kendler heard a hand clap around what sounded like a gun. His pistol?

"LofAl in design," Atla-Eron said. "Cerise, please convince our visitor."

The woman struck. Again pain erupted in Kendler's lower back. He groaned, unable to contain the knifing agony. His hope had been in vain. Cerise was an expert. She had pulled her first punch. Something told him that even with the second punch, she had yet to display her full abilities.

Still, Kendler did not answer.

"Cerise!" Atla-Eron ordered.

Double explosions racked Kendler's body as the woman's fists pounded his right kidney, then the left. His legs went liquid, trying to collapse under him. Cerise's companions tightened their hold on his arms, keeping him flat against the wall.

"Harem Reve," Kendler repeated.

"I'm afraid you must convince him of our sincerity, Cerise," Atla-Eron replied.

"Turn him around," the woman ordered.

Kendler relaxed, preparing himself for an opening. The two men turned him to face the woman. He stared at Cerise. No sadistic smile moved her lips. Nor did her face betray the slightest hint of enjoyment. All he saw was cold determination. What she did was a job, something that must be done. That she might kill a man in the process appeared to be of no concern to her.

She stepped toward him, presenting the opening he hoped for. Kendler's right leg jerked high and kicked at her midriff.

Just how expert Cerise was became painfully apparent. Her own foot lashed out in a source block that struck where his thigh met his groin. The flat of her palm hammered into his forehead. The back of his head slammed into the wall. Her other hand shot out, again striking his brow. A small cut opened. Blood seeped from the wound into his right eye, partially blinding him with its burning viscosity.

Again she struck, driving a spear hand into the hollow of his throat. Before he could gag, she sank a fist into his solar plexus, then plowed a knee into his groin.

Her two companions released his arms. Kendler crumpled to the floor, moaning. His body drew into a ball, attempting to hide from the pain coursing through it.

"Give him a few minutes to consider what you've shown him," Atla-Eron said. "Then I'll ask my questions again."

Clamping his eyes tightly shut, Kendler fought through the agony. He sank within himself, closing off throbbing muscles and raw nerve endings. He floated with alpha awareness, gathering the psi forces within his brain. Carefully, he reached out, blending himself into Cerise's thoughts. If he could control her, he could free himself.

He weaved into her consciousness, cautiously extending

154

tentacles of his will to melt with hers. He built for the moment he would exert himself and command her mind.

Any doubts he held about Atla-Eron and his companions being Kavinites were erased as Cerise's thoughts became his. The woman and the three men were a team sent to exploit the *Nayati*, to direct the masses against the present government, as he and Caltha had suspected. But there was more.

He probed deeper. Cerise, Atla-Eron, and their two companions were also ordered to locate the source of the *Nayati*.

Shock railed through Kendler's awareness. They were not responsible for the psi-induced insanity. The Kavinites knew no more about it than he did.

"Merger!" He heard-felt Cerise cry in alarm. "He's a merger!"

In an instant of uncertainty stemming from his discovery, Kendler lost control, revealing his presence within her mind. He exerted himself. Too late! Mental barriers, the result of months of anti-psi training, flew up before him, thrusting him back into himself.

". . . take your time," he heard Atla-Eron say to the woman when he once more opened his brain to his senses. He found himself pinned against the wall again. The false prophet stared at him. "Lofgrinist, I will have your secret. Before you die you will tell me how you control the *Nayati*."

Cerise came at him again. Her fists, her fingers, her feet, and her legs extracted every ounce of agony they could without killing him. Atla-Eron, ever calm, repeated his questions over and over. When Kendler did not answer, Cerise returned.

After an eternity of eternities, Kendler fell gratefully into the security of unconsciousness. For an instant, Caltha's image floated in his mind. He smiled. At least she had been spared this. The *Nayati* was her problem now.

He let himself slip, tumbling into the surrounding blackness, knowing the four Kavinites would eventually revive him. When they did and at last realized his ignorance, they would kill him.

EIGHTEEN

An invisible force buckled under Kendler's feet, forcing him up the well. He struggled against it with all the strength he could muster. It persisted, directing his hands to find handholds in the glass-smooth wall.

He screamed and raved against the unseen power. When that brought no surcease, he pleaded and begged, whimpering to be shielded from the pain that awaited him when he completed the ascent. Still, he crawled like a spider upward, ever upward. His hands lipped over the well's wide mouth. His legs scrambled after them.

And there *was* pain.

Needles of white-hot light stabbed into his eyes when their lids fluttered open. He clamped them tightly, preferring the blackness.

Or did he?

The darkness no longer sheltered him from the pulsing aches that throbbed within every centimeter of his body. He tried to roll from the pain. The effort only made things worse. He rocked back and forth in a nauseating rhythm over which he held no control.

"Doctor! Doctor!" A woman's voice ripped a chasm in the silence. "He's coming to."

Feet scurried somewhere in the distance, then moved closer. A hand lifted his wrist, feeling for his pulse. He cursed and was answered by an unsympathetic chuckle.

"Kendler, can you hear me?" a man's voice inquired.

"No," he said to the echoing voice. "Can't hear anything, especially you."

Again the chuckle. Kendler forced his eyes open. Beyond the diminishing needles of searing light, he saw a man's head hovering above him. "Who the hell are you?"

The man smiled and chuckled the irritating chuckle. "Dr. Armon Tayib, physician to the Lofgrin Alliance embassy in Ban-Dorit, Morasha."

A chest now visible below the man's head expanded with his pronouncement. Kendler allowed his eyes to drift closed. "Go away. Let me sleep."

"Afraid the drugs in your system won't allow that." The doctor chuckled again. "Besides, you've had enough sleep for the past week to—"

"Week?" Kendler's head jerked up. His gaze darted about. Nothing was familiar. Though he was aware that he lay slung in a Morashan hammock.

Then he remembered—the Pyramid of Isal, Atla-Eron, Cerise.

"You're a lucky man," Dr. Tayib said. "The Kavinites did a thorough job."

"Where the hell *am* I?" Kendler glared at the physician.

"The embassy's infirmary." Annoyance creased Tayib's face. "You had a broken nose, damaged kidneys, a shattered femur, five broken fingers, a concussion . . ."

The doctor took sadistic pleasures in presenting a minute recounting of all the injuries Cerise and her expert hands had inflicted.

"In fact, I don't believe there's a centimeter of your body that hasn't been in the regenerative unit during the past week," Dr. Tayib said. "As I said, you're a lucky man."

"I don't feel that damn lucky," Kendler replied. "I hurt!"

"A few aches and some stiffness are to be expected. Only minor discomforts that will pass as soon as you've started your exercise program." Tayib chuckled again.

Minor discomforts? A few aches and some stiffness? Kendler groaned. From head to toe, he felt as though he had lost an argument with a pile driver.

"At the moment, you're experiencing some mild distress from a stimulant I gave you to hasten your awakening,"

Tayib continued. "It will pass in a half hour or so. After that you can get up and walk about a bit."

"Walk?" Kendler shook his head. The physician bandied around terms like "minor discomfort" and "mild distress" as if he thought his patient's pain were a casual joke.

"Maybe even run some. It will help get your body back into a well-toned condition," Tayib said. "You're perfectly healthy, Mr. Kendler, just out of shape from your week's rest."

Tayib made the recovery sound as if he had been luxuriating at some exotic tourist resort.

"I've other matters to attend now." Tayib stood and turned to the door. "I'll check on you this evening. Meanwhile, I believe you have a visitor outside."

Kendler's gaze followed the physician to the door across the room. He opened it and said, "You may come in now, Ms. Renenet."

Caltha pushed past the doctor and stopped when her eyes met Kendler's. Behind her, Tayib winked at his patient, then left them alone.

"Are you okay?" Caltha moved toward him in hesitant steps.

"I feel—"

"You look good." Her steps quickened, but remained uncertain.

"The doctor said—" Kendler tried to edge a word in.

"I didn't think you'd make it." She came faster, almost in a trot. "They were so slow in getting you back to the city."

"I'm—"

"You *do* look good, and the doctor said you're perfectly healthy, and all you need is exercise." She stopped beside the hammock. Her gaze nervously moved over him. Her hand rose toward his arm, then hesitated. "I didn't—"

"Shhhhh." Kendler raised a finger to her lips to shush her.

She stared at him, even more uncertain and nervous. "Nils, I—"

"Shhhhh." He shook his head. She swallowed back her comment. He smiled. "Now take a deep breath . . . no, three."

She complied.

"Now, let's start over." His smile widened. "Now repeat after me. 'Hello, Nils. It's a bright and sunny day, and I know you've been feeling like death warmed over. So, I thought I'd drop by and add a bit of cheer to your miserable existence.' "

"Hello, Nils . . ." She stopped abruptly, her eyes narrowing. "Dammit, Nils Kendler!"

158

"Hello, Caltha," he continued his teasing. "You're quite right. I do feel like death on an afterburner. It's really quite nice of you—"

"Dammit, Nils! You *deserve* a kick in the cubes!" She stared down at him, infuriated. "For a week, I didn't know if you were going to make it. Now you lie there as if nothing had happened to you, as if it were all a joke . . . as if . . ."

If it was possible for someone to throw herself atop a person in a hammock without physically climbing into the sling, that was what Caltha did. Her arms encircled his neck, and her mouth pressed firmly to his.

Kendler's own arms opened and closed about her, hugging her tightly to him. He ignored the aches and pains that continued to send hot needles into his body. The feel of her was good, so real, so alive.

All too soon, their lips parted. Caltha's head tilted back slightly. He gazed up, his eyes unable to soak in enough of her. Slowly, his fingertips rose to her face to trace its delicate features, to memorize her feel, the smooth texture of her skin. Then he eased her back to him, his mouth covering hers.

"This wasn't supposed to happen." Her lips never left his, but brushed softly at his mouth.

"I know." He cradled her face in his palms. "I keep telling myself I really don't like this fantastic woman. . . ."

She jerked back, her gaze riveted to him. "You do?"

"Mmmm hmmmm." He smiled, his arms closing around her. "The trouble is, I stopped listening to myself about ten days ago."

She came to him again, her kiss brimming with passion and joy. Their hands caressed, assuring one another with their soothing touch.

"Since my husband's death, I've told myself I don't need anything, anyone, except Paul and my work. There's always someone willing to bundle for a night if sex is what I want," she whispered. "Nils, I . . . I'm not sure . . ."

He pressed a finger to her lips. "No one's pressing you. There's time."

He said it, and he meant it. But in that instant, he recognized he did not want there to be time. He wanted her now. He felt his own commitment and wanted her to share it.

He pushed the thought aside. He looked into the lovely face that hovered above him. There was time, he could wait. He

159

grinned at Caltha and winked. "You know, we've got nothing to do with this. It's all Kate Dunbar's fault."

She slipped from his arms and stood. An estranged expression clouded her face for a moment, then an almost smile touched her lips. Kendler gazed at her, unsure what passed through her mind.

"I think I owe you a thank you," Kendler said.

"What for?" Her strange expression vanished, and she smiled at him.

"I don't know how you did it," he said, "but I think you're responsible for my being alive at the moment."

She winked. "You wouldn't let me go into Isal with you, so I did the next best thing."

It hit Kendler. "You opened yourself to me!"

She nodded. "You didn't order me not to."

"You devious little . . ." Kendler began.

"Actually, you should thank Ome," Caltha continued. "The minute you encountered Cerise and her playmates, he ran to the embassy for help. I didn't think he'd get back in time."

Kendler stared up at her. She had been with him through the whole ordeal. She had felt every blow Cerise had delivered, shared his agony. He took her hand and squeezed it.

"Ome had the good sense to summon the local authorities as well as Ambassador Lore," Caltha explained. "If Lore hadn't brought Dr. Tayib with him, you wouldn't have survived the trip back here."

"Atla-Eron and his crew?"

"In Morashan custody," Caltha replied. "Lore and the ministry have been meeting for the past five days to decide how to diplomatically handle the situation. They're working on the fine details. The final results have already been determined. The Kavinites will be off-planet by the end of the month."

Kendler smiled. They'd won this round. Future rounds were just that, a part of the future. It made no sense to ponder their outcome. In the end, that cosmic accountant would balance the columns. The players did not matter, only the constant balance needed to maintain a peaceful existence for the majority.

"Ome is back with his family," Caltha said. "Apparently his father has plans for him within the government once Morasha joins the LofAl. In a few years, that young man will be heading the ministry."

A half-forgotten memory erupted to the surface of Kendler's

thoughts. He tried to lever himself up within the hammock. "The Kavinites aren't responsible for the *Nayati!*"

"I know. Remember?" She reminded him of their mental link that night in Isal. "I've also probed Cerise and her two friends. They're all ignorant. The Kavinites were just trying to take advantage of the situation. They still believe we control the *Nayati.*"

"Do the locals know that?" he asked.

Caltha shook her head. "Lore thinks it best to take advantage of the Kavinites' mistakes. We look better if the Morashans believe Atla-Eron was responsible for the *Nayati.*"

"And the *Nayati*?"

"There hasn't been one since the night Atla-Eron called his followers to Isal," she replied. "Twice this week I've sensed the foreboding darkness that precedes a *Nayati.* Then it faded away."

Kendler lay silent, attempting to fit the pieces together and come up with a rational picture of the situation. If the Kavinites were not behind the *Nayati,* then who was?

"We've conducted a thorough search of Isal," Caltha said, anticipating his next question. "Nothing, absolutely nothing."

"It doesn't make sense. I would have staked a year's pay that the *Nayati* emanated from the pyramid," Kendler said.

"Nothing makes sense about this assignment." Caltha glanced at him. "Least of all us."

"I'm not sure about you, but I make sense." He grinned. "If you make any further remarks about the senior member of this team, I'll put you on report."

"Mother Kate Dunbar wouldn't care for that," Caltha answered. "She was adamant about this partnership working."

Kendler laughed. "I'd like to see Kate's reaction if you called her 'Mother' to her face."

"She'd probably give me a hug and a kiss. My mother is really quite a loving woman." An impish light danced in Caltha's dark eyes. "But, I warn you, she won't tolerate you bad-mouthing her only daughter."

"Daughter? Kate Dunbar . . . mother . . . you?" An invisible sandbag slammed atop his head. It took a moment for the spinning daze to clear. Caltha had not said "Mother Kate Dunbar," but "Mother, Kate Dunbar." He had missed the comma. "Kate Dunbar's daughter!"

"Neither one of us denies the relationship." Caltha smiled, apparently enjoying the effects of the bombshell she had just lobbed his way. "However, neither of us goes out of her way to broadcast the fact either. It tends to make people nervous if they know they're working with Kate Dunbar's daughter. Mother, as you know, believes in efficiency first."

Kendler shook his head slowly from side to side, trying to accept Kate and Caltha as mother and daughter. He took a deep breath, unsure he wanted to hear the answer to his next question. "Your father?"

"Gilmer Kingscript," she replied simply.

A second sandbag fell. Before his retirement two years ago, Gilmer Kingscript had chaired the LofAl Council for four consecutive terms. The name was synonymous with political power.

"It was a five-year bond contract," Caltha said in response to his punch-drunk expression. "Their lives took different directions, and they separated when the contract expired. However, I think that five years meant more to both of them than they'll openly admit. Neither has taken a bond-mate since the separation."

Kendler continued to stare at Caltha. Kate Dunbar and Gilmer Kingscript—it was a lot of weight to drop on a person.

Caltha coyly ran a hand across his chest in a most provocative and suggestive manner. "Having second thoughts, senior member? Getting cold feet?"

"Contacts in high places won't scare me off, Ms. Renenet." He reached up and pulled her to him. Suddenly he laughed.

Caltha stared at him, perplexed by his reaction. "Hey, I thought you were about to kiss me."

"Sorry." He managed to control his laughter. "It's just that I suddenly realized I've fallen in love with the boss's daughter."

"There should be no problems." Her lips teased at his. "As long as you see that the boss's preference for young men doesn't run to one Nils Kendler."

Her mouth opened to his when he hugged her to him.

NINETEEN

"Enough!" Kendler sank to the public garden's green lawn. He stared defiantly up at Caltha.

"Nils! Tayib said you were to do five klicks a day for the next two weeks." Her hands rose to her hips. "You've got to get your muscle tone back. We haven't done two kilometers yet!"

"Which is more than I intend to do tomorrow." Kendler wiped the sweat from his forehead. "Exercise is fine, but I refuse to have a heart attack in the process. Tayib has had a year to accustom himself to this heat and humidity. I haven't."

"You delight in being stubborn." She sat down beside him. The relief on her face told him the Morashan climate was getting to her also. She shook her head in mock disgust when he smiled at her.

"Have I told you I think you're beautiful?" He reached out and took her hand.

"No." Her disapproving frown faded to a soft smile. "Tell me."

"Remind me when we have more time. Right now, I've got to finish my five kilometers." His expression dead serious, he started to rise.

"Nils Kendler!" Caltha grabbed his wrist and jerked him back to the grass.

He turned to face her, innocently questioning her sudden action. She laughed. "Mother always told me to steer clear of the hired help."

"Hired help?" He eased her to him. His mock anger evaporated. "I do love you."

"And I . . ." Caltha's eyes widened. Furrows ran across her forehead.

"Caltha?" Kendler's arms tightened around her in concern. "Caltha?"

"Can't you feel it?" She gazed at him in disbelief.

"Feel what?" Then it was there, the darkness, the foreboding sensations that swept the emotions prior to the descent of a *Nayati.* "Fight it!"

"No," she said firmly and closed her eyes.

"Caltha, don't!" Her body went limp in his arms, muscles flaccid as she slid into alpha awareness.

The darkness passed. It lifted, leaving him with only a cold chill of what might have been.

Caltha's eyes opened. "Dammit! It's gone. I couldn't get it. Didn't have time to focus."

He stared at her, unable to accept what she had attempted. "What if the *Nayati* had erupted? Are you totally out of your head? It would have seared your mind . . . or killed you." The realization that he might have lost this woman he had just found prickled his body with cold sweat.

"It's a chance one of us had to take. Better me than you," she replied.

"I'll decide what chances we take, and when we take them." His fear transformed to anger.

"No. You would have done exactly what I did, if you'd thought of it." A firm determination permeated her words and tone. "I'm not a crystal figurine that requires your protection. If anything is to exist with us—this assignment— you and me—it has to be on an equal basis. You *and* me; not just *you.* I've fallen in love with you, Nils, but it won't work any other way. If you can't accept that, then it's better to get it out in the open now. We both need to know."

He stared at the ground. She was right. Maybe she had been right all the time. This was not supposed to have happened. The Psi Corps was no place for love. If it continued, things would only worsen. Whenever either of them went on assignment, the other would have to live with the haunting doubt that he or she might never return. Sooner or later, one of them would plead with the other to refuse an assignment. And sooner or later, he or she would agree. Or worse, go to flee the confining grasp of the other.

Love did not conquer all. It only asked questions, a myriad of questions, all needing answers before a final commitment was made.

"Nils, do you understand?" Caltha looked at him, doubt in her eyes.

"You're right. Any other way won't work." He nodded. "You're also right about needing time to think things through."

His answer was not what she had expected. He saw that in the veiled hurt of her eyes. Yet she reached out and touched the back of his hand. "We have time. No one is pressing you."

He winced inwardly, remembering speaking those same words to her yesterday in the infirmary.

They sat silently, neither apparently knowing where to go from there. Mentally, Kendler ran through every profanity he could dredge up in three languages. It did not ease the coiling spring that twisted within his chest. Moments ago, visions of a life with Caltha at his side had drifted lazily through his mind. *Daydreams*, he realized. Now reality intruded, the reality of who and what they were, the responsibility they had both accepted when joining Psi Corps.

Despite the cosmic accounting of their superiors, despite the political maneuverings without heed to the individuals who lost in the attempts to maintain a balance, despite the emotional calluses he built to ward off the cynical aspects of his life, there remained within enough of that eighteen-year-old Nils Kendler to keep alive the belief that he could somehow effect changes through the genetic quirk that provided his psi talent.

He glanced at Caltha. Surely the same thoughts must be passing through her mind, or had. After her husband's death, she had made the choice to join the corps rather than burying herself in a life devoted to her son, as so many parents, man or woman, would have done.

"Caltha, I *do* love you," he said.

"And I love you. That's what makes it so damn hard. If we didn't love one another, we'd be back at Suletu's bundling, enjoying a few nights together, then going our separate ways." A sad little smile tugged at the corners of her mouth. "If that's what you want, I'm agreeable. I think those would be quite pleasant nights. We might even come away with a few memories."

"Are you asking me to make a choice?" he asked.

"Presenting alternatives, for myself as much as for you," she answered. "Like it or not, relationships between two people always have terms, whether it be a contract bond, marriage, or a one-night bundling. Only a fool would walk into an arrangement without knowing the terms."

"As you said . . ." The words froze in his throat. Darkness swirled within his head, its gloom blanketing his consciousness. Stronger than moments before, the foreboding sensations lashed toward the edge of *Nayati*. Kendler fought it, locking the insanity from his mind.

"Ohhhhhh . . ." A whimpering cry drew his attention to Caltha. He cried out. She lay on her back, writhing. Her eyes were closed. She had opened herself to the psi force.

Terrified at the thought of her mind cauterized by the surge of *Nayati*, or even worse, he rolled to her. His arms encircled her shuddering body. "Fight it! Dammit, Caltha, fight it!"

She did not respond. The darkness swirled and twisted. Yet, *Nayati* did not descend. For a desperate instant, he considered merging with her and joining the struggle that raged within her brain. He shoved the thought away. The psi currents that churned about him could penetrate his mental barriers before he ever reached alpha awareness. Helpless, he clung to Caltha.

It subsided.

Caltha's quaking quieted to a tremble that slowly passed. Her eyes pushed open. "The Pyramid of Isal . . . it's coming from Isal."

Kendler's fear and anger faded as what she'd said sank into his head. "You did it?"

She smiled up, then pulled his head to her and planted a joyously wet kiss on his mouth. "I did it! At least part of the way. It's coming from Isal. The pyramid's image is reflected again and again in the emanations. I'm certain it's there."

"It?" Kendler asked "What is *it*?"

"I don't know." She shook her head. "Even open to the force, it remains dark and confused. Isal is the only clear image that came through."

"But you said Isal had been thoroughly searched," Kendler said.

"I know, I know. We missed something," she replied. "I

don't know how, but we missed something. Nils, we have to go back to Isal. If the source of the *Nayati* is still operational, it can still tear this planet apart."

"Then, you think it's some form of psitronics?"

"I don't know." Caltha stared up at him. "But we have to go back."

"We'll meet with Lore and tell him what you've learned." Kendler rose. "He can arrange for us to reenter Isal. We don't want the Lukyans accusing us of desecrating their holy pyramid."

He reached down and helped her to her feet. For the time being, the unanswered questions concerning their future would have to wait. They still had an assignment to complete.

TWENTY

A closed session with the Morashan Planetary Ministry and twenty-four hours later, Caltha and Kendler stood within the lower passageway of the Pyramid of Isal. Sunlight entering from outside the circular entrance penetrated the interior darkness only a few meters. The torches they carried did little better.

"Do you feel it?" Caltha whispered, as though afraid of disturbing the pyramid's ancient silence.

Kendler glanced over his shoulder while they made their way down the narrow corridor. "Feel what?"

"It's like a gloom before a *Nayati,* only weaker. Almost a distant echo," she said. "Do you feel it now?"

Kendler concentrated. Nothing touched him. "Can you pinpoint the source?"

"It's too faint . . . too weak and muddled," she said.

"Deeper?" Kendler suggested.

"Yes . . . no . . . wait." Caltha paused, closing her eyes. When she opened them, she shook her head. "It suddenly grew stronger, as though it sensed our presence. I think it's coming from farther into the pyramid."

Holding his torch ahead of him, Kendler took Caltha's free

hand and started down the corridor toward the still-glowing light of the Kavinites' suspensor globes.

"What is the possibility of running into a jungle denizen that's taken up residence in here?" Caltha asked.

"Slim," he answered. "Isal's interior is similar to a cave. The temperature is too cool for jungle life forms. Insects shouldn't come in more than twenty-five meters."

Reaching the first dogleg, they placed their torches on the floor. Kendler still leading, they started up the sharp incline.

"Nils, it's stronger." Caltha stopped halfway up their climb. "There's a desperate quality about it. I can't put it into words. It's not coming to me in images or words, but . . . moods. It's like the cry of a wounded animal."

Caltha shoved ahead of him, nearly sending him tumbling to the foot of the incline. She did not notice. Her gaze focused on the landing above them.

Kendler followed close on her heels. With each step, Caltha's feet slipped in the fine dust that covered the incline. He tensed, arms extended to catch her should she lose her precarious balance. Though he admitted that if she fell back, there would be little chance of halting her. Likely as not, one misplaced foot would leave them both lying at the bottom of the passage.

Despite her less than sure footing, Caltha reached the landing. She slowly turned, as though trying to locate the source of the emanations. Her eyes darted between the opposing corridors. "It knows we're coming. It's desperation is growing. Can't you feel it?"

"Nothing." Kendler could not feel the slightest tingling of psi contact.

"My God!" Caltha's face twisted in horror. "It's dying, Nils. It's dying!"

She pivoted toward the passage leading to the chamber in which Atla-Eron had held Kendler captive. Then she twisted to the other corridor. Her body trembled. Confused panic worried her face.

"Caltha . . ." He reached for her shoulder to calm her.

She shook off his hand and darted down the corridor on their right. "Hurry, Nils. Please hurry!"

Kendler moved after her as she ran down the straight passage, then disappeared around a sudden angular turn. Her voice echoed back to him. "Nils, in here. It's in here!"

He rounded the corner and stepped into a chamber twice the size of the one Atla-Eron and his companions had used.

His gaze shot over the interior. It did not differ from the rest of the pyramid except in size and its granite ceiling. The generator for the projectors lay beside the entrance. Other than that it was empty. As in the other sections of the pyramid the walls were unadorned.

Caltha stood at the room's center, balled fists pressed to her temples. She stared at the ceiling and turned in uncertain circles.

"It's here, Nils. I can feel it." Her voice came in sobbing heaves. Tears streamed down her cheeks. "It knows we're here. It's dying. Nils, it's dying."

"Where?" Kendler's eyes surveyed the chamber once again. Nothing. "Caltha, where is it?"

"Gone." She stopped her turning. "The emanations are gone."

Kendler moved to her. "We'll wait until they begin again."

"No." She shook her head from side to side. "They're gone forever."

Caltha's expression said she did not misjudge the situation. He sensed the almost tangible presence of the loss she felt. Something, an indescribable something, had been found and suddenly ripped from her. Sorrow haunted her features, and new tears welled from her eyes.

"Could you pinpoint it?" he pressed.

She could not speak, only shake her head.

Kendler slowly turned and once more scanned the chamber, seeking—something. The ceiling was bare. The walls were empty. The floor held nothing but a layer of dust, disturbed only by the footprints of Isal's recent intruders.

His gaze returned to Caltha, then shot back to something half glimpsed in the far corner of the chamber.

"Nils?" Caltha asked. "What is it?"

"I don't know." He crossed the room and knelt. He *had* seen it. Disappointment flooded him. It was only an insect, a centipedelike creature that had mindlessly wandered into the pyramid.

"Did you find anything?"

He rose and turned to her. "Nothing, just an—"

Insect! He swirled back to the wormlike arthropod. Jungle insects should not penetrate the pyramid this deep. The temperature was too cold for them.

"Nils?"

There was no time to explain. The centipede was dead or dying. Something this small could not be the source of the

Nayati—but there was nothing else. Kendler tried to ignore Caltha's desperation and convince himself the creature's brain capacity, if it had a brain, was too small for the psi torrents. But there was nothing else within the chamber.

There was only one way to be certain. If he was not too late.

Kneeling, Kendler closed off his senses and reached out to merge with the centipede. He met no resistance from the creature's sensory input. There was none. Life remained, but only a flicker. Death lay but seconds away.

He threaded his awareness deeper into the insect's consciousness, if the vague stirrings he touched could be called consciousness.

Death!

It boiled up and encompassed the psiotic. An overpowering tidal wave flooded Kendler's mind. He did not struggle, only accepted, allowing the psi torrent to wash through him.

In that acceptance, he understood and found the source of the *Nayati*. Imcomprehensible in its full force, Kendler now felt and grasped the emotions that had driven a planet mad—loneliness and sorrow. No, sorrow was not correct. It was sorrow, but more, or less; it had no correlation in Kendler's emotions. "Death sorrow" was the closest he could come to labeling it. Yet, it was not a fear of dying or death, but a sorrow of disembodiment, a lack of union with . . .

He could not grasp the alien concept. Consciousness weakened as death continued to drain the creature. Kendler pushed deeper in an attempt to overtake the dwindling sensations.

Awareness.

It sensed his presence within its mind.

Kendler reeled again. The creature's thoughts rushed out in a weak stream to greet him. He had not entered the mind of some arthropod, but the fully realized consciousness of an intelligent being during its last seconds of life.

He was making Man's first contact with an alien intelligence!

The loneliness, the "death sorrow," evaporated in an emotional fountain of joy and relief. Kendler probed, seeking to define the creature's thought, to neatly place it within his own scope of reference. It evaded him. Only dominating sensations radiated about him, as though emotion took physical form and caressed him.

Friend.

The single human word penetrated the undefined emotions and stabbed into the psiotic's awareness like a steel spike. He accepted the skewering pain and opened himself to the ever-weakening emanations. It, the . . .

Erna.

. . . had sought him. Realization crept into Kendler's consciousness. Its cries, the *Nayati*, had been for him, a summons from a dying friend.

Complete . . . done, Kendler read the emotions painfully shape into human thoughts he could comprehend. *The task is yours.*

Relief flowed from the Erna. The "death sorrow" was completely gone, and Kendler sensed its willingness to surrender life to death. Burden and agony gone, it could accept disembodiment from . . .

It still evaded the psiotic. *What task?*

Kendler sank deeper within the alien mind, groping for answers. Confusion swirled about him, a moment of flickering uncertainty. A reaction to his question? Kendler did not know. Death moved ever closer, threatening to claim the Erna before he found the answers.

Pain once more stabbed in the psiotic's consciousness. Weak and dim, but fully formed, the image of a pyramid blossomed in his mind.

Like a transparent overlay, the image slid atop the memory Kendler carried within his mind. Detail for detail, the images melted together—the pyramid Kendler had glimpsed from the Retrieve timestream. *How? Why?*

Contentment radiated from the alien mind, as though the image of the pyramid answered all questions. But it did not; nothing was answered. Kendler allowed his bewilderment to flow out to the Erna. The warm contentment continued to envelope him. Still, he probed, searching for anything that would clarify the creature's message.

Friend, the thought-word came weak and distant, barely discernible. Then nothing.

Kendler pulled back, retreating from the inevitability that clouded the Erna's awareness—death. He sensed the creature clinging to one last moment of life to allow him time to escape from its consciousness so that he would not share its transition from life into disembodiment from . . .

"Friend." Kendler's lips formed the single word when once more he opened his mind to his own body. "Friend."

"Nils," Caltha called to him.

He felt her, his head in her lap, her soft, cool fingers

cradling his face. He opened his eyes to find her hovering above him. He smiled, his fingertips brushing her cheek.

"Did you find it?" She gazed at him, questioning. "Did you find the source of the *Nayati*?"

"We found it," he whispered, finding no strength for more than a whisper. The sudden full realization of his merge, what he had encountered, slammed into his mind. "And we lost it. We were too late, Caltha. We came too late."

The *Nayati*. The word echoed in his mind. The irony of all that had occurred on Morasha knotted his gut. Not the Kavinites, or some unknown evil source, but a "friend" was responsible for the mass destruction on the planet. The *Nayati* had been the death cries of a dying alien, a friend that sought to summon him to its side.

Kendler closed his eyes and sucked in a steadying breath. He could not escape a sense of impotence, of shortcoming. He prided himself on his psi ability, yet he had failed to interpret the Erna's cry for help, to understand the message contained in that cry. Had he grasped the *Nayati*'s meaning sooner, hundreds, perhaps thousands, would be living this day. He looked up at Caltha, seeking comfort.

She stared at him, unable to comprehend the sorrow that ached within his chest. But he could not speak. In time, when he had absorbed all that had happened, he would explain. Now, he mourned. He had found what Man had searched the stars to discover—only to share the death of a friend.

TWENTY-ONE

Kendler strung the hammock, his only souvenir of the Morasha assignment, between two trees on the east side of his Lanatia mountain cabin. Retrieving a tumbler filled with a highly potent concoction of fruit juices and five jiggers of rum from the foot of one of the trees, he carefully deposited himself within the webbed net. He took a large swallow, closed his eyes, and sighed with contentment.

A cool breeze blew up from the valley below, carrying the fresh scent of the forest around him. The hammock swayed in a gentle rhythm. Kendler smiled and sipped at the drink again.

All of today, perhaps all of tomorrow, he considered, would be spent doing exactly what he was doing at the moment—absolutely nothing. He experienced no guilty twinges over the inactivity. He deserved the rest.

After filing his report on the contact with the Erna via tachyon communiqué to Lanatia, he had spent a month in prison—officially, isolation. He and Caltha had been locked in separate quarters during the two-week flight back to Lanatia. Kate Dunbar did not want to risk the slightest mention of alien contact leaking to anyone until both field agents were debriefed.

Debriefing. Kendler took another slug from the tumbler. Debriefing was a misnomer for another two weeks of isolation on Lanatia while teams of specialists tested, diagnosed, probed, jabbed, delved every centimeter of his mind and body. When they were through, they started again, milking every sensation, thought, and emotion from him that he had felt while within the Erna's dying mind.

Only two hours ago, Kate Dunbar had walked into his room at Psi Corps Headquarters and given him two days of R&R. She refused to answer any questions concerning the Erna and her teams' conclusions. Nor did she mention Caltha. Kendler knew better than to ask. He would be told about each when Kate Dunbar deemed it necessary for him to know.

Kendler had left headquarters in a rented skimmer. An hour's flight to the cabin and a half hour to prepare drink and hammock, and he was ready to while away two days doing as little as possible and keeping Kate Dunbar as far from his thoughts as he could until he walked into her office for an early-morning meeting forty-eight hours from now.

Removing the Erna from his thoughts would not be as easy. For a month, his waking hours had been haunted by the dead creature. His few moments of contact with that alien mind replayed over and over in his mind like a loop of spetape. He could still feel the emotions that welled around him to form the sensation of "friend."

And the task? It made no more sense now than it had four weeks ago. Yet the Erna had left it for him to complete. Its contentment and relief that he would perform as needed still nagged at him, adding to his confusion and frustration.

Kendler took another overly large sip from the tumbler. Before his taste buds could fully savor the tangy fruit flavor, he slugged down yet another healthy swig. He did not want to get drunk, just reach a nice alcoholic haze that would obscure the Erna and the unknown task it had placed in his lap.

And most of all, the alcohol would ease the sorrow, the loss of a friend he had only glimpsed in the creature's dying seconds.

The soft hum of a skimmer intruded into his mental meanderings. Reluctantly, as though looking up would give credence to the aircraft, Kendler opened his eyes. A small metallic-blue four-passenger craft scooted over the treetops toward the cabin. His eyelids drifted together. *Weekenders heading for the resort on the other side of the mountain.*

The skimmer's steady hum increased. He glanced up once more. It hovered above the cabin. *Damn!* He rolled from the hammock when the craft started its descent. He downed one last swig from the tumbler in the hope of shoving aside the niggling suspicion the Psi Corps was about to elbow its way into his free days.

Walking to the far side of the cabin, the psiotic stood and watched the blue skimmer sink to the ground beside his rented vehicle. The craft's engines died and a door swung open on its side. A wide grin split his doubtful frown.

Caltha stepped out, her own grin greeting his. Her feet barely touched the ground before she was running. Then she was in his arms, hugging his neck, her mouth pressed firmly to his.

"Mmmmmmmm," she sighed when they parted. "A month is a hell of a long time. I'd forgotten how good that was."

"Is," he corrected and returned the kiss with equal enthusiasm."

"I don't think I've ever seen someone who looks so good," he said when they drifted apart again. They stood there, allowing their eyes to soak in one another. "Damn, but you *are* beautiful!"

"A month of being locked away didn't seem to hurt you any either." She nodded to the half-drained tumbler he held. "Think I could get one of those?"

Kendler wrapped an arm about her waist and led her into the cabin. "When did Kate release you?"

"A week ago." Caltha seated herself on an oversized sofa while he mixed fresh drinks for both of them. "Despite all the interrogations, I didn't have much to tell them."

"What I had didn't seem to be convincing." Kendler handed her a cool glass and settled beside her on the couch. "Any hint what the official decision is going to be?"

Caltha shook her head. "Kate's keeping tight wraps on this. Outside the debriefing teams, Ambassador Lore, and ourselves, the Erna is nonexistent."

"Why?" He watched her shake her head again.

It did not make sense. Kate had every detail of the contact. She also had the Erna's body, neatly preserved during the return voyage to Lanatia in a regeneration unit.

Caltha reached out and took his hand. "I told Kate about us."

Kendler was not sure an "us" existed, but he did not say anything. "What was her reaction?"

"She mumbled something about my taste in men and prima donna psiotics," Caltha replied. "Then she kissed and hugged me and asked what our plans were."

Uncertain how he was supposed to react, Kendler slowly sipped at his drink.

"I told her that she had kept us locked away from one another for four weeks and that we hadn't had time to talk, let alone think about the future," Caltha said.

Kendler had thought about the future. Even with the problems he foresaw, the possibility of a future without this woman was far dimmer. "Have you made any plans?"

"A few, but they all depend on you." She paused, giving him the opportunity to comment. Kendler sat and listened. "To begin with, I'd like you to meet Paul."

"We can't have a future without that." Caltha's young son was definitely part of any permanent relationship they might share. "Why didn't you bring him with you?"

"I left him with his grandmother," Caltha said. "I wanted to talk with you first."

Grandmother! Kendler was just getting accustomed to thinking of Kate Dunbar as a mother.

"As for us . . ." Caltha hesitated, her eyes meeting his. For a moment silence hung embarrassingly heavy around them. "We don't know unless we try. The problem is, I don't see how two prima donnas can even consider . . ."

"I'm willing to try," Kendler slipped in.

Caltha's gaze remained on him. "Starting this weekend?"

"Starting now."

He drew her to him. Their lips touched, a gentle kiss to confirm mutual commitment. He sensed an instant of hesitation. His palms read a shivery tremble that suffused through her body. The hesitancy faded. She nestled in his arms, her womanly contours so definable beneath her clothing.

The passion of their embrace grew, their mouths opening to their tongues. The awkward uncertainty of that first moment melted, soothed by the assurance of stroking hands and fingertips.

Holding one another, they rose from the sofa. Kendler's fingers ran down the static strips of Caltha's clothing. The clasps hissed softly when they opened. Caltha's hands answered, touching the static clasps of his clothes.

She eased from his arms and stepped back. "Clothes should be designed to melt at times like this. They're too clumsy."

There was no clumsiness as she slipped from her clothing to stand unashamed before him. Nor did she display a trace of embarrassment while his gaze caressed her nakedness. If anything, he caught a gleam of pride in her dark eyes.

Shedding his own clothing, Kendler moved her. His open palms rose to caress the uptilted cones of her breasts. With a coy, taunting smile, she sidestepped his embrace and stretched atop the sofa's cushions, opening her arms.

He came to her. Love, desire, need swirled in a wonderfully aching core as he eased into the enveloping warmth of her body. She clung to him, her mouth covering his. Bathing in her luxury, his hands calmed her tremblings and soothed away doubt. Her fingers replied with tender intimacies of their own. Minutes, hours, they held no meaning. Time lost itself in the gentle rhythm of their union. They gave themselves to one another, rising with mutual love and need.

"Open to me." In her voice, he sensed the mounting passion of his own desire.

He did as she requested, his mind flowing out to merge with hers. Uninhibited, she bared herself to him. Thought, emotion, and sensation rushed to surround him.

She opened herself to his mind.

Like crystal mirrors that stood facing one another, their minds lay naked. She was he; he was she. Yet their individual identities remained. Their minds reflected an infinite kaleidoscope of love and sensation that flared in a consuming mental and physical maelstrom.

Slowly, ever so slowly, they withdrew, neither wishing to break the melting of flesh and thought that united them. Side by side, they held tightly to one another, basking in the satisfaction of the love they shared.

Kendler closed his eyes and breathed in the feminine fragrance of the woman cradled in his arms. For the first time in his life, the future held no doubts.

"We'll make it," he whispered. "We'll make it."

Paul's gaze never left the two Cretaceous monarchs as the threesome walked around the exhibit amid a steady crowd that circled the Retrieve display. Kendler watched the boy. He could see Caltha in her son's features, the bright eyes, the small nose, and hints of sensuality to the mouth that would be a sure attraction to the opposite sex by the time he reached puberty.

But the boy's hair was as blond as Caltha's was black. And Paul seemed taller than the normal seven-year-old. Kendler suspected he would be taller than his mother in a few years.

Paul glanced up at Kendler, grinned, then returned his full attention to the carnosaurs. Kendler smiled; the awe reflected in Paul's youthful eyes was not restricted to the children. The two carnosaurs awakened something within adults jaded to the wonders of the galaxy. The dinosaurs seemed to be a focal point, a reminder of a common past humankind shared.

"The crowds have been like this since the exhibition opened," Caltha said, squeezing Kendler's hand. "The other LofAl planets are bidding to be next in line for the exhibit."

Kendler's smile widened. Now that the LofAl clamored for the exhibit, the council would be hard pressed to deny Retrieve funding. With Earth's past open to them, Retrieve had the capability of supplying a never-ending series of exhibitions to tantalize the Alliance's populace.

Perhaps not infinite, Kendler admitted, but enough exhibits to milk the needed funding from the council and breathe life into Jon Beamin's dream of transforming a dead ball of clay into a Terran historical park.

"Can we go around again?" Paul stared up at Kendler, his eyes wide and pleading. The boy then turned to his mother to repeat his appeal.

Caltha shook her head. "Nils was kind enough to bring us here. I don't think we should intrude on his time any further."

The boy was obviously disappointed. Kendler reached down and placed a hand on his shoulder. "I'll make a deal with you, Paul. I know some of the people who run this show. I believe I can arrange for us to see these two at feeding time, when there are no crowds around."

Paul's face brightened with a certain relish. "At feeding time! Tomorrow?"

"I'll have to make a few calls to set it up, but I think we can arrange it for tomorrow." Kendler smiled. "I'll call your grandmother tonight and give her the details."

"You're on!" The boy grinned widely at the prospect of viewing the carnivores' gory meal.

Moving with the crowd, they exited the exhibit and caught

a skimmer-bus to Kate Dunbar's apartplex. A liftshaft floated them up to the Psi Corps director's penthouse.

If Kate Dunbar was cold and calculating in her role at the helm of the corps, she was the exact opposite with her grandchild. Kendler watched the woman with Paul out of the corner of an eye while Caltha and he prepared drinks. Kate listened attentively to every detail of the exhibition visit before calling Caltha to shuttle her son to bed.

"It won't take long." Caltha kissed Kendler's cheek. "Paul never argues longer than ten minutes before he's resigned to the fact that he must go to bed." Caltha turned to her son, then glanced back. "Be careful of Mother. She's only tough as Psi Corps director. As the mother of an only daughter, she can be hell incarnate if she wants to be."

Kendler's cool confidence dissolved with Caltha's words. He stared up to see Kate give her grandson a goodnight kiss. He could almost forget the woman was Kate Dunbar—*the* Kate Dunbar. *Almost.* He sucked in a deep breath as Caltha and Paul left the room, then gathered the drinks and joined Kate.

"Mmmmm, that's good." Kate took a short sip and motioned him to a chair. "Damn sight better than the servos mix."

Kendler nodded and took a swig of his own drink, deeper than he should have. He felt like an adolescent squirming under the appraising eye of his first date's parents.

"You could really make points with Paul," Kate said. "If he knew you were responsible for capturing those two overgrown lizards, you'd be an overnight hero."

"Points like that seem to have a way of tarnishing," Kendler said. "Sooner or later, children discover heroes are human. Better to begin as a human."

Kate smiled, approval in her eyes. "Have you and Caltha bundled yet?"

No subtlety, no beating around the bush—the question came out of nowhere, calculated to jerk the rug out from under his feet. Kendler laughed aloud at her directness. "Don't you think that's a question you should ask Caltha?"

"Mothers and daughters have an awkward time talking about sex," Kate replied. "But no matter, you've answered my question. If you hadn't hopped into bed, you would have said 'no.'"

Kendler studied the Psi Corps director. He recollected that strange little expression Caltha had worn when he had

180

suggested her mother held the responsibility for the unexpected love that grew between them. Had Kate purposely arranged the unprecedented partnership for reasons outside corps efficiency? Kate Dunbar—mother, grandmother, matchmaker. The possibility amused him, but he could not give it credence.

Kate sipped slowly from her drink. "Bundling's good. I don't approve of a woman's involving herself with a man she hasn't slept with. What a woman and a man share in bed isn't everything, but unless it's good, there isn't much chance for anything else to work."

Before Kendler could reply, Caltha walked into the room. She glanced at the two of them, as though making certain everything had gone smoothly in her absence, then crossed the room and sat on the arm of Kendler's chair. "What have you two been talking about? I get the feeling I walked in at the wrong time."

"I've been prying into your sex life," Kate said, ignoring her daughter's irritated expression. "And from the color to your cheeks, I'd say Nils passed the test."

Caltha looked at Kendler, demure. A heavy silence hung in the room.

"Why don't you two get the hell out of here?" Kate shattered the uneasiness. She called for the house computer to open the door. "You don't want to spend half the night entertaining me. And I don't feel like being entertained."

"Mother, are you sure?" Caltha asked.

"Hell, yes," Kate answered. "Now get out. You're wasting time I'd planned to spend on myself."

Neither Caltha nor Kendler protested, but left. An hour's skimmer flight back to the cabin, then a few quick calls to arrange for the private tour of the Retrieve exhibit in the morning, and Kendler found himself snuggling beside Caltha in his Morashan hammock beneath the Lanatian stars. Shortly thereafter, he discovered his first assessment of the webbed sling had been totally wrong. Not only was it designed for restful sleep, but it was more than adequate for lovemaking.

TWENTY-TWO

Kate Dunbar sat behind her desk shuffling through several stacks of manila folders. With a disgusted shake of her head, she dropped the files and looked up.

Her gaze moved between Caltha and Kendler. The Psi Corps director bit her lower lip and sucked at it. "Despite the debriefing teams' battery of interrogations, tests, and interpretations, we have been unable to translate whatever message or messages you received on Morasha. At the same time, they could find no evidence the experience was artificially induced. As far as you two are concerned, the Erna was real."

"As far as we are concerned?" Kendler caught the woman's careful phrasing.

"And as far as I'm concerned," Kate added. "But I'm not the LofAl Council, nor am I the debriefing teams. Several of their members contend the Erna's message was a hallucination somehow artificially induced, or perhaps self-induced, due to the strain of the assignment."

Doubt? Kendler stared at the woman, confused and bewildered. Awe, joy, fear—anything but doubt. He had not expected this. Humankind had searched too long for another intelligence with which to share the universe.

"I repeat, *I* believe you." Once more Kate's gaze moved between her daughter and Kendler. "Neither of you is given to self-induced hallucinations. And I don't believe the Kavinites have the capability of producing the psi hysteria Morasha experienced."

"But?" Caltha added Kate's unspoken condition.

"We have no physical evidence." Kate leaned back in her chair. "Nothing to take the council. Hell, I refuse to take this anywhere on the word of one man. I, along with the corps, would be laughed into oblivion."

"What about the Erna's body?" Kendler asked. "That's hard physical evidence."

"Evidence that you encountered an alien life form." Kate shook her head. "On Morasha there are thousands of alien life forms, and we've no proof any of them are intelligent. There's no way to demonstrate the carcass you brought back here ever held intelligence. It's a dead bug, a misshapen centipede."

Kate pointed to her computer terminal. "We can't tell anything definite about the carcass. You can call up the report before you leave, if you want. A team of three xenobiologists have been unable to locate a brain or anything that resembles a central nerve plexus."

Kendler cursed, not bothering to disguise his disgust. He understood the need for caution. But they were burying the truth in bureaucratic compost. The Erna had been real. It had existed. It could not be shoved aside, tidily filed away under a label of "alien arthropod."

"What about what I felt?" Caltha asked. "Doesn't that support Nils?"

"What did you feel?" Kate turned to her daughter. "A bit of gloom, a fear of dying? You didn't make contact. I doubt that you had the ability. If Nils's story is correct, it took a merger to touch the Erna's dying consciousness."

Caltha stiffened, but said nothing.

"What about the pyramid? The Erna impressed an image of a pyramid onto my mind," Kendler said, reaching for straws. "It was the same one I saw on Earth. There has to be a connection."

"That and my belief in your capability is why I'm willing to take a few more steps before the Erna is forgotten." Kate paused and turned to the computer. "Gustaf, dim the lights and give us the pyramid presentation."

The computer immediately responded. A projection of a pyramid appeared at the center of the room. Kendler had never seen it before.

"After you returned from Earth, I put a team on your pyramid request. They managed to assemble this presentation from various library sources throughout the Alliance. Surprising how many of these damn things Earth had," Kate said. "Tell Gustaf to stop the display if you see your pyramid, Nils."

The computer flashed another pyramid into the room. This one had a long flight of stairs leading to its apexless top. Behind him, Kendler heard Kate giving Caltha an outline of his Retrieve venture.

More pyramids came and went. Many appeared to belong to different time periods and a variety of cultures. Kate had been right, their Terran ancestors definitely had an affinity for pyramidal structures. Did they all have the religious significance that Isal held for the Morashans?

The computer image faded, and yet another pyramid formed before the psiotic. Kendler sat up, pushing to the edge of his chair. "Gustaf, hold this one."

"Nils?" Kate asked. "Do you recognize it?"

"I don't know." Kendler studied the projected image. Unlike the one he had seen, the capstone was missing, as was the smooth limestone veneer that covered the building stones. Yet there was something familiar about the structure. "Are there any other views?"

Gustaf answered with a series of twenty different projections. The last was an artist's conception of the pyramid as it had stood before the ravages of Man and time. Both capstone and veneer were in place. The desert around the structure varied little from the scene Kendler had seen from the Retrieve timestream.

"Gustaf, the lights," Kate called. The lights flashed on overhead. The Psi Corps director grinned widely. "I think we've just found a needle in a haystack. Gustaf, profile the pyramid."

"The Great Pyramid of Giza, also the Pyramid of Gizah, Khufu or Cheops, was the largest construction of Man, and was considered one of the eight ancient wonders of Earth," a deep and definitely male voice answered from the computer. "The structure stood amid eight other lesser structures on the Egyptian plain of Giza. An exact construction date was never determined by Terran historians. It was generally accepted that the Great Pyramid of Giza was built during Egypt's Fourth Dynasty, between 2720 B.C. to 2560 B.C. An estimated thirty to fifty years were required to construct the structure."

Kendler listened while the computer recounted how 2,600,000 limestone and granite blocks, weighing from two to seventy tons each, had been used in the construction. Each block was hewn so accurately that joints were never more than half a millimeter wide.

"That's as good as we can do with the most sensitive instruments today," Kate said. "It took two tons of pressure to cut the stone used for Giza. We can do it with a diamond bit or energy beams. The ancient Egyptians had neither. Nor is history clear on their methods for cutting the stone blocks."

She added that the limestone was thought to have been quarried a few kilometers from the pyramid site, but the granite had to be transported from over eight hundred kilometers away. "Quite impressive when you remember the Egyptians didn't have our terraforming equipment, just slave labor. If ten stones a day were laid, it would have taken more than six hundred years to build the Great Pyramid. The methods used to transport the stone blocks and then manhandle them into position apparently had been the subject of considerable debate among Terran ancestors."

When Kate finished, Gustaf began again, noting the pyramid measured 240.4 meters in length along each of its four faces and originally rose to a height of 146.7 meters. The structure's base covered an area of 540 ares and weighed more than five million tons. Its volume was more than a quarter of a million cubic meters.

The figures did little to impress Kendler. He had seen the pyramid.

"The Great Pyramid of Giza was built at the junction of ancient Upper and Lower Egypt," Gustaf said. "Historians generally believed the pyramid was constructed as a tomb for the Pharaoh Khufu. However, a body was never discovered within the structure. Nor were hieroglyphics, emblems, inscriptions, or statuary found inside the structure. All these were necessary for the transition of a soul into an afterworld, according to the religious beliefs of ancient Egyptians."

"Isal held no markings or decorations on its walls," Kendler said, remembering he had felt it strange a religious monument should be so bare when he first entered Isal.

"Other theories concerning the Great Pyramid of Giza's purpose include an astronomical observatory, an artificially created hill used as a giant road marker for desert caravans, a temple for initiating acolytes into a now forgotten religious order, a mathematical coding of scientific facts, or a coded history of the human race, both past and future," Gustaf continued.

"A mathematical code?" Kendler asked.

"The pyramid is based on a ratio of phi and pi," the computer answered. "For centuries metaphysical researchers and theologians plotted and calculated the structure's angles and measurements, attempting to unlock undefined mystical secrets supposedly contained within the pyramid. The Great Pyramid of Giza's interior passages and chambers also were a part of this undeciphered code."

Kate's voice came from behind Kendler. "Apparently our ancestors never considered the possibility that a structure built to the Great Pyramid's dimensions would naturally provide this relationship of phi and pi."

"An accidental relationship rather than one purposely codified in the structure?" Kendler asked.

"Exactly," Kate answered. "A logical conclusion when one takes into account the fact that pi was not discovered until the Greek civilization and phi centuries later."

"As originally constructed, the pyramid was covered in a limestone veneer two point five meters thick," Gustaf began again. "The veneer was stripped to help rebuild the Egyptian city of Cairo after a series of earthquakes in the thirteenth century. The missing capstone remains a mystery. No record remains of its removal."

"Enough, Gustaf," Kate said. The computer immediately went silent. Kate looked at Kendler. "Giza drew the most interest from my researchers."

Kate shuffled through the folders on her desk again. This time she came up with the one she searched for and tossed it to Kendler. The folder was tabbed in bold type THE GREAT PYRAMID OF GIZA. Kendler opened it. The first several pages within were various diagrams showing the pyramid's dimensions and the corridors within from a variety of angles.

"During the twentieth century, popular interest in pyramids reached a peak on Earth," Kate said. "A majority of this popularity can be traced to metaphysical research in a then Terran superpower called Russia. When a pyramid is built to

Giza's proportions and aligned so that the four faces are positioned to face the true global directions, the structure is supposed to produce a mystical energy within."

Kendler flipped through more of the folder's pages. "Does this energy exist?"

"As far as my researchers have taken it, there seems to be something generated within a pyramid. It seems to be akin to electromagnetic energy, but that's not definite," Kate said.

Kendler's eye was drawn to an item in the folder. "Apparently, Terrans had a long history of believing in this mystical energy. The names for it listed here take up a quarter of a page—life energy, bioplasmic energy, odie force, prana, mana, magnale, n-rays, animal magnetism, psychotronic energy, bioenergy, chi, and Kirlian energy." *Kirlian?* Kendler glanced up at Kate, a questioning look on his face.

The Psi Corps director nodded. "The same energy field that surrounds all life forms. Our ancestors also called it an aura."

"What is this Kirlian force supposed to do?" Caltha asked.

"Not sure yet. My researchers have only duplicated some of the old Terran experiments," Kate said. "It seems food placed within a pyramid shape will dehydrate but not spoil. Seeds tend to germinate quicker within the structure, and plants watered with water left in the pyramid for several days seem to mature more rapidly and be healthier."

"It says here that pyramids were used for meditation," Kendler said, reading the folder. "Supposedly they promoted some type of inner tranquillity."

"There were also pyramid-shaped razor-blade sharpeners, and two countries used pyramid-shaped containers to retard spoilage in milk and yogurt," Kate said. "All of which is interesting and in all likelihood one of those freaks of nature that have absolutely no value to us. Except for the fact that the wavelengths of this pyramid energy and that of certain psi wavelengths are the same."

"The same?" Caltha's voice was filled with disbelief.

"My researchers had the same reaction," Kate said. "However, that didn't alter the fact the waves match curve for curve."

"Which psi wave lengths?" Kendler asked.

"It depends," Kate replied. "There appears to be a correlation between the sun and the energy produced. During the day, the wavelengths are that of a psi sender. At night, they are that of a receiver."

"A psi amplifier," Kendler thought aloud as he grasped the structure's possible application.

"Exactly," Kate said. "Presently, we're experimenting with psiotics enclosed within pyramids. The results are not definitive, and probably won't be for another decade. However, early results indicate some psiotics' abilities are enhanced while inside the structure. The best results have been achieved with receivers and senders. In some incidents, their abilities have tripled."

Kate paused. "On the other hand, others have shown no increase of their powers within a pyramid."

"Still, the Erna might have used Isal to amplify his psi energy," Kendler said. Even without amplification, the alien produced psi emanations that exceeded those of any human mind.

"There is also the possibility you encountered an Erna prior to Morasha," Kate suggested.

"The pyramid on Earth . . . Giza?" Caltha asked.

Kate nodded. "I've had a cruiser orbiting Lanatia for the past week. It's waiting for someone to find out."

"Meaning me?" Kendler's excitement rose.

"Caltha and you," Kate said. "It took two of you to find the Erna. I don't think it would be wise to break up the team."

"What about Retrieve?" Kendler asked. "Have you told them what we're searching for?"

"No," Kate said with a shake of her head. "They raised eyebrows and did their best to find out what we're after, but I dodged them. It came down to the fact that they owed me a favor. They agreed to transport you to any time period without questions."

"It will be sticky," Kendler said.

"It's always sticky," Kate replied. "It's a matter of getting used to walking on flypaper."

"When do we leave?" Caltha looked at her mother.

"There's a shuttle waiting to transport you to the cruiser the moment we're through," Kate answered. "I've got the necessary recording equipment aboard the shuttle that you'll need to document your time jump and any contact with the Erna. Though I prefer a living alien."

"I have to make arrangements before we can leave," Caltha said.

"They've been taken care of," Kate replied. "Paul will stay with me."

Caltha turned to Kendler. She grinned, apparently sharing his excitement.

"A skimmer is waiting below to take you to the shuttle," Kate said as the two psiotics rose. "Good luck. Bring me back an Erna."

TWENTY-THREE

The shuttle dropped to Earth. Kendler stared down at the sphere that rushed up to greet the craft. He tried to imagine the dead terrain below once more alive with carefully controlled pockets of the planet's past. He could not.

Humankind's inability to cope with itself had almost brought an end to existence on this planet. That same intolerance came close to wiping the species from the cosmic account ledger during the Century Conflagration. Even at the moment, the human animal maintained a precarious balance. One misplaced step could plunge mankind into another interplanetary confrontation that could conceivably wipe Man from the slate.

The stars burning in the void beyond Earth drew his attention. Which one or ones belonged to the Erna? How long had it taken them to crawl their centipedal bodies from the slime and reach the stars? Why had they remained hidden from Man for so long? Man's violence? Or did they conceal their own shames, an ancient culture rotting at its core?

His gaze moved to Caltha. Her excitement was obvious. He recalled his own expectations when he had first ventured to Earth months ago. Just as vivid was the disappointment when he viewed the lifeless landscape that surrounded Retrieve Base One.

He turned back to Earth and closed his eyes.

After a half hour of uneventful descent, the shuttle settled to the ground within the Base One force shield. Gathering their holographic and audio recording equipment, the two psiotics disembarked. Jon Beamin waited for them outside the craft.

After a round of polite introductions and greetings, Beamin pointed to the equipment. "What's that?"

Caltha explained. Beamin listened, then rubbed his chin. Kendler noticed the Base One director did not inquire into their reasons for needing the recording devices.

"I don't know," Beamin eventually said while they walked toward the Retrieve complex.

"Don't know what?" Kendler asked.

"It's bulky." He paused, then shook his head. "You'll understand when we get inside."

Within the complex, Beamin hastily led them into his office. He settled behind his desk and motioned for them to take a seat. "To begin with, Retrieve and the Psi Corps have determined that December 8, 2123, is the optimum time for the jump-down. To put it simply, it came down to a matter of energy conservation."

December 8, 2123—the day Earth died. An eerie chill ran up Kendler's spine. Caltha and he would walk Earth the day humankind decided to destroy itself.

"The only problem with the jump is that you'll only have two hours in which to complete your work," Beamin said. "Our mutual superiors have decided two hours is sufficient for your task and will give you less opportunity to attract the attention of Earth's inhabitants."

The Base One director paused and took a deep breath. "Daily tourist journey to view the Great Pyramid of Giza. Arrangements have been made for you to join one of these tourist tours. Getting within the structure is another problem. By 2123, the Great Pyramid was sealed with an iron gate to keep sightseers out. The entrance was also under twenty-four-hour guard."

Beamin opened a desk drawer and pulled out a small box containing explosive discs. "The way you handle the guards is up to you. These will take care of the gate."

Kendler's gaze shot to the director. He could not believe the man would consider using explosives on a structure of such historical significance.

"I've thought of everything we could do to save it," Beamin answered the psiotic's unspoken question. "We presently haven't got the facilities to handle the mass. But we might in the future. So restrict your explosive use to the entrance gate."

Caltha and Kendler nodded their assurance.

"In the past four weeks, I've sent back three two-person teams to reconnoiter the period for you," Beamin continued. "Our computer holds the sleep-learning programs that will provide you with the necessary language and logistical information."

"What about period dress?" Caltha asked.

"Authentic," the director said. "My teams have brought back costumes for both of you, as well as local currency. However, the major problem does concern the clothing."

Beamin punched his intercom and ordered their costumes brought to his office. He looked back at Kendler and Caltha. "To establish an effective time corridor, there must be both a receiving and transmitting station. For the majority of our operations, this base and the field bases form the needed links. Time jumping won't work any other way."

Something did not make sense to Kendler. "But you have to establish field bases."

"Correct. We do that by sending back individuals, each equipped so that he is virtually a miniature base. The best we've been able to manage is a personal power source that's operational for a week," Beamin said. "Usually two persons can establish a field base within a week."

Caltha glanced at Kendler, her expression as blank as his own.

"Think of time travel as a matter of two electromagnets. Their polarity either repels or attracts. A traveler represents one of those magnets and this base the other. The traveler must carry a power source to maintain his polarity. When the polarity is the same, he is repelled from Base One back into time. When the polarity is opposite, he's attracted toward now, 'real' time."

"Since no field base exists where we're going, we'll have to wear some type of power pack," Kendler said, and Beamin nodded.

"I don't see the problem. You already have the equipment," Caltha said.

"Our present power units are heavy and bulky," the Base One director answered. "When a traveler is destined for a prehistoric period, the awkward bulk doesn't matter. But for the time you're going, it's simply a matter of current styles. You can't suddenly appear in a manner that will attract attention. To function, you have to blend in."

The door to the office opened, and a man walked in carrying two garments over an arm. Kendler grinned. The predicament was immediately apparent. Both garments were made of some transparent material that clouded to translucency over the vital sexual areas.

"As you can see, these give us little or no area in which to hide our equipment," Beamin explained with a shrug of his shoulders. "However, it was quite common for both sexes to carry pouches in which to place personal items. These pouches were usually worn over the shoulder by means of a strap."

Kendler noticed the newcomer held two pouches in his other hand. He opened a flap on one to display Beamin's power source hidden within.

"Each of these weighs two kilos. We've managed to weave transparent monofilament wiring into the garments that will establish a polarity field around the wearers," Beamin said. "The pouch straps connect to the shoulders of the clothing via a terminal that will complete the circuit."

Beamin lifted one of the pouches and pointed to a small electric torch concealed beside the battery, noting they would be needed once inside the Great Pyramid of Giza.

"Ten minutes prior to depletion of the power source, a warning buzzer will sound. Hit this switch and return to Base One." He pointed to a silver toggle switch atop the unit. "Five minutes later, the polarity will reverse automatically, and you will jump up ready or not."

The director sank back in his chair. "Now, I believe you can understand why I was troubled by the recording equipment. There's just no place to conceal it in these garments."

Kendler nodded. "But you'll come up with something."

Beamin frowned and released an exasperated sigh. "We'll see."

Kendler had no doubt that he would. Either that or face Kate Dunbar.

"If Beamin weren't waiting for us in the next room," Kendler said in his recently sleep-learned Hebraic, "I'd find some way to talk you out of that and make love to you."

193

Caltha beamed. She coyly turned before him to display her jump-down attire. Kendler grinned and allowed his gaze to take in her alluring nakedness beneath the transparent fabric. Ancient Terrans definitely had something in their mode of dress. The clothing was designed to titillate; it did that. Once he had read that the human body clothed by the merest obscuring veils was often more provocative than when it was nude. He had doubted the statement until now.

Caltha's gaze languidly traveled over him. She made no attempt to hide the approving smile that upturned the corners of her mouth. She sighed. "But Beamin *is* waiting."

Outside the dressing area, the Base One director stood impatiently. "Ten minutes until jump-down. Place these around your necks."

The man handed them what appeared to be gold medallions, explaining they were miniaturized holo cameras. He then placed gold bracelets in their palms. "Audio recorders. Both units draw power from the packs. However, they should not affect your stay by more than two seconds."

Caltha and Kendler placed the bracelets around their wrists while they followed the director into the control room. Beamin directed them to stand on the grid at the room's center. Unlike before, no glass canopy slid from the ceiling to envelope Kendler.

"Remember the ten-minute warning," Beamin said as he walked behind the control console. "If possible, begin your return when it sounds."

"If possible." Kendler listened to the man call out the countdown.

Abruptly Kendler's world quaked and shattered. A man caught in an energy sling, he hurled . . . up? down? forward? He did not know. He could not orient himself to the sudden onrush. Unlike his two previous journeys, he did not move within a timestream. He was the head of that stream while it rammed through time's barrier into Earth's past.

The hurling stopped. Caltha stood beside him, eyes wide, face pale. For several pounding heartbeats, neither moved; they stood staring at each other with uncertainty. Then their gazes tentatively inspected the surroundings. Kendler released an overly held breath. He recognized the scene around them from their sleep-programming—an alley behind a Cairo tourist agency.

"Our transportation to Giza should be around that corner." He pointed to the alley's exit. "Ready?"

Caltha took a deep breath and nodded. As Beamin had promised, an electric GEV bus was poised at the curb outside the agency. Giving their names to a guide who leaned against the vehicle's door, they waited until he checked their names off a passenger list, then stepped inside.

Here and there greeting smiles met them while they moved down an aisle between two rows of seats. Music blared from a small black radio a youth held to his ear. He glanced up as they walked toward him and winked at Caltha before returning to the music.

Forty passengers in all. Kendler studied each of his fellow tourists, and thirty-eight of them were ghosts. His eyes turned from them, unable to linger on their faces.

Gratefully, he sank beside Caltha on a vacant bench at the back of the bus. The backs of the passengers' heads were easier to accept.

What is past is past. It did nothing to ease his disquiet. He wanted to stand and scream out a warning, to save them from the inevitable death that awaited them this day.

Caltha took his hand and squeezed it tightly. "Anything we could say or do would only endanger our purpose for being here. Think of the Erna."

Kendler looked at her and managed a weak smile that could not erase his uneasiness. He sat within a bus filled with dead men, phantoms. Before the day ended, humankind's existence on Earth would take an irreversible step toward total oblivion. And there was nothing he could do to stop it.

The guide stepped onto the bus and seated himself in the driver's couch. The bus rumbled to life. There was a metallic grinding, as though gears ate at one another. The vehicle lifted from the ground to lurch forward and wind through a maze of crowded, narrow streets. Kendler closed his eyes to let the ghosts outside go by unseen.

Forty-five minutes after their jump-down and ten miles west of the city, the vehicle stopped beside the Giza complex. Caltha and Kendler rose and exited the bus with their fellow tourists. The dry desert heat enveloped them.

That same awesome power of ancient things Kendler had sensed while standing in the shadow of the Pyramid of Isal suffused through him as he gazed on the Giza complex. Two gigantic pyramids and six lesser ones stood overlooking the palm groves of the Nile Valley from the Giza Plain. Guarding the structures was the crouching Great Sphinx. Kendler's attention focused on the largest pyramid with its missing apical stone.

He glanced at Caltha. "Feel anything?"

"Nothing." She shook her head as they moved with the group toward the base of the Great Pyramid of Giza. "Nothing at all."

In a group, the tourists skirted the crumbling steplike blocks of the structure, making their way to its northern face and the two guards standing to either side of the locked entrance. Kendler glanced at his watch. An hour remained before they had to return to Base One.

While the guide prattled on about the size, weight, and age of the Great Pyramid of Khufu, the tourists formed a line and slowly took their turn gazing through the grated gate into the pyramid's interior.

"Any ideas on how we're going to get inside?" Caltha whispered.

Kendler sucked at his teeth. "There's no way to get at the guards with all these people around." His eyes nervously shot to his watch again.

"God!" A woman screamed. "My God!"

The youth with the radio held it above his head, turning its volume up to full blast. A woman's voice crackled over the overloaded speaker.

"I repeat, we have confirmed that the Sudanic capital of Khartoum has been destroyed in a nuclear attack. It is believed a retaliatory attack has been . . ."

"They've done it! They've finally done it!" The woman ahead of them screamed. A man beside her grabbed her shoulder and swirled her around. His palm cracked sharply against her cheek. Her hysterical cries stopped, muted to uncontrollable sobs.

". . . while no action is expected to be taken against our nation, the government has declared a temporary state of emergency. Citizens are advised to take immediate precautionary measures. Civil authorities are presently manning all National Defense Centers. I repeat . . ." the radio droned on.

"The bus!" The guide called to his passengers. "Please return to the bus. There is a defense center just within the city. We can be there in ten minutes. There is no need for panic."

Caught in the realization of a lifetime of fears, the tourists ignored him. They turned and ran.

"Please! There is no need to panic," the guide shouted.

For a moment, the man stood staring as though unsure what to do. Then he ran after his wards. The panic was infectious. One of the pyramid guards bolted after the guide.

Kendler watched the flight for a few moments, then turned to Caltha. "Plant the explosives. I'll take the guard."

"We've been noticed." Caltha tilted her head to the remaining guard. He approached, rifle leveled at them.

Kendler dropped to his knees. Closing off his senses, he reached out and touched the guard's mind. Easily he blended with the man's consciousness. He found the fear he knew would be there and molded it. Creating images of blossoming mushroom clouds and flesh melting from the bone in a nuclear inferno, Kendler weaved his thoughts into the mind of his target.

There was no need to dominate the guard's mind. The images were enough. The man threw down his weapon and ran screaming toward the bus. With one last terrifying vision for impetus, Kendler withdrew and flowed back into his own body. He opened his eyes to find Caltha running to him.

"Stay down!" She dropped to his side and covered her head.

Kendler threw his arms over his head. The first disc went off, exploding the desert stillness. Three other explosions followed on its heels. Fragments of blasted limestone showered over them, biting at arms, back, and legs.

The echoing rumble died. Caltha and Kendler pushed to their feet. A cursory examination of one another proved neither sustained more than a few minor cuts from the debris. Kendler glanced at the now retreating bus, then pivoted to the open entrance of the Great Pyramid of Giza.

Extracting the electric torch from within the power pack, he squatted before the meter-square entry passage. The light beam cut through the interior darkness. Even with its ages of thorough exploration, the structure appeared to have seen no more use than Isal. And as with Isal, Kendler could detect no ornamentation on the walls.

"Thirty minutes," Caltha said behind him. "I still can't sense anything."

On hands and knees, they entered the pyramid, crawling thirty meters down a descending passage before the ceiling opened to reveal another passage slightly larger than a meter square. Still on all fours, they crawled more than a hundred meters up the steeply inclined ascending passageway. At its top, a horizontal passage led them into a gable-roofed room commonly called the Queen's Chamber.

"Anything?" Kendler shot a glance to Caltha.

"Nothing. I can't feel anything." Her voice was strained. Her expression reflected a mounting desperation as their jump time rapidly ran out. "The King's Chamber?"

Grabbing her hand, Kendler pulled her back into the horizontal passage into the pyramid's Grand Gallery, a stepped corridor two meters wide, eight and a half meters high, and forty-nine meters long. A buzzer blared, echoing off the polished limestone walls. Ten minutes until they were jerked back to "real" time. Together they ran up the inclined passageway.

Reaching the top of the Grand Gallery, they moved through an anteroom and into Giza's largest chamber, the King's Chamber.

"Nothing." Caltha shook her head. "Nils, I'm going to open myself."

He did not like the idea with jump-up ready to snatch them from the heart of the pyramid, but he nodded. Caltha closed her eyes as his arms went around her waist for support. Seconds later her lids blinked open. She stared at him.

"It's not here," she said softly. "The Erna's not here."

Kendler released her. Numbly he turned around, gazing about the immense chamber. The Erna had to be here. "Are you sure?"

"Nils, there's nothing here," Caltha answered. "Nothing at all."

"It can't be . . . it just can't be." He twisted around again, searching for any clue. "Caltha, it placed an image of Giza in my mind before it died. It has to be here."

Before she could reply, a quaking tremor ran through the floor of the chamber. The massive blocks of limestone and granite around them groaned, their faces shifting against one another. Again a tremor came, as though the earth had grown tired of carrying the massive burden and now sought to shed the pyramid's weight.

Kendler reached out and pulled Caltha to him. He sensed the quaking stemmed from other than natural sources. Somewhere beyond the protecting walls of Giza, a mammoth fireball erupted to prove the Egyptian government wrong. The Sudanic military had taken retaliatory measures.

The image of the bus and its passengers trapped in that blinding inferno flashed through Kendler's mind. They were dead or dying. That he could have done nothing to save them, that what was past was past, did not ease the anguish. It made no sense—insanity never made sense.

"Nils!" Caltha cried, her voice racing through the octaves in high-pitched panic.

She vanished from his arms, leaving him holding empty air. A fraction of a second later, he once more found himself hurled by an invisible sling, rushing toward Base One as his power pack pulled him back to the security of his own time.

TWENTY-FOUR

Kendler felt Beamin's irritation emanating across the desk. Yet the man contained it. Neither his voice nor his manner displayed the slightest hint of agitation. Which meant the director had not been pushed to his limit. Kendler was prepared to push beyond that limit, if that was what it took to get what they wanted.

"Retrieve isn't a haphazard operation. We operate on a tight schedule. Base One services thirty field bases," Beamin explained in a voice just short of condescension. "Because of your two-hour jump yesterday, three field bases had to delay jumping up important data and experiments. You put them twenty-four hours behind schedule. What you're now asking would suspend our operations for a week!"

Beamin's expression pleaded with them to withdraw their request without further discussion. Neither Kendler nor Caltha answered the man.

"You can't go time hopping in search of . . . whatever in hell you two are looking for," the Base One director said. "If I had an idea of what you expected to find, maybe I could justify tying up our operations for a week, but . . ."

"Dammit! We've been over this at least ten times. We're seeking the force that almost wrenched me from the timestream." Kendler made no attempt to conceal his own growing anger. "We need at least a week to work our way back through the history of the Great Pyramid of Giza."

Beamin tapped the computer terminal on his desk. "There's still no evidence that an exterior force affected the timestream."

"But you said it's never happened before or after Nils's jump-up," Caltha insisted. "Something had to make it happen then."

Beamin refused to concede her point. Instead he punched up a computer display. "Here's a graph of the jump-up." His finger touched an angular valley in an otherwise straight line. "This represents a period from 4000 B.C. to 1000 B.C. That's three thousand years. A week wouldn't be enough to pinpoint the instant you supposedly saw the Great Pyramid of Cheops."

Kendler refused to give in. The Erna had to be somewhere in Earth's past waiting for him. He toyed with the idea of telling Beamin everything, then shoved the thought away. Likely as not, the director would totally reject their request without hard evidence of the Erna's existence. He had to take another approach or admit failure.

"If I can pinpoint a date, would you agree to a twenty-four-hour jump-down?" Kendler's eyes narrowed when he stared at the man.

"A week, a day, I can't tie us up that long without clearance from Lanatia," Beamin replied. "The most I could justify is another short jump."

"Two hours then," Kendler said. "Another two hours?"

"An hour," Beamin countered. "Give me an exact date and I'll give you an hour."

"Both of us," Kendler answered. "Both of us have to make the jump. It's essential."

"The time?" Beamin asked dubiously.

"2500 B.C.," Kendler replied. "That's the very bottom of the graph's valley."

Beamin sank in his chair. "Every seventy-two hours, we shut down Base One to do a complete systems check. We give ourselves eight hours to complete the work. However, the procedure normally takes six to seven hours. I'll let you have whatever time is left of those eight hours after all the safety checks have been run."

Beamin glanced to the chronometer on the wall. "The next check is twelve hours from now."

Twelve plus six equaled eighteen. Kendler did a quick mental calculation. "We'll be waiting."

Three hours into the systems check, Caltha and Kendler walked into the control room and leaned against a wall, out of the way of the technicians and engineers busily running their analyses of the Retrieve equipment. Beamin noticed the pair, but only gave them a disgusted expression and a shake of his head as a greeting.

"Great to be wanted, isn't it?" Caltha smiled and winked at Kendler.

He took her hand in his. The closer the jump came, the less he believed his own logic. What assurance did they have that the Erna would be waiting for them? For that matter, that the Erna had ever been on Earth?

"Why so gloomy?" Caltha squeezed his hand. "You did the best you could."

"It's a case of the 'what-if's,' " he answered. "Mainly, what if we blow this."

"We won't." She smiled. "If we don't locate the Erna this time, we will eventually. The Erna knew you, remember? It called you 'friend.' "

"We had to have made contact prior to Morasha," he said, trying to convince himself.

Still, he could not be certain the Erna had called him "friend." That was his own definition for a sensation, an alien sensation he could easily have misinterpreted. The Erna had been dying; it could have mistaken him for something else.

Kendler recalled the waves of doubt and confusion that had flooded from the creature when he had not recognized it.

The Erna's image of the Great Pyramid of Giza overlaid his mental image of the structure flashed in his mind's eye. It was the only thread that linked him to the creature. A thread that stretched thinner the more he thought about it. The Erna could have drawn the image from his own mind and fed it back to him, seeking some common denominator between them, a relationship between Giza and Isal.

Above all, the nagging worry rose, the worse of his fears. Could a creature live the five thousand years needed for them to meet on Morasha?

"I don't care for your attire this jump," Caltha said. "I prefer you ninety-nine percent nude."

He smiled at her attempt to relieve the tension. His gaze moved over the coarsely spun robes they wore. At best, the garments were only a rough approximation of the clothing of the era they were to enter. The time they had been given to prepare did not allow for anything but makeshift costumes.

Beneath the rough-cut robes, they wore the same power packs they had carried on the previous jump. They also wore the recording devices Beamin had given them for the first jump. Faced with as little as one hour of effective time for the jump, they had not wanted to weigh themselves down with their own bulky equipment.

"Kendler?" Beamin's voice cut into the psiotic's thoughts. He looked up to see the director signal him. With Caltha at his side, Kendler walked to where the man stood behind the control console.

"We'll be through here in another two hours," Beamin said. "Looks like you'll get a full two-hour jump."

Caltha squeezed Kendler's hand and grinned.

Despite being prepared, the jolt of being slung back into time caught Kendler off-balance. The force of the jump slammed at his body from all angles while threatening to rip him limb from limb in the same instant.

When the exterior hurricane stopped, he stood amid the Egyptian desert once again, sun-baked sand seeping over his sandaled feet. Before him rose the Great Pyramid of Giza in its full splendor. Slabs of limestone veneer, smooth and polished, covered its sides. Atop its apex rode a capstone, a perfect pyramid in itself.

"Feel anything?" He turned to Caltha. "Caltha!"

She stood swaying, eyes bulged, mouth gaping in a sound-less scream. Her hands clutched her head as though to protect it from an unseen bludgeon. She jerked around to face him, panic, fear, desperation in her eyes.

He reached for her. Her arms flailed at him, and she backstepped. Abruptly, her face went blank. Her eyes rolled upward to display their whites, and she collapsed to the sand.

Before he could step toward her, it hit him. Like the full fury of a Morashan *Nayati*, it invaded his mind. Kendler reeled to face Giza, fighting the urge to close himself off from the overwhelming psi storm.

The capstone glowed, flaring in an actinic glare. The stone melted. *No, dissolved!* Confusion and panic railed within the psiotic's brain as he denied the message of his own senses.

Wave after wave of forced washed through his mind. *Too strong!* He sensed its purpose—a greeting, a welcoming, a joyous uniting. *Too strong!* Pain, burning pain, sizzled within his skull. Kendler tried to open his mind, to project the agony back upon its source, to penetrate the ceaseless barrage of joy. His meager efforts melted, stillborn in the face of such power.

Light, pure and white, now engulfed Giza's heights. It flared like a bursting star, crystal beams skewering the sky in dazzling array. In the batting of an eye, it vanished, faded and disappeared. *No.* A single glowing orb remained, floating like a beacon or cyclopean eye above the now capless pyramid. The globe floated downward toward him.

The joyous chorus of union rose to a soul-shattering crescendo. He screamed; the naked power broke against his mind like a thousand tidal waves. Closer the orb came. In it . . . something. He could not discern the silhouetted shape held within.

Pain!

Kendler stumbled, clutching his head. Joy overloaded his senses. He fell to his back in the sand, writhing. Unconsciousness rushed upward to swallow him. Gratefully, he accepted it; anything to escape the brain-devouring joy that seared within his head.

A mental hand caught the nape of his neck, halting his descent into mindless oblivion. He floated in limbo between consciousness and unconsciousness. Sorrow suffused through his being. *Within? Without?* He no longer distinguished one from the other. The force now merged with him, matching itself to every cell of his brain.

Still the sorrow enveloped him, but with it came an understanding. The sorrow was an apology for the pain it brought, sorrow for misjudging the strength of the greeting. A quiet calm filled the psiotic, an assurance there would be no further agony, that it would protect his mind and body.

Caltha?

Kendler felt it sense his anguish over his fellow psiotic's safety. The force around and within him moved. Caltha stood within. It merged with her mind; they stood there as three, as one.

Again he sensed its movement, probing, dissecting, assimilating their memories, conscious and subconscious.

Sorrow returned.

Kendler recognized this churning sadness. He had felt it once before in the Pyramid of Isal, radiating from the Erna's dying mind—the "death sorrow." The force had located his memories of Morasha! It saw a reflection of itself. Within his mind, it saw its own future, its death. More, it saw the destruction and the thousands of human deaths its dying cries would cause on Morasha. Its railing horror, cries of protest, and the terror of an inescapable future and the havoc its dying would produce quaked through Kendler. Then, as on Morasha, he sensed its resignation to the inevitable, acceptance of its preordained task.

Task?

It did not respond. Deeper it probed, recognizing him as the entity it had attempted to rip from the timestream.

Erna?

Friend. The sensations Kendler had experienced on Morasha once more rippled gently through his mind, soothing and calming him. *Friends.* It repeated its message to include Caltha.

Erna? Kendler asked again.

There were no words, no thought-speech as with human beings, who communicate abstracts with concrete symbols. Yet, the answer still came in emotion, intangible sensations, rushing images.

Erna . . . I am/of the Erna.

It sensed his questions before he did, answering them before they formed in his mind. Kendler accepted, opening himself to the barrage that swirled into his brain.

Ambassador/explorer/seeker, the Erna's concept remained alien to Kendler. Yet he felt the creature's purpose—to find other intelligent beings who might unite in the glory of the universe with it. Erna . . . he saw the race of creatures—beings of pure energy—who called themself Erna. Erna . . . he saw the single creature who now floated above his unconscious body enclosed in a globe of light. Erna . . . he saw the individual and the race; they were one and the same. Its present centipedal body was but a physical form to be easily perceived by biological life forms, a simple body to assure its contacts of its peaceful intent.

The never-ceasing torrent of images raced through Kendler's mind. *Too fast!* The Erna did not, or could not, slow the maelstrom. Kendler grasped what he could.

Pyramid. The alien incorporated the human term and flashed images of Giza and the not yet constructed Isal. The images transformed, solarized visions of flowing energy streams. Kendler saw the streams eddy around the Erna, feeding its physical form. The psiotic saw and understood.

The structure focused the Kirlian energy and nourished the alien; the energy was the Erna's life force. With its own mental power, controlling matter and energy, the creature constructed a pyramid on each planet where it detected sentient life and waited. . . .

Kendler's perception slipped; the meaning evaded him. It waited until the race developed psi abilities? Until the race understood the secrets of such energy? When this occurred, it greeted the race with its offer to join the Erna among the stars.

A record? A history? The alien sensations overwhelmed Kendler, slipping through his mental grasp before he recognized them. Giza and Isal filled his vision once more. He saw their passages, their purpose. His mind reeled. The pyramids stood as a warning to humankind, a stone record of the Erna's arrival on-planet. *More!* The structures also predicted the moment of the planet's destruction.

No, Kendler accepted the Erna's meaning. *Foretold, not predicted.*

Isal foretold Morasha's destruction! In that instant, he understood the task the Erna had given him in its dying moments. He was to unlock Isal's meaning and warn the planet's inhabitants.

The Erna moved within his mind again, assuring him the task would be completed. Again, it brought forth images of the pyramids. Both stood shrouded in night. Brilliant beams of light leaped from their apexes into the starry skies. Simultaneously, Kendler followed them beyond the galaxy until they intersected. Before his mind's eye, the Erna, the race, opened to him, waiting for him to join them.

The pyramid was more than a warning. It was a beacon, a signpost for humankind that pointed the way to the Erna. *When?* He suddenly realized that beacon was useless unless he knew when to follow the light, the position of heaven's stars.

Again the Erna incorporated human thought-speech. *Midnight . . . solstice.*

The joy rushed back, permeating the core of Kendler's being. The sense of "friend" was there, but greater was the Erna's realization of purpose. Tears welled in Kendler's closed eyes. The Erna thanked him for pointing the way to the future, for defining the task that had until now been veiled by its inability to discern its own future. Gratitude flowed about the psiotic, bathing and washing over him.

Morasha—he felt the pain as the Erna transformed its thoughts from liquid beauty into cold, hard thought-words. It confirmed their future rendezvous, an assurance of commitment to a task and a death that would separate it from the union of the Erna, a disembodiment from its race.

Friend—once more it surrounded and nestled Kendler. He felt the gentle hand holding him slip away. *Friend.*

No! We must talk!

The psiotic raged against the unconsciousness that reached up to drag him downward. *No!* The Erna was gone. Kendler drifted into the blackness, the Erna's invitation to join them among the stars echoing in his mind.

TWENTY-FIVE

The power pack's warning buzzer pulled Kendler from the blanketing darkness. He forced his eyes open and groaned. His head pounded as though his sinus cavities were packed with concrete. Despite the Erna's gentleness, its uninhibited greeting had left its marks on his brain.

The Erna!?!

Kendler rolled from his back and pushed to his knees in the desert sand. Two meters away, Caltha lay on her back. She stirred, moaning softly. Crawling beside her, he lifted her head into his lap. Her eyes opened and she pressed her palms to her temples.

"Our friend certainly had a loud voice," she murmured. In the next instant, she bolted up, amazed disbelief on her face. "I heard him . . . we heard him. Nils, the pyramid . . . we have to warn Morasha . . . we have—"

"—to get back to Base One, then the cruiser." He rose and reached down to help Caltha to her feet. "Our power packs are about to jerk us back to 'real' time."

He looked to the Great Pyramid of Giza. Except for the limestone veneer, it now stood as it would throughout humankind's history on Earth. Even minus its apical capstone, the structure towered above him, its mass dwarfing the psiotic.

"Do you still feel the Erna?" Caltha looked up at Kendler.

He shook his head. "It's gone . . . to Morasha, where it waits for us."

"It couldn't leave us like that." Caltha's eyes grew wide. "It couldn't."

Before he could react, she closed her eyes. His arms went around her as her body went limp. While she drifted in alpha level awareness seeking a friend they would never meet again, Kendler lightly kissed her forehead. There had been no reason for the Erna to remain. It had probed their minds in a matter of seconds, then it had opened to them. Nothing more could be said. It went to prepare for its final task.

Caltha's eyes fluttered open and tears trickled down her cheeks. Her arms encircled his neck, clinging. His own embrace tightened about her as they shared the joy and loss of having been touched by the power of the stars. They still held one another when the time sling caught them in its grasp and hurled them toward the future.

Kendler carefully secured the door to their cruiser cabin. Returning to his bunk, he extracted the holotape from the medallions they had worn. Sitting beside him, Caltha removed the spetape from their bracelets.

"I don't think Beamin bought our story," Caltha said while she fed a reel of tape into a recorder. "This is out of your bracelet."

Kendler nodded and placed the holotape from his medallion into the projector. "Beamin knew something happened. But he had the sense not to make an issue of it. He realizes any official word about our jump has to come from Lanatia."

"I feel guilty about keeping him in the dark," Caltha said. "He did put his neck on the line when he allowed us to make an unauthorized second jump."

Beamin's risk had not been that great, Kendler thought. The Base One director knew he would have had to face Kate Dunbar's wrath if he had not assisted them. Still, Beamin and Retrieve had made the contact possible. "We'll see that Kate gives Retrieve its share of credit."

"And make sure Beamin receives credit for the decision on the second jump," Caltha added.

Beamin did not strike Kendler as a man who put much weight in personal publicity. However, the media exposure might give the man an opportunity to promote his Earth park project.

"Ready to look at what we've got?" Caltha rose to flip off the cabin's lights.

Kendler tapped the switches on the recorder and projector when Caltha sat beside him again. A rushing blur streaked through the center of the cabin. It took a moment for Kendler to recognize his own jerky movements as he acclimated himself to the Egyptian desert. The image sharpened and a miniature Great Pyramid of Giza floated in the middle of the air. Abruptly, there was another blur, then Caltha came into view. She staggered back, clutching her head.

"The Erna had just made contact. I was afraid you were going to do something to break that contact." Caltha chuckled, as though she had just realized nothing he could have done would have endangered that mental link.

Again the image blurred and focused on Giza's heights. The apex glowed, dissolved. Caltha gasped and squeezed Kendler's hand. Once more, the psiotic watched the globe of light descend from the pyramid toward him. At the center of the orb floated the centipedal body of the Erna.

"This was when I passed out," Kendler whispered.

The holographic record continued. The globe hovered a meter above Kendler's unconscious body, as best as he could judge. Posing for the mechanical eye atop the psiotic's chest, the Erna slowly revolved, allowing the holocamera to view its alien body from all angles.

The recorder that had sat silent during the viewing suddenly came to life. A sound that Kendler could only describe as music—the very heart of music, its core, a living core—surrounded and caressed him.

The Erna floated higher into the air. Something drifted upward to join it in the glowing globe.

"How did it do that?" Kendler recognized that something floating beside the Erna—himself! "How did it get me into the air without disturbing the camera?"

"You?" Caltha shot a perplexed glance at him. "That's me!"

Kendler stared at the hologram. It was not Caltha in the air, but himself. "Are you sure you see yourself?"

"Yes!" she answered. "I know what I look like."

Kendler grinned. Only time would confirm the migrant thought that moved through his mind. But at the moment, he was willing to lay a year's salary on the line that time would prove him correct.

A soft glowing light appeared on the forehead of the figure floating beside the Erna—Kendler for Kendler, Caltha for Caltha. A similar light surrounded the Erna's small head. The two glows slowly drifted from the two creatures—man and alien to melt together in a flaring star.

The Erna's music rose again. The feeling-word "friend" formed in Kendler's mind as strong as when the Erna had merged with his mind—as it would with anyone who viewed and heard the tapes. The song of the Erna rose to an engulfing crescendo.

The tapes ended; darkness and silence filled the cabin.

A minute, an hour, Kendler did not know how long Caltha and he sat without speaking. The message in the symbolic melting of minds and the Erna's song was clear as it had been when the creature touched his mind—the invitation for humankind to join the Erna in a fellowship of the stars.

Later, they examined Caltha's tapes. They were identical to Kendler's. Again both psiotics saw themselves floating beside the centipedal alien. The message remained loud and clear.

"Nils," Caltha's voice broke the cabin's silence, "we've got to transmit this. We have to share it with someone."

Kendler nodded mediatively, then came to life. "Damn! We have to tell Kate about the Pyramid of Isal!"

"Will she believe us?" Caltha stared at him when he switched on the lights. "We still have no real physical evidence."

"I believe the Erna gave us all we'll need." Kendler retrieved the tapes from recorder and projector. He quickly explained his theory about their seeing themselves on the tapes.

A smile curved Caltha's lips. "It has to be that."

"Only one way to find out." Kendler opened the door to the cabin. "And that's to transmit these to Lanatia."

Despite the speed of tachyon communications, it took a week for Kate Dunbar's answer to reach the cruiser as it made its way back to Lanatia. Kendler and Caltha stood before a vidcom screen in their cabin and waited for the Psi Corps director's image to appear.

"Incredible, magnificent . . . any superlative you can think of doesn't describe what you've brought back," Kate said when the screen came alive. "Nor does it describe the pride I feel for you two."

She paused to glance at a sheet of paper in her hands. "First, you were right about Isal. Using the calculations you gave us based on the Erna's mathematics, Isal predicts the destruction of Morasha in twelve standard months. It also might interest you to know our astronomers have observed fluctuation in Morasha's sun. They calculate it will nova in twelve standard months.

"I can't give you anything definitive on the recordings until my staff has the opportunity to study the real items." She hesitated as though searching for the correct words. "Do you realize everyone who has viewed your transmission has seen himself floating in the air beside the Erna?"

Again, Kate paused. "If you realize that, we are open to any speculations on the methods the Erna used to achieve that effect.

"My congratulations on a job well done, once more," Kate said. "On a personal level, Nils, give my daughter a hug and a kiss. And, Caltha, do the same to Nils."

Kate winked most suggestively as her image faded.

Kendler immediately switched the vidcom to transmission. "The Erna's manipulation of holographic images was noted. No speculations on its methods, but we suspect it found a way to provide the hard evidence you required in the only possible method available to it and still complete its task on Morasha."

He paused and looked at Caltha to see if she wanted to add anything. She shook her head. Kendler concluded, "Should arrive on Lanatia in four weeks, then your staff can take a look at these tapes. Now, I've got to deliver a hug and a kiss."

He switched off the vidcom and turned to Caltha. She grinned, stepping into his arms to receive the promised kiss.

"Mmmmm," she sighed when they parted. "That was definitely not a motherly kiss."

"Maybe I should try again?" He did.

"Still not motherly." She smiled, an impish light flashing in her dark eyes. "It might take a day or two for you to get it right. But I'm not in any hurry."

"I was thinking more in terms of a lifetime," Kendler answered.

"Pair-bonding? A bond contract?" Caltha looked up at him. "Are you prepared for that big a step?"

"I was considering an old-fashioned Seker marriage," Kendler replied. "That is, if you're not opposed to alien customs."

Caltha's lips parted, but he stifled her words with another kiss. "I don't want an answer now. I want you to think about it. And I want Paul included in this decision."

Caltha nodded, then returned his kiss.

TWENTY-SIX

Kate Dunbar shoved away from her desk to sit back in her chair. She heaved a deep breath and eyed Caltha and Kendler. Surprise? Shock? Kendler could not read the woman's expression, if that deadpan look could be called an expression.

"Hmmmmm." Kate selected a freeform briar pipe from the rack on the desk, took her time to pack the bowl, and lit it. After exhaling a small cloud of blue smoke, her eyes returned to the pair. "Hmmmmm."

Kendler suppressed the urge to rub the sweat from his palms. He told himself Kate's decision did not matter. But the truth was their future with the Psi Corps hinged on the utterance of one word from the woman across from him. He sensed Caltha's tension as the weight of the moment sat squarely on their shoulders. From the corner of his eyes, he saw her doing her best not to squirm in her seat.

"Marriage, hmmmmm." Kate's gaze seemed to pin the two psiotics to their chairs at the same moment. "Perhaps it's time the Psi Corps experimented with a permanent team. The results might prove interesting."

"The Psi Corps? The results might prove interesting?" Caltha glared at her mother. "Is that all you can say? I said Nils and I have decided to marry!"

"It might be just the thing for a new assignment I have been considering," Kate continued, ignoring Caltha. "It could provide a certain stability to the project. We'll talk about it further later. Right now, I want to cover the items I brought you here to discuss."

Caltha snorted with disgust and slumped in her chair. Her face tightened in exasperation. A nervous relief rippled through Kendler. Kate had just given her approval of the marriage, something unheard of with the corps. He caught a delighted glint in the older woman's eyes. He turned his head away to hide an amused smile that crept to his lips. Within her own agency, Kate Dunbar would not be bested, not even by her own daughter. Perhaps especially by her own daughter.

"I thought you might like to know that evacuation of the Morashan population is presently underway." The Psi Corps director puffed at the pipe several times, then blew a thin stream of smoke above her head. "Relocation will be complete in six months on a newly discovered Earth-type planet in the Ound System."

Four months prior to Morasha's sun's going nova, Kendler thought. Not much leeway for anything to go wrong, but the Erna had given them the chance to rescue the Lukya society from the fury of an exploding star.

"The LofAl Council has also approved funding for an educational program for the Morashans," Kate said. "When they arrive on their new homeworld, they will have the benefit of technologies lost to them for centuries."

Kendler smiled. When Ome eventually filled his father's seat in the ministry, the world he would help govern would have shed its ignorance to stand with the other LofAl planets as an equal member. He doubted the Morashans could shake off the confinement of the Lukya religion in that time, but superstition would not leave them susceptible to cheap technological tricks like those used by the false prophet Atla-Eron.

"Gustaf, the projection display," Kate called to her personal computer. In response, the windows shuttered closed and the lights dimmed.

Kendler watched as a globe of softly glowing light appeared at the center of the Psi Corps director's office. A shadowy figure slowly materialized within the heart of the globe. Kendler gripped the arms of his chair in an almost subconscious action.

"What is it?" he heard Caltha ask.

"You tell me," Kate replied. "Take your time."

Kendler scooted to the edge of his seat, unable to take his gaze from the blurred image. His fingers tried to dig holes in the chair's upholstery. Something about the unfocused projection irritated him. His eyes narrowed to slits in an attempt to bring out the features on the face he stared at.

"What do you see, Nils?" Kate asked.

"A man," he answered. "A blurred man. I can't make out his features. Also, the projection is affecting me on an emotional level. I'm experiencing an undefined anger . . . almost a loathing."

"Caltha?" Kate asked.

"I see a vague image of a woman," Caltha replied. "Like Nils, looking at it evokes an anger. What are we seeing?"

"Gustaf, they've seen enough," Kate said. She smiled at her two field agents when the lights came back on. "That was our tenth attempt to duplicate what was found on your holotapes of the Erna."

She paused to relight her pipe and take a couple more deep puffs. "I'm still trying to understand the technical details. Basically what was found on the tapes is what appears to be a visual code that evokes the mental concept of 'self' within the human mind. Thus, every person who views the tapes sees himself in the air beside the Erna."

"And the anger we felt?" Caltha asked.

"The human brain doesn't care for anything to screw with its self-image," Kate said with a chuckle. "This attempt to duplicate the Erna's code provides just enough of the signal to tap that common 'self' concept in every human being's mind, but not enough to bring the image into focus. We subconsciously read 'self' but the conscious mind denies the signal because it isn't complete. The anger and loathing stems from that conflict. Our brains reject a twisted self-image."

"All of which is interesting, *but*?" Kendler asked.

"This, along with the original tapes, has been presented to a closed session of the LofAl Council," Kate said. She paused, then grinned widely. "You brought back the hard evidence needed to convince them that the Erna is real . . . that an intelligent civilization waits for Man to join them."

Caltha turned to Kendler, her grin as wide as her mother's, as wide as his own. He took her hand and squeezed it tightly. The pressure of Caltha's answering grip left his knuckles aching. He recalled his first impression of this diminutive woman. Caltha was anything but a fragile China figurine.

"What's the next step?" Caltha turned back to Kate.

"Immediately, it's to release the tapes to the public," Kate replied. "The council wants public backing for what they have in mind. Or for what I put in their minds."

"But the Kavinites will learn about the Erna," Caltha said.

"Exactly," Kate said. "When we offer to let them in on the project, they will jump at the opportunity. The Erna might have provided us the means to begin tearing down the artificial barriers that separate humankind."

"What project is this?" Kendler asked dubiously.

"*Seeker* . . . a journey to the Erna's homeworld," Kate said nonchalantly.

"When do we leave?" Kendler could not contain his excitement.

"Fifteen years, if everything runs smoothly," Kate said, her gaze drifting between the two psiotics. She smiled.

"Paul will be a man," Caltha said softly. "Fifteen years?"

"Which is just as well," Kate said. "While I love my grandson, I don't relish playing mother while you are off exploring the stars. Being a mother once is enough for any woman." She looked at Kendler. "If you don't believe it, try it sometime."

"But why so long?" Kendler asked. "A cruiser could be ready within a month, or sooner if you pushed it."

Kate laughed and shook her head. "Obviously you didn't grasp what the Erna showed you. The *Seeker* crew won't be headed for any place in this galaxy, but for REV90732P."

The psiotics stared at the Psi Corps director.

"REV90732P," Kate repeated. "For centuries it was thought to be an echo galaxy, a radio phantom. But that's where the vectors the Erna gave you lead. Even with proposed modifications in our present tachyon drive, which should square the obtainable speeds, the journey will take another twenty years."

Twenty years! It slowly sank into Kendler's head. From Caltha's look, the thought had the same numbing effect.

"Gustaf, give us the *Seeker* proposals," Kate said to the computer.

Again the room darkened. A holo of a metallic orb floated within the office.

"The *Seeker*," Kate said, unable to hide the pride in her voice. "It was originally designed as a mobile naval command base shortly after the *Roscoe Turner* was destroyed and war appeared imminent. The council later canceled the funding necessary for its construction."

Kendler studied the dimensions that flashed over the orb. Five kilometers in diameter, it was patterned on the ancient L-5 colonies of the Sol System. The projection changed to a cross section of the proposed craft while Kate explained that ten to twelve years would be required for the *Seeker*'s construction and an additional three years for flight testing and equipping the ship.

Kendler's gaze moved over the multilevel interior of the *Seeker*. It would be a small world, including farming land, parks, and recreational areas as well as the normal fittings of a spacecraft. Built around the propulsion and energy core, the ship would be a series of spheres each built around a small sphere every hundred to two hundred meters. An artist's concept of the command level blinked before Kendler.

"The *Seeker* will carry a full crew of two thousand persons," Kate said. "Included in those will be ten four-member Psi Corps teams."

"I assume the assignment you mentioned earlier was this," Caltha said. "Nils and I will be members of one of those teams . . . won't we?"

"Nils and you will head the command team," Kate answered. "That is, if you want it."

Kendler glanced at Caltha. He saw her nod approval in the glowing light of the holographic projection. He smiled. "We want it."

"Don't be so hasty," Kate said. "We're talking about thirty-five years devoted to one project, twenty of them within a metallic world hurling through tachyon space. That's the first leg of the journey. It'll take another twenty years to make it back. That's fifty-five years in all. Almost two-thirds of your life will be gone."

"But we'll have established contact with the Erna," Caltha said.

"I hope it will be worth it," Kate replied. "The next few years of your lives are going to be sheer hell for two people accustomed to field service. To begin with, your brains hold the key to communicating with the Erna. I plan to pick every bit of information they hold. When I've got that, we'll start over just in case something slipped by. Then we'll do it a third and a fourth time."

Kendler remembered the month of debriefing after they

had returned from Morasha. He cringed inwardly, knowing it had been only a sample of what they could expect now.

"With what we can get from you and what we decipher from the Erna's music and its visual code, we'll be prepared for two-way communication when we find them." Kate stared at the two.

Kendler and Caltha looked to one another again, then nodded their willingness to Kate.

"If we're lucky, that portion of the project will be complete five years from now. Then begins the administrative work," Kate continued. "You will be personally responsible for screening every applicant for the voyage. If a tenth-level grease monkey has latent psi abilities, I'll want to know about it. In fact, every member of the *Seeker*'s crew should be a latent psiotic atop whatever other qualifications he or she happens to have."

It did not sound that complicated on the surface, until Kendler thought about it. There would not be a few thousand applicants seeking a position on the vessel, but a few thousand from each planet in the Alliance.

"It will also be your responsibility to create and train the Psi Corps teams aboard the *Seeker*," Kate said. "That in itself should be a full-time job for any five people."

"You aren't scaring us off," Caltha said firmly. "It's what we both want. We've had time to discuss it. We knew an expedition would be sent, and we know we want to be part of it."

Kate nodded and pursed her lips. "And I knew what both your answers would be. I just wanted you to know what it was going to be like. A few months from now, I don't want to hear any complaints to the effect that you weren't warned in advance of the crap you'll encounter."

"You've warned us," Kendler said. "Now, when do we begin?"

"Monday morning," Kate replied.

"That's only three days from now. . . . The wedding?" Caltha looked at her mother.

"Unless you plan to postpone the services for fifteen years, I suggest you move the date up," Kate said with no consideration for the plans Caltha had made.

Caltha's mouth opened, then closed as though she realized there was no use in arguing with the woman.

"Are there any other questions?" Kate looked at both of them.

"I'd like another look at the *Seeker*," Kendler said.

"Fine, but you'll have to do it without me." Kate rose and walked to the door to her office. "I've got to prepare things for the celebration tonight."

"Celebration?" Caltha turned to her mother.

"Engagement . . . or wedding party, whichever," Kate replied. "I had Jon Beamin jump up some vintage Terran champagne for the occasion while you were on Earth."

Caltha's eyes grew wider. "You knew all along?"

Kate winked and called back as she left them alone, "Hell, it didn't take a mind reader to see what was in your minds."

Kendler laughed as he rose and pushed his chair beside Caltha. He leaned to her and gave her a quieting kiss. "Some mother you've got there."

"She's not my mother; I disown her." She smiled mischievously. "But she will be your mother-in-law, my love."

"Hmmmmm?" Kendler winced in a mock grimace, then smiled when Caltha returned his kiss. "Ready to take a second look at the *Seeker*?"

Caltha nodded, and Kendler called for the computer to project the display once again. This time his gaze traced every line of the proposed ship, attempting to commit it to memory. Fifteen years and the ship would be a reality. What was fifteen years compared to the centuries it had taken humankind to find the Erna? It was but the batting of a sleepy eye before it opened to see a new dawn.

Caltha reached out and took his hand, squeezing it very tightly.

ABOUT THE AUTHOR

A native Texian, Geo. W. Proctor was raised in the pine woods and red clay country of East Texas, on his parents' farm for breeding and training thoroughbred race horses. Before beginning his writing career, he worked briefly as a television cameraman and spent five years as a reporter with a major Dallas daily newspaper.

A longtime enthusiast of science fiction and fantasy, Proctor made his first story sale in 1972. Also a "weekend painter," he has sold paintings which appeared in a national fantasy periodical.

Proctor and his wife Lana presently live in Arlington, Texas, a suburb between Dallas and Fort Worth.

GREAT ADVENTURES IN READING

The Legends of the Old West
Live On in Fawcett Westerns